GALLOWS POINT

DAVID EBRIGHT

WELCOME TO THE WORLD OF JACK RACKHAM AND HIS THIRD ADVENTURE

STAUGUSTINEPUBLISHING.COM 2018

GALLOWS POINT IS DEDICATED TO

the memory of my wonderful parents . . .

my wife, Deb – who is always there . . .

and my grandkids – I love being your "Pop"

THANK YOU

DEB (my awesome wife) – incredible photographer, motivator, beta reader, and best friend (love you lots) – AKA "Nan" – my inspiration

CHRISTIAN BENTULAN – Cover artist extraordinaire. A young talent with a brilliant future and incredible work ethic – **WWW.COVERSBYCHRISTIAN.COM**

CRISTI TAIJERON at Endless Horizon Designs for her work on layout, design, publicity and marketing. Also an outstanding author and publisher – she really "gets" pirates! **WWW.ENDLESSHORIZONDESIGNS.COM**

GALLOWS POINT

1
TRAVELERS

RACHEL COULDN'T BREATHE as she spun helplessly through brilliant pulsing light. Overcome with fear and despair, hysteria building as the sensation of a crushing weight intensified, her arms twisting in an unseen grip, skin burning hot then cold, stretching, separating from the tissue beneath, pain so intense, she nearly fainted.

Mercifully it ended. Tears streamed down her cheeks. Her heartbeat slowed. She wrapped her arms around herself rocking rhythmically, inhaling great gulps of air through racking sobs. Several minutes passed before the pain finally subsided and she opened her eyes, flexing her joints and muscles while her chest heaved with sharp spasms.

She found herself lying on a bed of leafy vegetation, damp against her skin, the sound of water flowing in the distance. Colorful birds screeched and flapped overhead. Monkeys chased one another through tangled vines above. The sweet smell of blooming flowers wafted over a gentle breeze as patchy sunlight filtered through a thick canopy of green, gently warming the side of her tear-streaked face.

Rachel rolled from her back to her side and finally pushed up onto her knees, steadying herself with outstretched arms; kneeling on all fours, head down, long thick blonde hair covering her face, nearly touching the ground. Several seconds passed. She stood, swaying briefly before pulling her hair back and surveying her surroundings.

She was alone in a dense jungle, near the base of a mountain. Several yards away a waterfall fed a small clear pool which emptied into a wide, bubbling stream. She shuffled slowly toward the pool, her body aching with every step. After peering in all directions, she eased into the water up to her shoulders, her body welcoming the healing chill.

This was her real-life nightmare. Calico Jack Rackham, a ruthless pirate, dead for nearly three centuries had somehow returned from the grave. He had used mind control to make her abandon her friends as they searched for treasure on one of the small islands in the Bahamas. Under his trance she had flown a seaplane across several miles of open blue water eventually crashing in the everglades when it ran out of fuel. From there he had taken her hostage to force her friend Jack, the pirate's own descendant, to follow to a place called the Valley of the Kings. He had told her they would travel in time to the year 1720 on a quest to rescue Calico Jack and his crew from the hangman's noose. Rachel leaned back, floating, staring upward, her ears underwater, blocking all sound, wondering when the rotting corpse of the dreaded pirate would appear. The tears flowed again as she remembered the horror of his fleshless hands wrapped around her wrists, dragging her roughly into the swirling green mist, to end up here, lost in a tropical jungle teeming with dangerous predators.

Refreshed, Rachel trudged cautiously through the jungle toward a clearing to the left of the waterfall. To her surprise, she found a small campfire crackling and glowing with something resembling chicken skewered above the flames. Stacked nearby was a pile of fresh fruit and beyond, a shelter made from thick bamboo covered with leafy fronds. Inside she found a hammock made of woven vines suspended three feet above the ground. She looked around, expecting to discover Calico Jack lurking nearby. There was no sign of him, but she knew he had left the provisions. She sat down next to the fire and helped herself to a piece of fruit. It was sweet and juicy, the taste a cross between a mango and a papaya. Next she tried the roasted meat, and found it tender and flavorful, much better than chicken. Full and exhausted Rachel climbed into the hammock. She had nowhere to run and knew that the worst of her nightmare was yet to come. For now, she needed rest.

A few hours later Rachel woke with a start to the sound of the now-roaring fire. She moved from the shelter and gasped at the sight of Calico Jack Rackham hovering inches from the flames, close enough that any human would have suffered severe burns. He turned slowly to face the makeshift hut as she inched her way outside.

"Avast, dear girl, it be such a pleasure to see ye in good health. Feelin' better are we?"

The pirate wore multi colored striped trousers stuffed into the tops of high black boots. His white ruffled shirt was bloody at the neck which was wrapped with a stained yellow kerchief. He wore a blue waistcoat with heavy brocade, his head covered with a bandana beneath a tri-cornered hat over his long light colored hair which was only slightly darker than his goatee which had been trimmed to a point.

Rachel's mouth moved but only a weak whimper of terror escaped her lips. The shaking started again and her eyes welled up. Her legs felt weak, on the verge of collapse and she covered her face with her hands trying to stifle a new round of tears. Finally, she cleared her throat. "Where am I?" she asked in a quivering whisper.

"Miss Rachel, take heart, I mean ye no harm. As to yer whereabouts, we be just a short trek from the Valley of the Kings and awaitin' young Jack and his able mate Kai to join us."

"W . . . what makes you think they'll come?"

"Both lads be makin' their way here now. 'Twas never me intent to bring ye here to be offerin' ye as bait, but the lad left me no option. Aye, he be such the stubborn lubber."

Rachel eyed the old pirate, hoping his clothes would burst into flames. "But what makes you so sure they'll follow?"

"Ye must know, lass, yer Jack be willin' to risk life n' limb fer yer sake. There be ne're a doubt 'bout that. Meself knowin' this, I sent me ship, *The William* to fetch the pair. 'Twill take them aboard soon. How did ye like the iguana, Miss Rachel? They tend to be quite tender n' tasty wee creatures, wouldn't ye agree?"

She gagged as she looked down at the leftovers still skewered on the sharpened stick. "How long will it take them to get here?"

"Oh, child, there be no way o' tellin'. Me ship'll get the lads across the sea; make no mistake of it, but me assistance ends there. A perilous journey awaits once ashore and the fate of all four of us rogues rests in their hands."

"What's that supposed to mean?"

"Alas, if they do not survive, we shan't either. There are but thirteen days remaining before ye must cross over."

"You mean cross over into the past."

Calico Jack's smile seemed almost warm as he looked directly into Rachel's emerald eyes. "Aye, into me past, to save me from the gallows and rescue me dear Anne Bonny and me unborn son and make fer us a new life."

The tears dried as Rachel, now resigned to spending several days alone with the pirate corpse, took a deep breath. "And you think Jack can survive and make this scheme of yours work? That's a lot to expect of a sixteen-year-old you know," said Rachel.

"Aye, 'tis true, but young Rackham is brave and

resourceful. He'll not fail."

"Sounds like you're trying to convince yourself more than me."

"He has the gift," said the pirate.

"What do you mean the gift?"

"When we was alone in the cave on Fishtail Cay, I granted him the ability to control minds. Once the lad learns to control its power, he shall become a dangerous mate to reckon with, able to command others to do his biddin' and bend to his will on matters great or small. He shall be, I must confess, nearly invincible."

"Jack would never want that kind of power! No one should want it. It would be … evil."

"Aye, in the wrong hands, it could very well be used for evil. Ye should know that Jack were given no choice. 'Tis true, he rejected me offer, but I convinced him 'twas for the best."

"I don't believe you," said Rachel. "You did something to him."

"The young man now bears the brand of Calico Jack. On that I'll say no more."

"And that's why I heard Jack's voice when I crashed."

"Aye."

Moored just offshore from Key Largo, Jack and Kai sat at the stern of *Reckless Endeavor* the hundred-year-old fully customized one-hundred-eighty-two-foot schooner owned by Jack's grandfather. The pair had been best friends since the days when five-year-old Jack started spending summers with his grandparents in St. Augustine Florida. Following in Pop's footsteps, they had already completed two successful treasure hunts, netting them millions in gold and gemstones. During the course of these adventures, each had risked his own life to save the other on more than one occasion. The bond between them was unbreakable.

"He said he wouldn't kill her,' said Kai.

"You ready to take the word of an evil dead guy?"

Kai sighed and rubbed his forehead. "No, but I don't see how we're gonna do this."

"We have thirteen days," said Jack as he stood from his seat at the gunwale. He was a big kid, six feet four inches tall and muscular at two hundred and twenty pounds, with long blonde hair and deep blue eyes.

"Yeah, thirteen days to cross the Gulf of Mexico, enter a foreign country illegally, find some tomb in the middle of a jungle and then . . ."

"I know, sounds impossible, but we don't have a choice."

"Shouldn't we ask Pop what he thinks?"

"No adult in their right mind would go along with this. He already suspects we're up to something. I feel rotten that he's wasting time lining up more search teams to look for Rachel in the Everglades when I already know she's not there. We have to move on this fast."

"It's not like you lied to anyone," said Kai.

"But I didn't tell anyone that I knew where she was either. That's just as bad."

"Yeah, like someone would believe the real story."

"We have to do this on our own."

"Jack, we can't run off and say nothin' to Pop."

"We'll leave a note. That's all we can do."

"When would we leave?" asked Kai.

"Half an hour."

"And the plan is?"

"Listen, Kai, you can bail on this if you want. I wouldn't blame you," said Jack.

"You're not leavin' me out of this, Rackham. What makes you think I want to miss out on chasin' a dead pirate and travelin' back in time?" Kai stood from his spot and ran his hands through his thick mop of curly dark hair. He was shorter by four inches and, although Jack outweighed him by forty pounds, he too was broad-shouldered and muscular.

"We might not make it. In fact, chances are pretty good we won't."

"Can you do this by yourself?"

"I don't know," said Jack.

"You could've said, 'No, Kai, I'm desperate, ya gotta help me'."

"But it's not fair to drag you into this."

"Rachel's my friend too. Think I want to see her die or disappear forever?"

"It's your choice. Just so you know the risk. Ever jump out of a plane?"

Kai laughed. "Yeah, right. You know I hate flyin'."

Jack didn't smile just cocked one eyebrow as he stared at his friend.

"You're serious. You mean like parachuting?"

"I don't see any other way to do it. I've gone over the map a dozen times. To get to The Valley of the Kings we've got to cross seven hundred miles of ocean, hike thirty miles of jungle, climb through two mountain passes and then follow a river for about fifteen miles. We can reach the coast by plane in three hours, and if we chute into the jungle, we can cut the hike way down. That saves us more than a week. Besides, we can't fly commercial, that would leave too much ground to cover and give Pop a chance to track us down."

"I assume you have somethin' arranged already," said Kai.

"Not yet, but we need to go to Key West and get started."

"Why Key West?"

"Key West is the closest small airport with planes that can cover that distance. There's got to be a pilot looking for a big payday that will take a chance. Since money is the one thing we have plenty of, that's where I think we need to go."

"Okay, I'm in. How do we get there from here?" asked Kai.

"I talked to a guy with a fast boat this morning. I offered him two thousand bucks to run us down there this afternoon. We have to meet him in less than an hour."

"So I guess you already wrote the note."

"I did. A courier is going to deliver it six hours from now. That's enough time to give us a short head start," explained Jack. "Hopefully, we'll be in the air before Pop chases us down."

"What kind of gear do we need?"

"I've packed most of it but we're going to have to buy some stuff."

"Like parachutes?"

"Like parachutes, climbing ropes, and food," said Jack. "We'll have to travel light."

"Uh, how 'bout weapons?"

"Nope."

Kai took a deep breath and shook his head. "Guess we better roll. We're runnin' outta time and it won't take Pop long to start lookin' for us once he gets your note. Still can't believe we gotta jump out of a plane. That's nuts."

"Yeah, it'll be my first jump too. Let's grab our stuff and get moving while no one's around to ask questions."

X

The boat was a forty-two-foot *Fountain Lightning*, a racing machine, capable of running across calm water at one hundred and thirty miles per hour. Jack and Kai arrived in Key West in less than fifty minutes. The boys combed the airport, looking for a plane and pilot for hire, but no one would take the pair of sixteen-year-olds seriously, despite their offers of a substantial cash payment. Time was running out. The letter Jack had written would be delivered to Pop aboard *Reckless Endeavor* within the hour, ruining Jack's scheme. The sun was fading when they stopped at a crowded gulf-side dock. "Looks like we're stuck," said Kai.

"I thought waving a pile of cash around would do the trick," said Jack.

"Probably thought we stole it and we're running away. No one would believe that guys our age could be millionaires. I have a hard time believin' it myself sometimes."

"Guess so but it's still the only way to cover that kind of distance in such a short time. A boat, even *Reckless* with its huge engines, would take too long."

"Maybe we'll have to get Pop to go with us after all. He could hire the plane."

"Forget it," said Jack.

"Don't tell him about the time travel part."

"It's too late. I explained that in the letter too."

"Well, you'd think that idiot pirate woulda helped us get there at least. He's the one needin' our help and we're stuck here on a dock. Can't you call him or whatever it is you do with that mind stuff he infected you with?"

"I don't know how to make the mind control stuff work or I might have tried it on a pilot. It's been two days since that creep branded his mark on my arm. It only seems to work when the scar burns bright red. Since he took her

...."

"I don't believe it," interrupted Kai.

"Seriously, it doesn't ..."

"I'm not talkin' about that. Look over there, where the sun's settin'. See that shape in front of the big red ball? I think our ride's here."

Jack looked west into the Gulf of Mexico where Kai pointed. There was a ship on the horizon sailing toward them at great speed. It was an ancient schooner with three masts, the sails tattered and stained, stretched and billowing as if filled by strong winds on a following sea, though the air was nearly still. The Rackham flag, crossed cutlasses beneath a white skull depicted on a black background, flapped from above the crow's nest. As the ship approached, ear-splitting cannon fire erupted from the port and starboard sides but no one in the bustling marina, other than Jack and Kai, heard the thundering explosions.

"Looks like we get to travel on a ghost ship 'stead of jumpin' out of a plane, but I'm not sure it's an upgrade," said Kai.

Jack let out a deep breath and looked up to the sky. "This is bad."

"No kiddin'."

"If we get on that ship, we're in Calico Jack's control. If we don't, we'll never see Rachel again. Both choices suck. What do you think we should do?"

Kai walked to an empty bench, plopped down and leaned forward on his forearms, his head tucked toward his knees with his hands clasped in front. After a short pause, he spoke up. "There's no choice, Jack. We have to take the ship. No one's gonna fly us there and we can't leave Rachel in no man's land with a corpse. Gotta take the shot, I guess." Kai smiled. "Probably shoulda had our wills prepared."

Jack laughed at that as the great ship nosed up against

the dock, coming to a complete stop with barely a bump, the sails still taut from a breeze that didn't exist. "This is going to be an adventure that we can brag to our grandkids about, assuming we live through it," he said as he reached for the duffle bag. "Better shove off."

"Didja notice that none of the people walkin' around us can see this monstrosity of a boat? Pretty weird."

"I think weird is just beginning, Kai."

⌒X⌒

"He's crossed the line now," said a red-faced Pop as he tossed Jack's note onto the deck.

"What are you grumbling about now? What line?" asked Nan.

"Jack and Kai are on their way to a place called the Valley of the Kings. If I recall, that's in southern Mexico near Central America, the former home of the ancient Aztecs."

"What? Why?"

Pop retrieved the note and handed it to Nan. "To rescue Rachel. Go ahead, read this, then I'll explain." He stroked his pure white goatee while watching Nan, waiting for her response.

Nan spread the paper out and read the handwritten letter. She looked up, her face nearly as red as Pop's, her blue eyes flashing. "He's crossed the line this time."

"I already said that."

"Explain this insanity to me. He says they have to travel back in time to rescue Rachel and keep Calico Jack Rackham from being hanged. What does all of that mean? "

"Better get Val out here so you can both sit down while I tell you how we actually met the ghost of Calico Jack aboard *Reckless*," said Pop.

"This is no time for tall tales. Save them for your books."

Pop shook his head. This ain't part of a novel, but it *would* make a great story. Took me a while to believe it myself . . . and I was there!" Once Val joined them on deck he explained about the two men that followed *Reckless* and how Calico Jack saved his life when the pair tried to board. He also told them that they found Fishtail Cay and that now over a ton of gold rested below-decks inside *Reckless Endeavor's* storage hold next to the engine room. He described, as much as he could, the Rackham Curse and Jack's new ability to control and read minds.

"We have to go find them," said Nan.

"Easier said than done. They have a big head start and I have no idea where they started from. Besides, if they go back in time, there's no way to follow 'em."

"So what do we do?"

"I think we travel to where it's likely to end."

"Why is that?"

"We can't intercept them in the middle of the Gulf and there's no way to find them in the jungle, but we do know from history where the hanging of Calico Jack Rackham took place."

"Rackham's Cay?" asked Val.

"Close. That tiny island is only a stone's throw from Gallows Point. Let's go grab something decent for dinner. Tomorrow we'll re-stock our provisions and fuel *Reckless* and our reserve tanks up so we can set sail for Jamaica day after tomorrow."

"Why not leave now? Aren't you the least bit worried about the kids?"

"Of course I'm worried, but according to the note, this rescue won't happen for nearly two weeks. They'll probably find Rachel, save Calico Jack and be back in St

Augustine ahead of us anyway."

"Then why are we going to Jamaica?" huffed Nan impatiently.

"Treasure hunter's instincts kickin' in? Maybe they return to the present wherever they happen to be geographically? Maybe they'll need help. The real answer? I don't know."

"As crazy as it sounds, I'll go with your logic," said Nan as she walked across the deck toward the cabin stairs.

~X~

Jack and Kai climbed aboard *The William* and walked across its splintered decks. There was no sign of a crew. The sails were little more than shredded rags and the large wooden wheel at the helm had only two spokes holding it together, and they were cracked.

"Jumpin' out of a plane's might've been safer than this," said Kai.

Jack turned from looking down into what was left of the hatch. "There's no crew aboard this pile of floating driftwood. He can't seriously think we can sail this thing."

"No one could sail this chum bucket. Better make up your mind what you want to do, we're leavin' port like it or not."

The ship reversed away from the dock at surprising speed, the bow turning quickly into the path of a luxury mega-yacht reversing its starboard engine to bring its stern about and come alongside the floating wharf. The boys braced for impact, grabbing at the rotted center mast. The yacht completed its turn, cutting through *The William* amid ship without slowing. There was no crash, no scrape, and no jarring collision as the yacht continued toward a pair of marina workers waiting dockside to grab the lines to be tossed from the yacht's deckhands above.

"Think I'm gonna puke. That boat passed through us like we were a fog," said Kai.

"We're on a ghost ship. What did you expect?"

"Well, genius, why'd *we* see it?"

Jack sighed. "How do I know? Guess we're supposed to."

"And we're supposed to sail this haunted shipwreck across the Gulf of Mexico by ourselves?"

"Don't think we're sailing anything, we're just along for the ride. Might as well quit complaining and get comfortable."

"That's it? Get comfortable? How do you know we're not gonna get ten miles offshore and sink to the bottom?"

"I don't know, but at the rate we're moving, we've already covered two miles and so far so good. We're too far out to sea to jump ship now. Lots of sharks in these waters," said Jack.

Kai reached absently at his thigh where a bull shark had bitten him the summer before.

The boys tossed their gear inside the battered cabin and climbed below decks where they found gaping holes throughout the hull. They could see the water rushing past the jagged openings but there were no signs of leaks and *The William* sailed swiftly through the warm waters of the gulf unaffected by wind or calm.

On day two of the voyage, Jack's arm pulsed as the angry raised flesh of the Rackham brand glowed red. He held his hand over the hideous skull and crossed cutlasses that had been burned into his arm, hoping to stop the pain, but as his palm clamped tight against his skin, his vision blurred and he found himself staring through a black tunnel and into the shadowed but recognizable face of Calico Jack.

"So 'tis yerself again, lad" boomed the pirate's voice. "And how be it with ye? I see ye be learnin' the ways of the brand."

"I don't know what you're talking about. My arm started burning and when I grabbed for it, you appeared. Where's Rachel? What did you do with her?"

"Ah yes, Miss Rachel. I take pleasure in sayin' that I be sure and certain that ye shall find the lass in good health and spirits and she anxiously awaits yer arrival. With that bit o' business out of the way, it be time for me to 'splain how ye use the brand to see things and control the thoughts of other lubbers."

"I already told you, I want no part of any mind control," said Jack.

"Ye have no choice in the matter. The quest ye have undertaken will test yer strength and bravery beyond the limits of most mortals. Yer new *ability*, once ye learn to use it, will not only prove useful, but necessary to accomplish the task and keep ye and yer friends alive. On this I swear on me oath."

Jack sighed and blinked his eyes, trying to break the spell. When he refocused, the vision of the pirate remained. "So how do I make this power work?" he asked.

"It be a matter of deep concentration, m'lad. Think of what ye want others to see or what ye be wantin' to make 'em do. When ye grasp the vision yerself, touch the brand and t'will be so."

"So you made the brand do that."

"Aye, t'was meself summonin' yer attention so I could give ye warnin' and instruction before ye reached land 'bout usin' the ...."

"The Rackham Curse?" offered Jack.

"Aye, The Rackham Curse, if that be what ye want to be callin' it," answered Calico Jack. "Now be so kind as to let me continue."

For the next several minutes, the pirate explained the workings of the curse and warned of the dangers awaiting the two boys. When the vision faded, Jack found himself sitting against the port side gunwale staring blankly at Kai who was standing with his arms folded across his chest.

"Guess you were talkin' to our dear dead friend," said Kai.

"Yeah. Pretty creepy. He explained how to use the curse. Said once we leave the boat, well, it's going to be tough getting to the Valley of the Kings." Jack's eyes narrowed as he stared at his friend.

"Whaddya starin' at?"

Jack felt the painful sting of the brand and touched it with his fingers while keeping his eyes trained on Kai. After a few seconds, Kai jumped from where he was standing, brushing and smacking at his arms and chest and yelling, "Get 'em off me. Get 'em off me!"

As Kai moved to jump overboard, Jack reached out and grabbed his friend by the arm. "Are you alright?"

Kai stared down, inspecting his chest. "Didn't you see 'em? There were spiders crawlin' all over me."

Jack nodded. "I saw them." He tapped the side of his head. "Up here."

"What's that supposed to mean?"

"I imagined them and made you see them too. I was practicing mind control."

"So I'm your guinea pig?"

"Sorry."

"You jerk. Had to pick spiders. You know I hate spiders." Kai continued brushing off his arms and chest. "Was it easy?"

"Yep."

"It seemed totally real. I could actually feel 'em on me."

"Sorry," said Jack.

"You said that already. Just don't do it again, butthead. Freaked me out," said Kai.

"I needed to practice. Spiders happened to be the first thing that crossed my mind. Captain Rackham said I'll have to use the curse to help us get through this quest. Thought I'd better try it out at least once."

"Got it. But no more spiders." Kai scratched again at his arms causing Jack to smile. "Did he tell you what we have to look out for? Any tips on how not to die?"

"He said the brand on my arm will burn if we go off course. Once we get deep into the jungle, we have to find a river and follow it to where he and Rachel are waiting. We're supposed to travel only during daylight."

"What're we supposed to do at night?"

"Camp out, I guess. Most of the predators are nocturnal, meaning they feed at night."

"I know what nocturnal means, moron. So we should stay huddled up in one place in the dark so we'll be an easy meal."

"A campfire should keep the critters away," answered Jack.

"Gonna be hot and humid travelin' during the day."

"Yep. It's going to be brutal."

On the third night, *The William* encountered angry seas with gale force winds and torrential rain. Jack and Kai worried that the rotted vessel would break apart but the ship sailed on unaffected and the decks and tattered sails remained dry through the storm while the wheel at the helm barely moved. The boys spotted land at daybreak on the fifth day, the ship sailing hard toward shore with no sign of slowing.

"Looks like our ghost ship's gonna make a crash landing," said Kai.

"Maybe we're supposed to jump overboard when we get to the shallows."

"Tough swim with that bag of gear. It ain't gonna float."

Jack ran to the bow, scanning the water on the lookout for submerged rocks or reefs. "I'd say we've got two minutes before we run out of water. Maybe we should move to the stern. If we feel the ship running aground, we'll jump off the port side."

"Why the port side?" asked Kai.

"The center mast is leaning toward starboard. If it snaps, it should fall to that side. I'm open for suggestions if you have something in mind but we're running out of time."

"Let's hold tight and see what happens."

The William cut through the breakers on a straight line, onto the wet sand, its prow poking out over the beach and stopped without a crash or skid.

"That was cool. Not even a bump," said Kai. "Guess we better get goin'."

Jack agreed and reached for the heavy duffel bag. As he hoisted the bag to his shoulder, the old ship shuddered and the masts crumbled into the surf.

"The ship's breakin' up, we gotta hurry," yelled Kai as he pushed Jack toward the gunwale.

The boys scrambled over the side, dropping to the sand below. When they were twenty yards from *The William*, they stopped and watched the old ship disintegrate into splintered beams and decking. The cracking and popping continued, even as chunks of the hull and deck drifted into the sea. Once offshore, a great plume of steam swirled upward from the water, and all traces of the ghost ship disappeared.

Jack knelt down and rummaged through the bag.

Whaddya lookin' for?" asked Kai.

"This," said Jack as he hoisted a small pouch attached to a leather drawstring.

"What's that?"

"It's the *Wind Jewel of Quetzalcoatl* that was part of the treasure. I don't want to leave it in the bag in case we end up ditching or losing it. This thing must hold some kind of power if Calico Jack wanted it so badly."

"But he's still got the *Serpent Dagger*," said Kai.

"Right, but I think the dagger is useless without the stone." Jack looped the drawstring around his neck, the large emerald now inside the pouch to hang against his chest. He held his hand up shading his eyes as he looked west. "We should try to get past those cliffs before nightfall."

Kai turned facing west. "I knew you were gonna say that. They're probably ten miles away."

"And a couple hundred feet high, maybe more. All rock." "We don't have climbing gear."

"We'll have to free climb and use our rope to pull the bag up behind us," said Jack.

"No way to hike around?"

"Nope."

"Figures," said Kai as he started trudging in the direction of the cliffs. "We're both gonna die. Hope you know that."

"Can't live forever," said Jack as he grabbed the duffel and joined up with Kai.

They reached the base of the cliffs by mid-morning and carefully searched for the area providing the best handholds. Jack tied off the straps of the duffel to a length of rope, and attached another rope to the end of the first before wrapping the other end around his waist. "If we've got to climb more than two hundred feet, we're going to have to leave the bag behind."

"If we gotta climb more than two hundred feet in this heat, we're buzzard food," said Kai as he started his ascent.

"Buzzard food," repeated Jack with a sigh as he reached for a crevasse in the rock face.

By noon, the temperatures hovered near one hundred degrees under cloudless blue skies. Slight breezes were rare. Time wore on, their muscles cramped painfully from dehydration, the water gone since the midway point of the climb, but they continued upward, reaching the top nearly four hours after they had started. Jack crawled to his knees, grabbed the rope, and hoisted the duffel from the ground below. Kai joined in to help as the bag bounced and swayed across the rocks. With the retrieval complete, the boys grabbed the remaining water from the bag, guzzled it down in a few seconds, and rested again in silence for several minutes.

Kai spoke up first. "I think we need to find more water and set up camp for the night."

"Should we set up here in the open or inside that tree line?"

"Inside the trees. We have to go that way to find water anyway."

"Looks like about a two-mile hike," said Jack.

"Then we'd better get walkin'. I'll carry the bag this time," said Kai as started moving west again. "At least we've got plenty of daylight left."

~X~

Calico Jack appeared from the shadows, causing an already jumpy Rachel to shriek. "Sorry me dear, never meant to give ye such a start," said the captain with a smirk.

"What do you want now?"

"Thought ye should know, yer friends be ashore and be makin' their way through the jungle now."

"How do you know that?" asked Rachel.

The dead pirate's lip turned up in a snarl. "'Tis for me to know, lass." With that, he moved back into the dense foliage, leaving Rachel alone by the campfire.

DAVID EBRIGHT

2
SHOOTING GALLERY

DURING THE DAY, they suffered through oppressive heat, humidity and maddening swarms of insects. At night, the bats, snakes and more ravenous insects, including blood-sucking mosquitoes the size of humming birds, came out. Soon after their long hike began, they learned to cover their exposed skin with mud to protect themselves from bites and stings, caking it on in thick layers across their necks and faces. The thick mud further reduced the harsh pain and swelling from previous bites. Kai's left eye had swollen shut but applying the black mud reduced the inflammation by half, leaving him a narrow slit to see through. They also learned to avoid contact with the ground at night or risk being gnawed by ants the size of a man's thumb as the frenzied creatures scavenged feverishly through the natural compost of fallen leaves and the decayed carcasses of small primates and rodents at the base of the trees.

They had covered nearly thirty miles by the end of the third day and, taking an early break, set up camp in a small clearing. As soon as the fire blazed and the palm hammocks were strung up, they boiled water and emptied pouches of instant soup into a small pot, before adding several strips of beef jerky.

"We're running out of food," said Jack. "There's no way to keep this pace up much longer without more protein and calories."

"What's left in the bag?" asked Kai.

"Enough grub for maybe one more day, a first aid kit, a few water bottles and the rope."

"Guess we'll have to learn how to hunt."

"We've got to find that river, maybe make a raft and fish for food," said Jack.

"The jungle's gettin' thicker. That's gonna slow us down big time."

"Maybe, but I think . . . did you hear something?" asked Jack.

Kai stood and walked to the edge of the clearing. He turned calmly facing Jack. Somebody's walkin' this way. I can see lights way back to the left. Hurry up, let's put the fire out before they see it."

Jack jumped to his feet and, using his hands as shovels, buried the campfire under moist dirt. Kai took the hammocks down, rolled them together and stuffed them under his arms along with the duffel. In less than five minutes, they had erased all of the most obvious signs of their presence and moved silently into the thick underbrush watching for the source of the noise to pass beyond their campsite.

Four men arrived in the small clearing vacated by Jack and Kai only thirty minutes earlier. Three were armed; the fourth had his arms bound behind his back. The prisoner wore a bloody white shirt torn at the collar, his face covered in bruises, one eye closed like an oozing plum. A man barked orders to the others in Spanish and the other two tied the prisoner to a tree on the west side of the clearing, ten feet from Jack and Kai. With their prisoner secured, two of the men set up camp and prepared a fire, making ready to settle in for the long night, while the third patrolled the perimeter sniffing for the source of lingering smoke and inspecting the flattened vegetation.

"What do we do now?" asked Kai.

"It's almost dark so I'm thinking we wait until they're asleep, cut their prisoner loose, and get out of here."

"How do you know that the guy tied up isn't the bad guy?"

"I don't. Not yet anyway."

"So how do we find out?"

"We'll ask him," said Jack.

"There you go. Why didn't I think of that?"

Two hours passed before two of intruders curled up to get some sleep. The third kept watch sitting on the ground in front of the fire with his arms wrapped around his knees, his weapon on the ground.

"Okay genius, they posted a guard. That changes everything," said Kai.

"Should we just move on and mind our business?"

"Can you use that mind control stuff on them?" asked Kai.

"I don't know if I can use it on three people at one time and since they're armed, now's not the time to experiment."

"I still think we're takin' a big chance lettin' that guy loose but hurry up and get this over with."

"Alright. Take the bag and walk west one hundred yards. I'll cut the guy free," said Jack.

Jack crawled to the base of the tree and stood carefully before reaching around with his left hand to cover the prisoner's mouth. In a whisper he said, "I'm cutting these ropes. Follow me into the jungle. Don't make a sound or you're dead. Got that?"

The man nodded his head, never taking his eyes off the now-sleeping guard seated next to the fire. After a few seconds, the man was loose, but remained completely still while Jack crawled off into the brush. Finally, the man turned away, crouched on all fours and silently followed in the direction that Jack had taken. He reached Jack and Kai several minutes later. Kai motioned for him to follow and the three traveled on in silence for nearly an hour. The mosquitoes were feasting on their exposed skin, the protective mud long gone, washed away by their sweat. They stopped to cake their faces and arms once more.

The man finally spoke. "Who are you guys? What are you doing in this jungle?"

Kai answered. "How'd you know we spoke English?"

"The big kid spoke to me in English, American, northeastern accent. You, on the other hand, have a slight trace of South Georgia – North Florida twang. Am I right?"

"Who are you?" asked Jack.

"I can't give that info. So what's your story? Two American kids in the middle of the Mexican jungle at night, miles from the coast."

"Can't give *that* info, but I'm hoping we didn't just let a drug dealer or gun runner loose by mistake," answered Jack.

"I'm an American ATF Agent, tracking weapons smuggled into Mexico from the U.S. I can't give my name, so you're going to have to take my word for it. I do appreciate your help. If those guys had had their way, I would have been shot and dumped in the middle of nowhere. Apparently, whoever runs the show for them wanted to learn what I'd found out so they were taking me in for what would have been a painful meeting. Bottom line, you two saved my life. It's your turn now. Tell me what you're up to and let's see if I can help."

"If we told you the truth, you wouldn't believe it. The short version is we're on our way to save a friend of ours who's being held hostage. If anyone finds out, well, she won't survive."

"So what I can I do to help?"

"Go in the opposite direction of us. We're headin' west," said Kai.

"If that's how you want it, fair enough, fellas. Good luck." After a quick round of handshakes, the agent moved off toward a thick stand of overgrowth. He paused and turned. "You guys have guts." With a brief wave, he disappeared into the jungle and Jack and Kai continued west, careful to remain quiet as they hiked through the dense foliage.

~X~

The brand on Jack's arm kept them on course but the lack of rest took its toll and Jack and Kai struggled as they hiked onward. They assumed the gun smugglers were busy scouring the jungle looking for their lost prisoner, while Jack and Kai pushed themselves to put plenty of distance between themselves and the abandoned campsite. Daylight was upon them.

"We're out of water," said Kai as he paused to massage his cramping legs. "I think I'm sweatin' half a gallon per minute."

"Yeah, we'll look for some soon. We're heading downhill and the jungle's not as thick. We should find a spring or something down below."

"Let's fold up that duffel now that it's mostly empty and use some rope to make it a backpack. My arms are achin', yours gotta be screamin'".

"Good idea," said Jack as he knelt to prepare the bag. "Wonder where the bad guys are? It's been pretty quiet, not that I'm complaining."

"Let's not try our luck. I'll feel better when we get some H2O into us and cover a few more miles," said Kai.

Jack knotted the strap and pulled the folded bag on over his shoulders. "Ready?"

"Suppose so."

They had walked and climbed downhill for another mile when they heard a ruckus from behind. Monkeys screeched and birds took flight from up above. Jack and Kai paused to listen. From not too far away came the sound of men stomping and rushing through the jungle, yelling to one another in Spanish. The boys turned and ran toward the valley, falling and sliding along the way. As they reached the bottom, the foliage cleared, revealing a wide expanse covered with rocks and boulders. It was a dry riverbed leaving no cover as they cut across the rocks to the opposite side. The voices grew louder and Jack's arm burned. He looked at the glowing red brand. They were off course. He stopped, turning slowly to see which way to go.

"What're you doin'? We gotta keep movin'. They're gonna catch us," pleaded Kai.

"We're off course," answered Jack.

"Who cares? They have guns. We can get back on the right path later. Right now we gotta find a place to hide."

Jack turned twenty degrees northwest and the burning stopped. He looked across the riverbed to see where the correct course would take them and smiled. "There's our hideout, Kai."

"What're you talkin' about?"

"There's a cave two hundred yards that way. We can make that."

They half-ran, half-stumbled across the riverbed, clambering up the loose rocks on the opposite side. When they reached the opening, chunks of rock pelted them as shots fired from across the dried up river nearly found their mark. They dove into the cave, rolling to the side as bullets raked the cave's entrance. They crawled back to the opening for a closer look. The three men were heading their way.

"It's a shootin' gallery! Ever been shot at before?" asked Kai.

Jack waved the flashlight's beam around the inside of the cave finally spotting a hole between the rocks. "Don't think so." He aimed the light at the hole and nodded. "You want to follow or go first."

"They're gainin' on us, already climbin' up the rocks," reported Kai from his lookout spot.

"In that case, you follow me," said Jack as he crawled away on all fours toward the gaping black hole. He stopped suddenly, causing Kai to bump into him. "There's probably bats down there."

"Yeah but bats don't carry guns."

"I can't see the bottom. Loop the rope off here and we'll scale down," said Jack.

"The bad guys will use it to follow us."

"So we take a chance and jump?"

Jack lowered himself hand over hand into the blackness, Kai trailing close behind, the rope swinging wildly, straining to support their weight. Sixty seconds into their descent, gunfire erupted, bullets pinging off the sidewalls of the vertical shaft. The boys stopped, flattening their bodies against the wall of damp rock, blindly hoping that the slugs would miss. All went quiet before they felt an upward tug on the rope.

"They're gonna climb down after us," whispered Kai.

"Or cut the …" Jack never finished the sentence and the boys fell into the blackness.

3
THE LOST RIVER

⌐THE WATER WAS SO COLD that their muscles cramped within seconds of their plunge, making it difficult to swim. The pair struggled to the edge, ten feet away, where they dragged themselves partway onto a narrow ledge to catch their breath. Kai rummaged through the bag, found another flashlight and aimed its beam over the sheer slime-covered walls of rock that surrounded them before shining the light toward Jack.

"I think we've stepped in it this time, Rackham," announced Kai.

Jack inched his way up to a standing position and reached down to help Kai. "You need to get all the way out of the water. Hypothermia might ruin your day. Come on, I'll move over."

Kai squeezed his way onto the ledge and stood. Like Jack, he rubbed his arms and legs briskly trying warm up and restore blood flow. "Ruin my day, huh. Well, we know there's got to be a way out; this water leads somewhere, hopefully not down."

"No way to swim around looking for an outlet, we wouldn't last ten minutes."

"Let's throw some of those food wrappers in the water and see if they're picked up by a current. That's how we find our way outta here," said Kai.

There was an outlet under the ledge, close to where

they stood. It was impossible to know how deep it flowed or if there would be places to surface for air along the way but climbing the sheer slippery walls of the cave to where they started was no option. They would take their chances underwater. Jack emptied the non-essentials from the survival bag and rolled it up tight before strapping it across his chest.

"Maybe I should go first, see if it lets out up ahead. No sense both of us drowning."

"Not happenin'. We stick together," said Kai.

Carrying dive knives and flashlights, they eased into the frigid water, filled their lungs with air and disappeared below the ledge and into the passageway.

There was no room to swim and they pulled themselves by hand over jagged rocks, through a space barely wide enough for their shoulders to fit, scraping the sides and top of the underwater tunnel. Finally, when it seemed there was no end, light beckoned. With the chill seeping into their bones and air running out, the boys shimmied through the final crevasse using the last of their strength. They surfaced inside an enormous cavern where they were caught up by the sweeping current of a fast-moving river. Fighting against the flow, Jack and Kai made it to the river's edge. Onshore, Jack sat up to take in their surroundings. Kai shivered alongside.

"This must be the river that we're supposed to find," said Jack.

"How do you know that?"

"The brand would burn if we were off course."

"Guess we'll go with that for now," said Kai as he looked around at the towering walls of sandstone. "Didja notice anything strange, bein' underground n' all?"

"It's daylight with no sky or sun over head," answered Jack.

"Yep, more weirdness."

"Pretty sure we're being watched too."

"You feel it? Thought maybe I was just bein' paranoid," said Kai. "Guess we'd better hike for a while and make up some lost time before we run out of energy."

"Too bad we can't make a raft and ride downriver."

Kai chuckled. "Yeah, like Huck Finn and Tom Sawyer."

"There's no sign of any trees to use, just a bunch of red-colored rock and some slimy moss, the Grand Canyon with a giant stone lid on it."

"Yep. Gonna be another long hike."

— X —

Rachel was bored. Calico Jack had left her alone except for brief visits at twilight. Now she looked forward to his arrival. After sunset, the pirate appeared.

"Ah, Miss Rachel, 'tis a relief to be findin' ye in such fine fettle. Will ye be needin' anythin', lass?"

She hesitated a moment. "Would you sit down and talk to me for a while?"

"Lonely are we? Why t'would be me honor an' pleasure to pass some time with ye."

"I want to know if you can see Jack and Kai. Are they safe?"

"Aye, a fair concern it be." The pirate moved toward the edge of the fire, across from where Rachel sat, and found a seat on a large rock. He smiled his blue eyes alert and piercing as he stared through the flames toward the sixteen-year-old girl. He started to speak but stopped abruptly as Rachel let out a squeal before reaching to cover her mouth with her hand.

Calico Jack stood, a look of concern crossed his face, but remained on the opposite side of the fire. "Whatever be the matter, dear girl?"

"Y. . . you . . ."

"Miss Rachel, trust that I mean ye no harm. I'll be takin' me leave so ye . . ."

"No. Wait. It's okay. I just can't believe . . . um, how much Jack looks like you," said Rachel. "You have the same features, blonde hair and blue eyes."

"Aye, the lad be a handsome devil fer sure," laughed the pirate. "But I daresay he be quite a bit bigger than meself."

Rachel smiled, trying to relax. "Are they safe? Are they still on their way?"

"You may be sure of it, lass. They be choice lads, though they had a time of it in the jungle. Ran across some scalawags they did, but outwitted 'em and found the river. They be makin' their way here even now."

"How long will it take them to find us?"

"Rest easy an' fret not. Might be a night or two yet to pass."

"But you can see them?"

"I be summonin' the images, aye."

"And Jack can do that too? He spoke to me through my mind while I was in the plane. He could see everything like he was there with me, you know, when I crashed, but there's been nothing since you brought me here."

"Aye, Jack still has the gift but I be blockin' his access to your mind."

"Why?"

The pirate's smile faltered. "Desperation drives him to this place on his mission to rescue ye. I be playin' on his sense of urgency and . . . fears."

"He's not afraid," challenged Rachel. "He's not afraid of anything."

"Not fer himself, dear girl, only for yer well bein'."

Rachel sighed deeply, remaining quiet for several seconds. "What are they doing now?"

"When last I . . . looked, they was approachin' the great city of the underworld."

Rachel waited for Calico Jack to explain. When greeted by silence, she changed the subject. "Why did you become a pirate?" she asked.

Calico Jack's face took on a sad, wistful look. "Aye, the sweet trade."

"The what?"

"Piracy. 'Twas known by many names but me favorite be . . . the sweet trade. A brash, raucous way of life, filled with adventure, sometimes violence, exhilaratin' to the very core. The call of 'Sails Ho', chasin' the merchant ships, the grapplin' hooks takin' hold of the prize, dividin' the booty, and the rum ... always there be rum."

"But knowing you would hang if caught, and obviously you were, why choose that kind of life?"

"What makes ye think it were a choice? I know how ye met young Jack an' how he rescued ye from that man what caught ye stealin'."

"That's not the same," said Rachel, plainly annoyed.

"Ah, but it is. Had the Rackhams not taken ye in, would ye have continued as a thief?"

"That man said awful things to me and . . ."

"You bein' a homeless orphan stole his money to get revenge, I suppose."

"I was hungry. He was a filthy creep. It was . . ."

"'T'was still yer choice, ye bein' desperate, hungry, angry, vengeful . . ."

Rachel interrupted. "It *WAS* my choice to steal from him and it was wrong. I could have gotten help, but I wanted to get even for what he said, so I did something terrible. No matter how you look at it, it was wrong and my circumstances and his . . . creepiness did not justify my actions. If Jack hadn't come along when he did, well, somehow you already know what happened, but things could have ended badly. There. Are you satisfied?"

"Ah, but look at how yer fortunes changed because of yer thievery."

"So you believe in taking whatever you want."

"Aye, and givin' no quarter along the way."

Rachel stood and walked around the fire, stretching her arms and legs looking off into the jungle, the sounds of the night intensifying. "So you have no regrets."

"I have many, lass. Tried, did I, to play the gentleman an' settle into the lubber's life. Gave up me piratin' for a time an' accepted a pardon from that rogue Gov'ner, Woodes Rogers. Me an' Anne wanted a family, but sadly t'wasn't meant to be."

"You mean Anne Bonny, the pirate?"

"One and the same but she weren't a pirate 'til we'd run off to go upon the account."

"Go upon the account?" asked Rachel.

"Another name fer the sweet trade, or piratin' if ye prefer."

"So tell me your story," said Rachel.

The dead pirate smiled. "Maybe another time, Miss Rachel. 'Tis a dreadful long tale."

Rachel sat down, spread her hands wide, motioning to the surrounding jungle, "I'm in no particular rush and, as you can see, have nowhere to go and obviously nothing important planned. Tell me everything . . . Captain Rackham."

Calico Jack turned to leave and stopped. After a pause, he shrugged out of his waistcoat, removed his cutlass and flintlocks and pulled his hat and bandana from atop his thick blond hair. He moved close to the fire, and held his hands out over the leaping flames. "Always loved a blazin' fire. Pity I can no longer feel its warmth." He stroked his beard absently as he locked eyes with Rachel. His eyes seemed warm and friendly, as if somehow a spark of life remained. "Me story," he said as he sat down. "Me story ye shall hear, because in a few days' time ye shall meet Calico Jack, the livin', breathin' Captain Calico Jack Rackham." His smile spread. "An' never were I able to say no to a woman, not in life an' apparently not even in death." He laughed, as he touched the kerchief covering the raw skin left from the hangman's noose. "A boy of twelve were I when first I put to sea . . ."

Kai looked down at his *Freestyle* dive watch. It was coming up on eight o'clock and, so far, there was no sign of nightfall. The path alongside the fast-moving river was wider now, the sides sloped upward more gently with scattered outcroppings of sagebrush and small scrappy trees. In the distance he could hear a steady static noise, which grew louder as they hiked along. He still couldn't shake the feeling of being watched. Twenty minutes later the sound had changed to an ear-splitting roar and Jack stood at the end of the pathway staring at a raging waterfall that dropped at least a hundred feet. It was useless trying to yell over the noise and the pair resorted to hand gestures. Jack pointed to a set of well-worn ladder rungs embedded in the vertical rock next to the gushing downward flow of white water and Kai shook his head no. Kai sighed when Jack knelt down to climb the rickety rungs.

After giving Jack a five-minute head start, he crawled across the edge of the rock, swung his legs over the side and felt around for the first foothold. Twenty steps from the top, far enough below the point where the water turned down from the riverbed above, Kai felt the heavy spill of the waterfall. It felt like fire hoses strategically aimed toward his head and ribs, something sinister trying to knock him from the rungs into the churning mist below. He continued on, tucking his head toward his shoulder to breathe through his mouth and squeezed his eyes shut against the pounding water, climbing downward by feel, one hand and one foot always in contact with the disintegrating rungs.

Several minutes passed, the pummeling water changed over to a heavy spray and his progress improved. He could see a wide flat surface below and Jack waiting, looking up. Finally his feet reached solid rock and he moved off to the side out of the heaviest of the waterfall's spray. After stretching his arms with some windmill motions and squeezing and opening his hands to make the cramps go away, Kai nodded to Jack, giving him the 'let's go' sign and took the lead.

It took a while to get far enough from the falls to communicate without yelling. Kai picked a spot off to the side, a flat spot below an overhang of rock a dozen feet higher than the pathway. He peeled off his soaked shirt before sitting down to lean against the smooth side of the rock face. "Well, Rackham, that was fun."

Jack wrung out his own shirt and laid it out on top of a small prickly shrub. "I keep wondering if we're going to have to retrace our steps to get home."

"There's a comforting thought. Of course if we succeed, Calico Jack isn't going to have a ghost ship to send us home on either."

"I thought about that too. Guess we'll deal with that

when the time comes."

"Well, if we don't die gettin' there . . . uh, where's the bag?"

"It's either at the bottom of the waterfall or somewhere downstream. I was partway down the ladder when the pounding water got to be too much. I had to dump it. There wasn't much left inside anyway."

"Maybe it washed up nearby. I'll walk down the trail and check. I'm gettin' kinda hungry and I think there was enough food left to get us through today," said Kai. "Didja notice it's not gettin' dark?"

"If it's going to stay light, do you want to keep moving for a few more hours?" asked Jack as he stood and shook out his shirt.

"Might as well."

They trudged on for three more hours, never finding the bag. "Guess we'll pull up a rock and get some rest," said Jack.

"Yep. Maybe I'll dream about a nice thick steak with a big old fat baked potato . . ."

Jack interrupted him. "Do you see that?"

"What?"

"Looks like something's burning up ahead."

"Let's check it out."

They found a campfire, food skewered and cooking above the flames and a pair of rolled up blankets each stuffed with fruit. An old flintlock sat atop the blankets.

"So you started as a twelve-year-old stowaway, traveled all over the world on merchant ships, were captured by pirates and decided to join them, worked your way up to quartermaster and eventually stole the ship from your last captain during a mutiny that you led," said Rachel.

"Aye but ye see, that rogue Vane weren't chasin' after . . ."

"You mentioned that, he didn't want to attack any large vessels but the men were restless for battle."

"No they wasn't lookin' fer a battle, dear girl, they wanted to take gold, fresh food, and rum from merchant ships, not fight. We was pirates, none've us wantin' to be floatin' at sea playin' hidey seek from the blasted King's navy. Methinks Vane wanted to give up the trade, gone soft n' timid he did. The men would have none of it an' so it was time to change n' give Vane an' his loyal mates what they was lookin' fer, peace an' quiet."

"So you marooned them."

"Aye, an' left them with full provisions, weapons, even a long boat we did. Didn't want 'em to die, child, but we was . . . pirates, not sailor boys."

"I guess I understand. It was the way things were done in those days," said Rachel.

"Exactly. It . . ." Calico Jack stopped looked up to the sky, his ear turned away from Rachel. After a moment he smiled and turned his face back toward the fire, a look of satisfaction on his face.

"What's the matter?"

"The lads be soon to join us, lass. They found the victuals I left for them and they now be restin' for the night." He stood from the fire and gathered his things. "My dear, Rachel ye should do the same. Rest plenty as the quest begins soon." The pirate donned his hat, slung his waistcoat over his shoulder, nodded and with a slight smile, turned toward the jungle. His shape vanished into the mist, as if pulled from where he stood.

X

Jack and Kai relaxed next to the campfire, using the blankets as pillows. Their meal had been tasty and filling. Kai busied himself checking out the old weapon. "You sure this is the one our not-so-friendly corpse carried?" he asked.

"He carries a pair and I'm positive that that's one of them," said Jack.

"Usin' it like a callin' card, huh?"

"I think he's letting us know we're getting close."

After a brief silence Kai put the weapon aside and sat up. "Still think Rachel's okay?"

"She's not the one I'm worried about right now, but yes, I think she's fine," said Jack.

"You're worried about everyone back home."

"Yeah, but mostly it's Pop. My note gave away too much information and I'm thinking he's going to try to find us."

"He's too old and too smart to chase us through a jungle."

"You forgot stubborn, Kai. That's the trade-off for old and that's why I'm worried."

"Let's get some rest. Pop's fine. Hopefully we'll find Rachel and Calico Jack tomorrow," said Kai as he leaned back and closed his eyes.

~THEY CONTINUED THROUGH the massive cavern. By mid-morning Kai noticed a brightly colored bird with a long sweeping tail circling continuously from high above as they hiked the path alongside the indigo-colored underground river. The bird's head was brilliant blue with a center streak of green that continued from the throat down across the middle of its wings which mixed with the color turquoise. Its chest looked like a perfectly shaped bib of blue ending in a semi-circular pattern bordering a full belly of crimson. The beak appeared to be made of gold when the surrounding light caught it at just the right angle.

Eventually the river widened, emptying into an enormous lake. At its center sat an ancient city made of stone, surrounded by great walls. Inside a towering structure spiraled upward, wide at the base, stepping back symmetrically to a flat narrow peak nearly two hundred feet above the other buildings. Carved into the stone were images of vicious serpents, their heads wreathed in feathers, their gaping mouths filled with threatening fangs. A pair of carvings, one on each side of where the arched gates would have stood centuries ago, depicted a great warrior king; arms stretched upward, one hand holding the sun, in the other, the *Serpent Dagger* of Quetzalcoatl.

There was no sign of activity from where Jack and Kai stood until a lone canoe drifted toward them in a straight line from the island to the edge of the bank in front of them. The boys climbed inside.

Kai spoke up first. "Think this is a trap?"

"Probably."

"Knew you were gonna say that. So this is some kind of forgotten Aztec city?"

"I'm guessing it's got to be Tenochtitlan. It used to be in the middle of Lake Texcoco but after Cortes conquered the Aztecs, the Spaniards drained the lake and built Mexico City.

"We're way south of Mexico City," said Kai.

"You're right. And none of this makes sense. I read as much as I could about the Valley of the Kings once I found out where Calico Jack took Rachel. Its history is created from mythology, so who knows what the true story might be."

They paddled toward the island, straying from their southerly hiking course. Halfway across Jack felt the slow burn of the brand on his arm. He dipped it into the river for a few minutes before telling Kai what he had read about the formerly grand Aztec city.

In 1519 a light skinned stranger reached the coast of Mexico. Hernan Cortes had crossed the ocean with 11 ships and more than 600 men. The Aztec emperor, Montezuma II, believed this strange visitor to be Quetzalcoatl, foretold in the legends handed down for centuries promising the sun god's return. For a short time the Spaniards and Aztecs lived together peacefully, until the Spaniards were fully recovered from their voyage and jungle march. Cortes forced Montezuma to give up control to act only as the symbolic leader of his people. Tensions escalated and, in 1520, war broke out.

Montezuma, at Cortes's urging, addressed his people from the palace balcony, begging for peace, but the Aztec Emperor was mortally wounded by a stray arrow. Immediately following Montezuma's death, the Spanish slaughtered the Aztec warriors and enslaved the survivors of the murderous rampage.

Within days, the Aztec population was reduced to only a few thousand. All seemed hopeless. Cortes had annihilated all potential threats from among the citizenry. His rule was brutal and extreme and the people suffered through deplorable conditions.

At noon on a summer day in 1522, a stranger appeared in the center of the city at the base of the great stepped pyramid. He wore a hooded robe that hid his face, hands and feet. Spanish soldiers were ordered to arrest him but as they encircled him with weapons drawn, he disappeared, fading into the solid rock of the massive structure. Taking advantage of this distraction, the Aztec people charged through the city, overwhelming their captors, butchering them in the streets. With most of the soldiers now dead or hiding in the jungle, they climbed the hewn stones of the great monument, eyes focused upward, searching for the mysterious visitor.

He appeared at the very peak, the hooded robe gone, revealing the head and upper torso of a snake, feathers jutting from around his neck, human hands reaching up toward the sun and fire escaping his mouth with every flick of his serpent tongue. The earth trembled under a blinding flash of light, followed by a catastrophic explosion. In that instant, the stranger, the people, the towering pyramid, and the great city itself, disappeared. King Quetzalcoatl had returned.

They jumped into knee deep water, dragged the canoe ashore and walked toward the city's main entrance. Other than the bird circling in the distance, there was still no sign of life. Inside the walls a vast city spread out before them with the great stepped pyramid in the center. A huge slab of polished yellow metallic rock, twice the size of a large coffin, lay at the base of the towering monument.

Kai looked around, and then turned to face Jack. "I think this is your lost city and this," he patted his hand on the massive yellow slab, "is one ginormous hunk of gold."

"Looks like gold. I think this is where they had their, uh, social gatherings, where they cut out warrior hearts and . . ."

"No way. You're makin' that up, Rackham," said Kai.

"The Aztecs, according to history, uh, practiced human sacrifice."

"I think we should get outta here then. This place is creepin' me out. Never shoulda jumped in that can . . ."

"It's a lost civilization. They're all gone. Disappeared five hundred years ago," said Jack.

"Yeah, well if you turn around you'll see they're back and don't look awfully thrilled to have company."

And there they were. Hundreds of them, armed with knives, clubs, long poles and a tool that looked like some type of hammer, all pointed at Jack and Kai.

"Thoughts? Ideas?" asked Kai. "We're outnumbered about five hundred to one. Whaddya say we come up with a useful plan. Maybe somethin' that'll keep us alive."

Jack kept his eyes on the restless crowd assembled two hundred yards away. "We still have an opening. Maybe we can outrun them, like we did with those zombies last summer."

"That was only four against two and they were dead guys. Slow dead guys. These odds really suck."

"I was kidding. Time to try The Rackham Curse, see how or if it works," said Jack. "What can I make them all think at the same time?"

"Make 'em think about anything but spiders."

Jack reached over with his left hand, covering the brand on his right arm and looked out over the crowd as they advanced slowly toward the pair. Thunder suddenly boomed and lighting flashed, accompanied by swirling winds. The mob retreated, shielding their faces with their arms against the creature now standing before them. Kai stared ahead at the half-man, half reptile, a ring of feathers surrounding the neck as its viper tongue flamed.

"You did it, Jack. You scared 'em off. Dude, that's incredible,"

"I didn't do it, Kai. Never even touched the brand. THAT is King Quetzalcoatl, the Aztec sun god, the real deal. I'm sure of it."

"Stop foolin' around."

The reptile-thing raised its arms and spoke to the crowd in a thunderous voice. Kai stared as everyone dispersed, walking backwards, never taking their eyes away from the half-human. As they retreated the reptilian creature turned to face Jack and Kai.

"Okay, you can make it go away now. The coast is almost clear," said Kai.

"I told you, I didn't make him appear. It's King Quetzalcoatl."

Kai laughed. "Okay, if you say so. Let's . . ."

The shape changed. A man stood in front of them, normal except for the way he was dressed. He wore a skirt-like wrap made from an animal skin and was bare chested with a thick collar of gold that extended to his sternum and across the top of his shoulders, both arms adorned with wide golden bands embedded with colorful jewels. He was tall, his posture perfect, his features sharp, a strong chin, prominent nose and eyes the color of onyx. His black hair was pulled tight against his scalp tied into a thick ponytail that reached his waist. Holding up his hand, as if demanding silence, he spoke. "You are not of this world. Leave or you will die."

Jack stepped forward a few paces. "You can speak our language."

"I speak every language."

"You sent the canoe, to get us to enter the city. Why?"

"To warn you."

Kai spoke up. "Jack says you're King Quetzalsomething. Is that true?"

"I am Quetzalcoatl. Now return to your homeland and tell no one of what you have found this day."

"With all respect, your highness, we have to continue to the Valley of the Kings to rescue our friend Rachel. She is being held by a, um, an evil spirit. He is demanding, in exchange for the safe return of our friend, that we travel back in time almost three hundred years to save him from execution." Jack looked at Kai and nodded before continuing. "We give you our word that no one will ever hear of your city from us."

The King walked over to Jack, to within a few inches of his face and stared upward into his eyes. He then did the same with Kai, though Kai kept inching backwards. Finally, he spoke, slowly, machinelike. "I must protect my people, no matter the cost. They have suffered much, nearly exterminated. It will never happen again. But I do believe you when you promise to keep the secret of my people. You are both honorable young men, brave with strong spirits. This quest of which you speak will surely lead to your deaths but I am confident that you will die bravely."

"We know the risk," answered Jack. "We're also not

ready to accept the outcome that you predict, again, with all due respect."

"We've been through life and death stuff before. We're used to it," said Kai as he tried to act brave and unconcerned.

"I anxiously await the outcome of your venture. I will accompany you to the Valley. Perhaps I can be of some assistance along the way."

"Well, King Quetzel, uh, Quexel, Qui … uh, I think that would be fine," said Kai.

"From this point forward, refer to me as Q," said the Aztec King, smiling now for the first time. "First, let us enjoy a feast before we begin our short journey." He turned from Jack and Kai and shouted out a series of orders before clapping his hands three times. Within seconds the city square bustled with activity, the Aztecs rushing about laughing and chattering excitedly in a language not heard by outsiders for five centuries.

~5~
THE WHEEL

~FOR HOURS THEY FEASTED ON jungle delicacies, exotic meats, desserts made from nuts, flowers and cane, and fruit juices that changed flavor with each sip. The Aztecs told stories, acting out key points for their honored guests with great enthusiasm as Quetzalcoatl interpreted their meaning. The mood was festive, enthusiastic, dominated by laughter and song. A party five hundred years overdue.

After the feast, Jack and Kai managed to sleep for a few hours inside a pair of small cave-like rooms on mattresses made of animal skins stuffed with dried sweet-smelling grasses. When they awoke, they found sacks stuffed with food for their hike. "Check these out," said Kai. "They have straps like the backpacks we use, with loop fasteners to keep 'em closed tight. Guess they haven't invented zippers yet."

"Wonder where King, I mean Q is hanging out. He said he wanted to go with us."

"Maybe he changed his mind. Notice there's no sign of any people?"

Jack laughed. "Partied out, I guess."

"Do we wait around or should we get movin'?"

"I think we're good to go. Q won't have trouble finding us."

They moved out of the city, climbed into the canoe

and paddled across the lake to the opposite shoreline. With the two barely ashore, the canoe spun and returned under its own power to the island city's shore.

"Guess we really didn't have to paddle," said Kai as they turned to go.

The trail was an easy walk for the first few hours turning more difficult as the path inclined, eventually becoming painfully steep and narrow as they exited the rocky cavern and entered the dense humid jungle. Finally the grade leveled out to a tangle of roots, vines and huge yellow flowers with petals the size of small cars. At last they reached a clearing where a narrow stream cut through its center. In the distance they heard a waterfall. From the sound they could tell it was much smaller than the one inside the cavern with its rickety ladder.

"Let's take a break," said Kai as he sat down at the clearing's edge.

"Good idea. I think we have to be getting close by now. Q said it wasn't too far."

"Yeah but he just waves his arms or slithers or does whatever when he travels. Did you see that bird up there? I think it's the same one we saw before."

"Didn't notice. We should probably set up camp soon. The sun's fading."

"Yeah, I'm kinda tired anyway. This seems like a good spot," said Kai. "I'll gather up some vines and leaves for the hammocks, you see what you can find for the fire."

From overhead came the sound of pitched squawking as the bird seen circling overhead soared toward them as if attacking. Jack and Kai dove for cover as the bird landed on a thick branch above where they had ducked. In seconds, the bird transformed into King Quetzalcoatl who stood with his arms crossed over his chest looking down at the boys. He laughed as he addressed them. "You are too close now to stop. Your friend waits near the waterfall next to a pool of clear water, a short walk from this place."

Kai's face lit up. "Q, you've been following us, pretending to be a bird?"

"Yes. The bird is known as a Quetzal, named after me, of course."

"And it just happens to have a solid gold beak," said Kai.

"Well, I am a king. Enough of this. I will lead you to your friend now. Another has just joined her. I suspect him to be the evil one that you spoke of. I will destroy . . . "

"Wait a minute," interrupted Jack. "I'm not sure how this works. He's my dead ancestor and he came back from the past to get my help. If you, uh, destroy him, does that mean I won't exist?"

"If he is already dead, you are probably safe," said Q.

"Let's not take that chance, just in case."

"As you wish."

◯—X—◯

"Miss Rachel pleased be I to report that Jack and Kai be arrivin' soon," said Calico Jack as he crossed to the fire pit from the jungle's edge.

"When?"

"In mere moments, lass."

"You're telling me this now? I look terrible!"

"Aye, after a week in the jungle . . ."

"I can't believe this . . ." There was a rustling off to her right.

"Rachel!" Jack ran past the pirate, wrapped his arms around her lifting her off her feet. "You're okay." He set her down, kissed the top of her head then grabbed her face in both hands and kissed her mouth, forehead and cheeks a dozen times.

"Ahem. You two realize you have an audience," said Kai, trying not to laugh.

"Kai!" Rachel let go of Jack and moved over to hug her friend. "You're here, finally, you're both here. I was so worried. I didn't think I would ever see either of you again. How did you find me?"

Jack walked over to face Captain Rackham. He held his arm out straight showing the brand of Calico Jack. "This kept us from getting lost. Didn't do much to keep us alive, but here we are. So what's the next step?"

"Right to business is it?"

"This business needs to be finished. Fast."

"Indeed it shall," answered Calico Jack, his left eyebrow raised in amusement.

The Quetzal bird landed on Kai's shoulder startling Rachel. "This is Q," said Kai. "He's one of us. Sort of."

"One of us?"

"He started following us a few days ago and yesterday decided to, uh, hang out."

"It's the most beautiful bird I've ever seen. The tail feathers, they must be three feet long. The beak . . . is it gold?"

"Gold? Uh huh. That's 'cause this bird's a king . . . uh, in real life," said Kai.

"King? What are you talking about, Kai?"

"Long story that'll hold until later. Looks like Jack wants to get this adventure goin' now, before he takes Calico Jack's head off. The two of 'em don't get along so well."

"Yes, let's get them separated before this blows up," said Rachel.

Kai walked over, nudging his way between Jack and

the pirate. Q took a three turn flight around the clearing before returning to land, this time on Rachel's shoulder. "C'mon, guys. Let's figure out what we're supposed to do so we can get home," said Kai.

"Okay. You're right. We need to get this done." Jack looked into the captain's eyes. "If you cross us . . . "

"Enough, lad! What gain'd there be fer me should I betray ye?" Calico Jack paced, clearly frustrated. "I should have asked ye to rescue me n' me crew 'stead of takin' Miss Rachel."

Kai shook his head. "Duh. Ya think?"

"Would ye have tried?"

"Honestly, I doubt it," replied Jack. "Rachel could've been killed in that crash. If that had happened, well, it didn't so . . . here we are. What do we do now?"

The pirate hung his head, clasped his hands behind his back, and paced again. He stopped and turned, facing Jack, Kai and Rachel. He removed his hat and tossed it absently to the ground before clearing his throat. "Indulge me, if ye please." His eyes turned upward, focusing on something distant. A mournful sigh escaped from deep inside before he spoke. "'Twas a gift . . . an' a curse . . . watchin' me son Jacob grow up from . . . where I were, an' me bein' dead an' all. His mum, me dear Anne Bonny, spent many a fine evenin' tellin' him stories of me, makin' him believe me to be brave n' mighty. She passed away one night, dreamin' she were at sea again, at me very side, 'board a ship ridin' low from the weight of its prize. A wonderful dream it were. An' years later, 'twas me sorrow to see me son pass on as well. Me son's children, and theirs, and theirs – born into the world to live and breathe . . . and die, generations of Rackhams for almost three hundred years. An' watch them all did I, them no longer knowin' a wee bit 'bout Calico Jack Rackham. Avast I watched yer grandfather, like so many Rackhams before him. His beard took to turnin' white 'bout the time his treasurin' days commenced. Aye, devil a doubt 'twas torture for me watchin' him from me . . . darkness whilst he studied charts n' journals. Then he found all manner of booty, an' built up his sizeable fortune, a true Rackham fortune. This man ye call Pop, traced his ancestry, he did, an' discovered his lineage included a certain pirate, namely me. An' then a new Rackham were born, a Jack Rackham. As ye grew up, he told ye tales of buccaneers, an' buried treasure, the high seas, an' Calico Jack an' how ye be me descendant. While ye were yet a wee lad, he found me copper plates engraved with directions to me own treasure. 'Twas then I started makin' me plans, believin' that at last, there be hope. Me help would come from one wee lad, another Jack Rackham, though ye ain't so wee no more."

An eerie silence fell over everyone as Calico Jack paused. He cleared his throat a few times, fidgeted, pulled at his kerchief, and adjusted his brace of flintlocks. Twice he opened his mouth to speak but stopped.

"I don't believe it," said Rachel.

"Believe what?" asked Jack.

"Captain Calico Jack Rackham here is getting choked up and sentimental about things."

"I don't believe it," said Jack.

"Rachel already said that," added Kai.

The three looked at the pirate. Kai finally spoke up. "So the deal is, you're a fraud. You actually care about the Rackhams and Rachel and now you're having second thoughts about this rescue scheme of yours because you know there's a chance we're all gonna die."

"'Tis true. An' I count ye equally as one to care 'bout, young Kai."

"Didja get tired of killin' people? Is that the problem?"

"You're having second thoughts? Really? All of us

came *this* close to getting killed these past two weeks because of you and *NOW* you're rethinking this?" asked Jack.

The captain looked down at his shifting feet, his hands clasped behind his back. Finally, he looked Jack in the eye, his chest puffed and chin pointed firmly, the picture of authority. "Aye, 'twas an unforgivable blunder. Ye shan't risk more on account of me."

Jack sighed. "We're past that now. Rachel's okay, we have help that you don't even know about and we're going to rescue you on the condition that you and Anne Bonny give up the pirate trade. Kai, do you agree?"

"I'm in."

"Rachel?"

"We've made it this far," she said.

"There you go, Captain Rackham. We have a rescue party assembled and, after some decent food and rest, we'll be ready to roll," said Jack. He turned to see Q nuzzling against Rachel's ear. "Q knock it off or I'll roast you like a chicken over that fire."

The bird turned from Rachel, raised his wings in a threatening gesture and let loose with a plume of fire from its open beak. Rachel shrieked and ducked off to the side causing Q to lose his grip on her shoulder which, in turn, changed the trajectory of the flame that streaked past Jack, missing him by inches.

"Come here, Q. It's okay, he didn't mean it," said Kai, his arm extended gently toward the bird. "Jack, you're forgettin' who you're dealin' with here, dude."

"Keep that thing away from me," yelled Rachel. "A fire-breathing bird. What next?"

"Uh, time travel . . . with a corpse and an Aztec King?" said Kai with a smirk as the bird landed on his shoulder.

"What manner of beast be this?" shouted Calico Jack.

"Relax, Captain. This is Quetzalcoatl, King of the Aztecs and the original owner of one *Serpent Dagger* that we're both very familiar with. He's a shape-shifter," said Jack.

"Show 'em," said Kai.

Kai was knocked to the ground as Quetzalcoatl made his grand appearance in a cloud of bright blue sparkling smoke. "You could have jumped off my arm first, you moron," said Kai as he got to his feet, rubbing his arm.

Quetzalcoatl stood, his arms folded across his muscular chest, his neck encircled with the thick necklace of gold, and the splendid bejeweled bracelets on his wrists which nearly covered his massive forearms. "I am Quetzalcoatl, the Serpent King of the Aztecs," he said as he looked at Rachel.

"We call him Q. It's easier," said Kai.

"W . . . w . . . well hi," said a clearly flustered Rachel.

"Perfect. He's gonna hit on your girl and she's gonna get all . . . wonky," said Kai.

"That's easy enough to solve," said Jack as he reached toward the brand on his arm. A moment later Rachel backed away terrified, stifling a scream. "It's okay," said Jack. "He won't hurt you. Stay with me or Kai at all times." He turned and raised an eyebrow toward Kai. "Right, Kai?"

Kai laughed. "Absolutely."

Later Jack would tell Kai that he had put the image of a worm-riddled carcass in Rachel's mind in place of the obviously attractive Aztec. Q, on the other hand, would never understand why she avoided him from that moment on.

Jack sat beside Calico Jack while everyone enjoyed a meal of roasted wild boar and fruit. The pirate had not joined the others at the great spread of food that Q had provided. Everyone knows dead men tell no tales, they also don't eat.

"So what can we expect once we get there?" asked Jack.

The pirate shrugged and looked away.

"That's it? You don't know?"

"Told ye, I did. I'll not exist in me present form once ye move into me real time. I won't know ye or yer friends, an' nothin' 'bout yer mission. 'Twill be livin' n' breathin' tryin' to survive an' save Anne an' me crew from hangin'. 'Tis all I know," said the pirate.

"But you know how we get back to your time from here."

"Aye, that I do, lad.' Calico Jack sighed heavily. "Once I show ye, an' ye cross over, well, reckon we won't be family no more."

"Yeah we will and still dysfunctional. When we meet in your time, I'll make you understand somehow. Maybe if I show you the *Serpent Dagger* and tell you about Fishtail Cay you'll know that we found your hiding place. That's when I'll explain that I traveled from the future to rescue you," said Jack. "There's also the Rackham Curse, don't forget. If I have to use it, well, that's only fair."

For the next thirty minutes they discussed strategy. Jack, Kai and Rachel would have to find clothing from that time period as soon as they crossed into 1720. Their cargo shorts, hiking boots, dive watches and T shirts would stand out as odd among the locals.

"Do you know someone that might be able to help if we get into trouble?"

"Port Royal be a den of thieves and cutthroats, Jack. Ye can't be trustin' anyone 'cept maybe . . ., nah, 'tis . . . well, maybe."

"Maybe what? Who?"

"Ah, he's but a lad, younger'n yerself."

"Can he be trusted?"

"Aye. He's got a good head on his shoulders that one and he be a hard worker, smart. Keeps his eyes n' ears open and his mouth shut, he does."

"Okay this is good. Where do we find him and what's his name?" asked Jack.

"His mum n' pap owns the sundry store next to me favorite tavern, The Devil's Elbow, on the west side near to the wharf. Always bought me provisions from 'em I did and that lad were right quick about loadin' me ship and leavin' me with nary a worry about him shortin' me. Each voyage I give 'im a gold piece for loadin' I did. Aye, tell the lad t'was Calico Jack what sent ye to him."

"What's his name?"

"Tinnermon. Bennett Tinnermon."

"Okay. So we look for this kid Bennett. What else do we need to know before we go?"

The pirate looked away and sighed before answering. "There be a vicious scalawag, the one what took such pleasure with the lash against me back. He's evil. Dare say he could be Beelzebub's Quartermaster, that one. The rogue has himself a thick ugly red scar down the one side of his face through his eye and mouth where a cutlass sliced him. Mind what I be tellin' ye now, stay away from that bilge rat, no matter what," said Calico Jack.

"We'll do our best. Time to get some rest, I'm beat," said Jack as he stood to walk away. He turned, then paused and stuck out his hand. "We're going to get this done."

Captain Rackham reached out, clasped Jack's hand between his own and managed a brief smile. "Aye, there be no doubt, lad, after all, yer a Rackham.

X

Calico Jack led the way as they left the clearing, walking on an angle toward the falls. He stopped to one side of the cascade. "Here we be," he announced. "Hold tight to the rocks, and slide in behind the water. This be where the time portal be hidden."

"Another cave," complained Kai as he squeezed his way into the opening.

It wasn't much of a cave, in fact, as it was not much bigger than a walk-in closet, barely enough space for the four of them to fit. Q was perched on Kai's shoulder. "It's all rock. What do we do now?" asked Rachel.

The pirate looked at the brightly colored bird. "Would ye mind showin' the way, your highness?"

Quetzalcoatl spread his wings, leapt from Kai's shoulder and flew straight through the rock. "Any questions?" asked Calico Jack as he turned and followed Q.

Kai was next, followed by Rachel and Jack. After several seconds of weightlessness and blurred vision, they found themselves standing in the middle of a lush garden in front of massive stone wheel. The face of the wheel was engraved with unfamiliar symbols.

Captain Rackham moved next to Jack and handed him the *Serpent Dagger.* "We shall require the use of the *Wind Jewel* for this step. Return it to the dagger when the deed is done."

Quetzalcoatl, now in human form and dressed as a royal warrior, stretched out his hand with his palm facing up. "I shall use the jewel to open the past."

Jack removed the gem from the leather pouch that hung from his neck and handed it over. He stared ahead as Quetzalcoatl turned to the giant wheel, placing the jewel inside an empty slot at the center. It was a perfect fit, as Jack expected. With no effort, Q spun the enormous stone in a counter-clockwise motion and stopped it at a series of now-flaming numerals. Quetzalcoatl looked over at the pirate and nodded slightly before removing the gemstone and handing it back to Jack. "It is time," announced the king.

Calico Jack approached the kids. "Me fate rests with me most able an' brave . . . friends. Forgive me roguish behavior these past weeks, 'twas desperation, though I find meself havin' second thoughts even now."

"You're not goin' with us?" asked Kai.

"No, lad. As I 'splained to young Jack, when the three of ye cross over, I'll not exist in this form or time. Alas, this old dead scalawag shall be of no help to ye."

"So this is it?"

"Aye."

"We'll come through for you, Captain Rackham." Kai put his hand on Calico Jack's shoulder and squeezed once before moving away.

Rachel felt a lump in her throat. The dead pirate had put her life at risk to get what he'd wanted, but had also taken good care of her in the jungle. She had gotten to know him, better than anyone, and knew deep down, Calico Jack Rackham was not the evil cutthroat he pretended. Her eyes filled with tears as she realized this would be a final goodbye. In an odd sort of way, she would miss him.

Sensing her thoughts, Calico Jack moved closer and whispered in her ear. "'Tis true what ye be thinkin'. Ne're was the time when Captain Jack ever took a life. On that ye have me oath. Now be off with ye, lass," he said with a sad smile.

Quetzalcoatl stepped to the right side of the wheel and gave it a shove. It opened with ease. Inside the gaping star-filled portal, bright constellations and planets moved as if choreographed, all beckoning, waiting to swallow them.

Kai and Rachel stood beside Quetzalcoatl at the entrance to time, waiting for Jack to join them. Jack approached his long-dead ancestor one last time. "We're ready to go. All I can promise is that we will do our best."

"Be well, Jack Rackham."

"Aye," answered Jack. He shook hands, turned and joined the others.

Q changed into a bird once more and perched on Kai's shoulder. The three took one last look at Captain Calico Jack Rackham before stepping into the waiting portal. With one spectacular flash, they were gone. The stone wheel slammed shut a moment later, the sound rumbling through the jungle causing birds and animals to scatter in panic. Calico Jack stood transfixed in front of the massive stone. Tears flowed down his rotting cheeks. Three teenagers now traveled in time, risking their lives, attempting a rescue mission on his behalf. Moments later he disintegrated. First the fingers dropped one by one, followed by the arms, the head and legs, his remains turned to ash, blown away by one strong gust on an otherwise windless day.

∽1720∾
PORT ROYAL, JAMAICA

DAVID EBRIGHT

~6~
BENNETT TINNERMON

~THE TRIP LASTED ONLY SECONDS. They stood in a thickly wooded area on a steep mountainside. "Now to figure out where we are and which way to go," said Jack.

Rachel spoke up. "Port Royal is like a peninsula. It's a narrow spit of land that runs from the main island into the sea."

"Been studyin' your geography?" asked Kai.

"Huh? No. Pop showed me. When we were sailing to the Bahamas he was teaching me how to stay on course and follow charts. He was telling me a little about Calico Jack and showed me Rackham's Cay on one of the GPS maps. I remember him explaining how Port Royal was wrecked by an earthquake and a tidal wave."

"Port Royal was the capitol for a long time. A lot of it washed into the sea when an earthquake and tsunami hit in 1692. People from our time call it the sunken city. As the story goes, Captain Morgan . . ."

"No. Don't even start with another hidden treasure story. We've got more money than we could ever spend and I'm tired of riskin' my neck," said Kai. "You need to spend more time playin' Xbox and cut back on all the history crap."

"Anyway," said Jack totally unfazed, "Captain Henry Morgan was a privateer, that's like a pirate but somewhat legal and he was one of the most successful. King Charles eventually made him a governor of Jamaica where he died in 1688, four years before the earthquake. As I started to say, it is believed that he tucked away a large part of his incredible fortune in one of the buildings that washed into the sea. Some estimate the value, based on current gold prices, at somewhere near two hundred million dollars."

"You're wasting your time. The Jamaican government allows no salvaging. Come up for air and even look like you're stickin' a dubloon in your pocket and you'll get tossed in jail for twenty years. Even I know that," said Kai.

"Can we get back to finding Port Royal?" asked Rachel.

"Sure. Let's forget about Captain Morgan, for now," said Jack.

"Let's get Q to fly over the island. Tell him what we're looking for and he can search from way up in the air," said Rachel.

Kai laughed. "Didja hear that Q? You're gonna be our spy in the sky."

The bird dipped his head so that he was eye to eye with Kai. "I'll be back," he said and flew away.

"I think that bird was mockin' me. Is it my imagination or did he just imitate Arnold Schwarzenegger?"

Jack shook his head, rolled his eyes and reached for Rachel's hand.

❧ X ❧

Q returned ten minutes later and shifted into his human form as soon as he landed. He pointed. "We must go six miles south to the base of the mountains and seven miles west to the city of Port Royal. The ship carrying Captain Rackham and his men has not yet arrived. There is a fortress in the city and suspect that is where the men in red coats will confine the captain and his crew."

"That would be Fort Charles and the men in red coats would be British soldiers," said Jack. "It's one of the few buildings that survived the earthquake."

"Let's start hikin'," said Kai.

They arrived at the edge of the bay as darkness settled in, Port Royal's lights visible in the distance. Now they needed to find clothes so they could blend in. Again, Q flew off on another scouting mission.

⤜X⤛

"Better hope we don't run into whoever owns these clothes," said Kai.

"Guess people were smaller in 1720. Look how short these sleeves are," said Jack.

"Quit complaining, you two. I'm the one pretending to be a boy," said Rachel.

"The boots are the worst. They're killing my feet. Q we need to find . . . aw, never mind."

"I can make them fit but no one may see the magic," said Q.

They all turned, facing opposite from Q. Seconds later the stolen clothes fit, even the boots. Kai started to ask, "How did you . . . ?"

Q shook his head; he was giving away no secrets. He walked into the shadows and returned with an armload of weapons, three flintlocks, powder, daggers, and cutlasses.

"What about you, Q? You dressin' like us or goin' around as a Quetzal bird?" asked Kai.

"I would rather fly so I will remain a bird for now.

Besides, I can change instantly into whatever I want whenever I want," said Q.

"Let's see," said Rachel.

Quetzalcoatl put on a brief demonstration changing from himself, to a well-dressed Englishman, to forlorn beggar, to a swashbuckling pirate, though the pirate had the head of an anaconda, Q's favorite snake.

"Shape-shifter. That's gotta be the coolest gig ever," said Kai

Jack checked his watch. "Getting late. Maybe we . . . I should get rid of this."

"Yes the timepiece would give your secret away. Yours as well, Kai," said Q. "I do think it best to get some rest before traveling much more, if you don't mind my saying so. At this hour you might raise suspicion among the locals. A mile from here is an abandoned shanty near the road to Port Royal which should be suitable and you can hide your things there."

~X~

They slept comfortably on sacks of cotton that had never made it to market. By daybreak they were on their way to Port Royal.

"So what are we supposed to do when we get there?" asked Rachel as they walked along.

"Keep our ears open, do some reconnaissance around the wharf and fort, maybe check out that Bennett kid, just investigate things," said Jack.

"We need to get inside the prison, see how it's laid out, how many guards are posted, when they change shifts, stuff like that," added Kai.

"You guys are going inside the prison?" asked Rachel.

"We'll have to sooner or later," said Kai.

"This is serious stuff. Somebody could get killed," said Rachel.

"Yeah. Us."

"We should split up to cover more ground. I'll check out the fort and the prison. For now, Kai can take the wharf and taverns. Q and Rachel you two find the Tinnermon kid and try convincing him to help us," said Jack.

"It would probably be best if we weren't seen together anyway," added Kai.

The foursome split up two miles from the fort. Jack used the side streets on the bay side of town, Kai cut across to the ocean side and Rachel, with Q flying overhead stuck to the main road going through the center of town.

Port Royal was clogged with carts, horses, goats and mules. Chickens darted in an out between the pedestrians, mostly fishermen, merchants and sailors. British soldiers, in tight groups of four, paraded through the streets intimidating the locals. Shopkeepers yelled out to the passersby, hawking their goods. There seemed to be a tavern for every man woman and child that scurried through the ramshackle settlement. The overwhelming stench of rotting meat, fish and raw sewage filled the air. Green-headed flies buzzed all around or feasting on the meat and produce for sale in the open marketplace.

Rachel, thankful that she had dressed like a man, tipped the front of her tri-cornered hat lower to help hide her face and continued dodging the merchants and livestock as she worked her way toward the west end looking for The Devil's Elbow, Calico Jack's favorite tavern. She heard a ruckus off to her right. British soldiers had surrounded a man waving a rum bottle as he struggled to stay on his feet. He yelled something that she couldn't understand just before one of the soldiers cracked the helpless drunk over the head with butt end of a musket. The man's knees buckled and he dropped in a heap face first. The soldiers laughed and went on their way. This was not a friendly place.

There it was, The Devil's Elbow, a two-story wooden structure that had never seen a drop of paint. Most of the balusters on the porch railing were broken or missing altogether and the steps leaned to one side. It was mid-morning and the establishment was packed. She continued on until she passed the tavern, no reason to pause in front of that raucous place. Looking around she spied the store. Compared to the other businesses along the main road, the place was well kept. Rachel walked past turned the corner and stopped. There he was, the kid she was supposed to find. He was behind the little shop loading heavy bags of something into a cart. It looked like hard work. Each of the sacks probably weighed close a hundred pounds. She stepped away and turned sideways, pretending to look at something down the dusty road. He was somewhere around fourteen, maybe a little older, not particularly big, just a shade under six feet and slender. He had medium length light brown hair tied back in a ponytail, intelligent brown eyes and clear features. His white shirt was soaked with sweat and he wore black pants tucked inside high leather boots. Rachel looked up, hoping to see Q. There was no sign of him. She would talk to Bennett Tinnermon on her own and hope for the best.

Rachel crossed to within ten paces. "Are you Mr. Tinnermon?"

The kid stopped and looked up. He thought he had heard a girl's voice, seeing the guy in the three cornered hat caught him off guard. "My father is picking up some goods down at the dock. Expect him back soon if you want to return later."

"Are you Bennett Tinnermon?"

"Yes, I am."

"Actually, I was looking for you," said Rachel.

"Me? Why?"

"You're a friend of Calico Jack Rackham?"

"Wouldn't say we were friends but I know the man," said Bennett.

"Well, he's the one that sent me to see you."

"He usually gives his provision orders to my father and I load everything. Besides that, I don't know him well at all."

"Did you know he's a pirate?"

"No surprise there. What do you want? I can give your order to Ma and she can tell you how much it will cost and then I can load your ship, just like I do for Captain Rackham."

Rachel thought about what to say next. The kid seemed smart and sure of himself, not likely to stop his work for long to make small talk, especially with a stranger. "Calico Jack was captured by the British. They're sailing this way with him now and intend to hang him for piracy. I'm here, along with some friends, to rescue him so he can start a new life with his family. He thought maybe you could help us."

Bennett walked closer to Rachel. "Well first, I have a few questions. Why would he think I could help? Why would he think I would want to help? And why do you sound like a girl but dress like a boy?" With his left hand he brushed the tri-cornered hat off Rachel's head and her long blonde hair fell loose past her shoulders.

She shrieked, grabbed the hat from the ground and ran for cover inside the doorway of the building, behind the cart. "You didn't have to do that, Bennett. I was going to tell you anyway."

"What are you trying to hide and who are you?"

"My name is Rachel, I'm from . . .   never mind that. Look around. You think it's safe around here for me to walk around alone?"

"Sorry, Rachel, I'll keep your secret, but I have to get back to work now. There's nothing I can do to help you or Captain Rackham."

"You don't even know what we need."

"What I don't need is to get my neck stretched for helping a pirate."

"That's not quite what we were going to ask."

"So what did you want me to do?"

"I'm not sure."

"That narrows it down then, doesn't it?"

"I guess we were hoping that if we needed a place to hide or food or something like that we could count on you. That's all I know," said Rachel.

"Who is we? How do you know Calico Jack is in custody and that Governor Rogers is going to hang him?"

"Because, well . . ." As Rachel stuttered trying to explain, Q swooped down and landed on her shoulder, startling both of them.

"I've never seen a bird like that! What is it?" asked Bennett.

"It's a Quetzal bird. This is Q, one of our friends. He's helping us rescue Captain Rackham."

"Look at those colors, and that tail. Is that beak made of gold?"

"Yes, it's solid Aztec gold, Bennett. There's a lot of stuff to explain about Q and my friends, and you probably won't believe me, but it's all true."

"How many are with you?"

"Three, counting Q."

"And you're going to take on an army of Redcoats to rescue a doomed pirate? Sorry, I don't see how you can manage that," said Bennett.

"We need to go inside the storage room. Q is going to show you a trick but I don't want anyone else to see it."

Bennett eyed the flintlock and the cutlass. "There's nothing worth robbing me for, so take your bird and leave."

Rachel handed him the weapons. "This won't take long. Trust me. You will want to see this. It will help you understand a little better."

"I'll watch this trick of yours from outside the door," said Bennett as he backed away.

"Fair enough. Let's go Q."

Rachel walked inside the doorway and turned to face Bennett who was leaning on the railing watching. She nodded to Q and the bird hopped from her shoulder to the floor and sat perfectly still.

"That's the trick?"

"C'mon Q, show him. It's the only thing I can think of to prove any of this."

Rachel joined Bennett at the rail. "Guess he's being stubborn."

There was no noise, no puff of smoke, no flash of light. In full view of Bennett and Rachel, Q changed to King Quetzalcoatl, his arms folded across his puffed out chest. Bennett stared wordlessly as Q changed into various creatures before their eyes. When he finished, and had returned to his human state, Q walked over to face the speechless teenager.

"I am King Quetzalcoatl. I am from the past. This is Rachel Lane. She is from the future. Soon you will meet her friends Jack Rackham, the descendant of our pirate friend who needs our help and Kai Mattison. They too are from the future."

"What do you mean the future?" asked Bennett.

"Three hundred years from now - the twenty first century, to be exact."

"That's impossible."

"So is changing from one creature to another. Do you want to see images of the future?"

"I don't know. No I don't think so," said Bennett.

"Very well, I thought you might want a glimpse of flying machines, and ships that sail beneath the waves and a wonderful game called baseball . . ."

Rachel interrupted. "Q, how do you know about that stuff?"

Q looked at her, confused. "I don't stay in the underground city all the time, Rachel."

"But really, baseball?"

He smiled. "I am very fond of the Dodgers."

Rachel rolled her eyes and smiled.

"Can you assist my friends?" asked Q. "You need not take any risk as they will make the rescue attempt themselves. Should you decide against getting involved, I would simply ask that you tell no one, even your parents, about this rescue."

"Please, Bennett. We need someone from this time and place to help us. We don't have much time and you're the only person that Captain Rackham had any confidence in as being honest, smart and resourceful," added Rachel.

Bennett looked down at his feet shaking his head. He took a deep breath and let it out slowly. "I'll try to help. But don't ask me to do something that will make the Redcoats put me or my parents in jail." Bennett looked from Q to Rachel and back to Q. "Uh, can you show me those flying machines now?"

❧ 7 ❧
FORT CHARLES

JACK ALWAYS LIKED BEING a big guy, until now. At six feet four inches tall he was drawing way too much attention. He stood nearly a head taller than most everyone in Port Royal and, as a stranger in a very rowdy town, it was only a matter of time before someone stepped up to challenge him to a senseless fight. He walked the perimeter of Fort Charles, looking for the most advantageous point to enter. It was not closed off to the public as he had expected, though there were guards posted all around. He decided to use the west gate since there was a stand of trees nearby. If he had to run, the trees would give him some cover. Jack ducked his head and hunched his shoulders and ambled inside the fortress.

Fort Charles was an imposing brick structure, situated on a bluff overlooking the harbor, cannons lining its parapet, the courtyard crowded with British soldiers, sailors, peddlers and beggars. The headquarters sat centered one hundred yards from the east wall, midway between north and south. Artillery sheds, small forges and three rows of barracks lined the west wall. Vendors had set up carts to sell their wares, positioning them at the perimeter away from the parade yard in the center. A three-rope gallows stood close to one of the arched entryways. It had seen heavy use. There were six sets of stocks and two racks, a sure sign that prisoners were kept somewhere nearby.

At last he spotted a pair of barred gates at the bottom of a set of stone stairs. The prison was part of a basement. He needed to get down those steps to see the layout and find an escape route. Two Redcoats stood guard at the gates and those guards would have keys. Jack would have to convince the men to open the gates and give him access to the prison. It was time to leave Fort Charles and find the only man that could help, the Governor of Jamaica, Woodes Rogers.

Kai watched the bustling activity along the wharf taking great care to avoid having to speak. His southern accent would never work in these parts and times. He'd overheard some British sailors talking about a certain Captain Barnet and his search for a notorious pirate who had had the audacity to attack and commandeer a sloop within sight of shore and the Royal Navy. Apparently Barnet had put to sea only two days earlier. To Kai that meant it could be several days before Calico Jack was captured and brought ashore. He noticed that most of the small ships and sloops were generally left unattended, the sailors and merchantmen more anxious to visit the taverns than worry about the security of their vessels. That, at least, was one discovery that might prove useful later.

He moved from the shadows ready to return to the shanty hideout when he spied a longboat approaching the bulkhead. Inside four black men, all chained together, sat hunched forward as if trying to hide while two men not chained and obviously in better condition, hoisted the oars and tied the small boat off to a piling. A large man with a thick red beard wearing a black waistcoat and filthy white ruffled shirt beneath it yelled out orders. The two men who had rowed the boat shoved the four prisoners onto the dock.

Kai noticed that the big man's left hand was missing, replaced by a menacing silver-colored hook. After struggling one-handed to climb onto the pier the man, sweating profusely and struggling to catch his breath, uncoiled a short whip and cracked it in the air, causing the four chained men to cower in terror. It was then that Kai saw the fresh lash marks on their backs. He knew then that these men were slaves and the man with the hook had to be a slave trader, arriving in port to sell the men off to the highest bidders. Kai's stomach churned as he decided there would be no sale if he could stop it.

Jack had no trouble finding the governor's mansion; it was the biggest and most ornate in all of Port Royal with sentries posted around the perimeter. He needed to see the man's face. His stomach grumbled as he sat down under a large tree where he had a direct line of sight to the grand entrance of the house. Two hours passed before the governor's carriage pulled up to the doors. The footman hurried to the side, placed a step stool on the ground and opened the carriage door. The governor and another man climbed inside and slammed the door slammed shut. The footman scurried to the front and hopped up into the seat next to the driver. The governor sat on the side closest to Jack, and after a deliberate ride down the winding driveway the pompous-looking man turned his head just in time for Jack to get a good look.

He was tired and hungry and the walk back to Fort Charles seemed to drag but the memory of Calico Jack's desperation and the fear in the pirate's eyes when speaking of the sadistic executioner made him push on.

By the time he returned, they had changed guards and the two watching the barred gates were fresher and more alert. He walked toward the pair, standing tall and appearing authoritative. When he was within twenty feet, Jack reached for his forearm and the Rackham brand. Both men stiffened a look of panic fell across their faces. He wondered how the governor would act in this situation. Jack decided that the man enjoyed authority, placing himself above everyone else and probably treated people like servants. He acted arrogant and impatient as he pictured the governor's face as he spoke.

"Unlock this gate, men. I have business to conduct. I shall also require one of you to act as my escort," said Jack.

"Yes, your Lordship," said one of the petrified guards as he fumbled with the keys.

"Hurry up man. I haven't all day to wait for the likes of you. Get this lock off immediately or you'll spend a night or two in one of the cells."

He turned to the other guard. "Let no one enter while I am inside. No one. Understand?"

"Yes, m'lord. No one."

It was a dank dingy place, smelling of rot and decay, with mold growing on the brick walls and water dripping from overhead. Thick rusted iron gates sealed the small cells. There were two torches in the corridor, one at each end, providing barely enough light to walk safely. Each cell, and there were only six, had four sets of chains and shackles attached to the walls, three feet above the dirt floors. The prison sat empty, making Jack wonder why guards were on station in the first place. He discovered that the entrance was also the only exit. At the end of the corridor at the base of the steps, he noticed a room with various tools on a bloodstained wooden table. On the wall hung a cat-o-nine tail, a short whip made with leather straps and pieces of bone attached to the ends, intended to cut through skin with each lash.

Jack addressed the guard. "I want six torches added down here along the corridor and get this place cleaned up.

Bring in clean straw and remove the shackles and manacles immediately. I want all of this done by sundown. Understand?"

"Yes, your Lordship. It will be done within the hour."

"Very good. What is your name?"

"Franklin Pennymore, m'lord."

"I will arrange for your promotion, Pennymore. I've seen quite enough. You will escort me upstairs to the west gate."

Jack stopped at the room where the tools were stored and removed the cat-o-nine tail. "This, I daresay, will not be needed."

Franklin Pennymore walked Jack to the west gate, still convinced that the man giving orders was Governor Woodes Rogers. Once past the gate, Jack dismissed the man and turned east toward the shanty hoping to find some food along the way.

~X~

Rachel and Bennett walked through town along the main road toward the shanty. Q circled overhead, keeping an eye out for trouble. They had collected a small supply of food from the back room of his parent's shop, and exchanged a bottle of rum for a hefty chunk of salt-pork. It would be enough to hold them over. Bennett could not contain his excitement about the flying machines of the future and was amazed to hear that Rachel and her friends had actually traveled in these contraptions called airplanes. Rachel didn't bother explaining the bad sides of it all, like airport check-ins or lost luggage.

They traveled two thirds of the way when they met up with Jack. Rachel made the introductions as Q landed and settled on Jack's shoulder. Bennett explained again that he was no fan of the Redcoats and was willing to help collect supplies and gather information, but he wouldn't put his parents or their business at risk trying to rescue a pirate, especially one that probably deserved hanging.

"How old are you?' asked Jack.

"Fourteen, sir," answered Bennett.

"Whoa. You don't need to call me sir. I'm only two years older than you."

"But you're . . . so big."

"I think people are generally bigger three hundred years from now - must be the water, or maybe the food. Man, I could go for one of Nan's shrimp wraps right about now," said Jack as he patted his growling stomach.

"You know Queen Nanny?" asked Bennett.

"Who?"

"Queen Nanny of the Maroons."

"The Nan I was talking about is my grandmother in Florida. Who is Queen Nanny?"

Bennett looked around before speaking. "She is the leader of the escaped slaves. Lately the Redcoats have been going on raids into the hills, trying to arrest her."

"I forgot this place was involved in the slave trade. What do you think about slavery, Bennett?"

"Me? I think it's terrible. My Ma says no one has a right to claim ownership of another human being. Besides, I believe that all men are created equal."

"Years from now a very important document called The Declaration of Independence will use those very words. My country, the one in the future, will go to war against the British Redcoats to win their freedom and become a new nation. Who knows? Maybe one day you'll go to America," said Jack.

"I would be very happy to leave this place," said

Bennett.

Jack changed the subject. "So what kind of food do we have? I'm starving."

Rachel smiled. "We've got something called salt-pork; some smoked fish, a dozen mangos, chopped sugar cane stalks, and a fruit called ackee."

"Okay, we'll make that work. How about Kai? Have you checked on him lately, Q?"

"The last time I saw him he was at the wharf. All seemed under control," answered Q.

"Think you could do a flyover and see if he's on his way back to the shanty?"

"Certainly." Quetzalcoatl flapped his wings and flew off toward the setting sun.

Bennett stopped walking and stared at Jack.

Jack noticed and laughed. "I guess it was kind of weird watching me talk to the bird."

"Yes, but hearing the bird speak was . . . oh, I don't feel so good," said Bennett.

Rachel walked over to him and put an arm around his shoulder. "It's okay, Bennett. You're going to see lots of weird stuff over the next few days. We're trying to help a bad man get the chance to be a good man. If you want us to leave you alone, we will. No hard feelings."

"No, I want to help. You seem like nice people, strange but nice. And I did like Calico Jack. He always spoke kindly to me and treated me like . . . like a man. It would be good to know that he got a second chance."

Jack started to speak but was interrupted by Q's flapping wings. The bird didn't land just transformed into the Aztec King as he touched the ground. "We must rescue Kai," said Quetzalcoatl. "I think he has just started a war with the men in the red coats."

"What did he do? Is he at the wharf?" asked Jack.

"Are we going to stand here while you ask questions or are we going to go help your friend?" asked Q.

Jack sighed, shaking his head. "Let's go," he said.

~8~
THE MAROONS

KAI PUSHED WITH HIS LEGS and pulled with his arms, his shoulder muscles pulsed in time with each powerful stroke as the oars flashed through the water. The pursuing Redcoats narrowed the gap, using two trained oarsmen in each of their longboats. It was a lucky thing they were shooting at him. Each time a volley rang out, the British had stopped rowing to give their marksmen a clean shot. The chop and distance, made hitting their target difficult. As Kai approached the shoreline the wood next to the starboard oarlock splintered, the sound of the shot muffled by the sound of the surf. *That's it he thought. I've got less than a minute to be onshore and running for the woods, or this mission is over.* He looked at the four terrified men cowering on the boat's deck, covering their heads, still chained together. No, he would finish what he started and help these men escape the slave master. The boat tipped and spun as they crashed through the surf.

Kai shouted out to the men to hurry and follow him into the trees. They didn't speak his language, but understood the sound of musket fire behind them. It took only seconds to reach the tree line where they plunged ahead into the thick foliage and climbed into the forested hills.

They ran hard uphill for ten minutes before stopping to rest. Kai walked several yards behind the men and listened for the soldiers. All was quiet. The Redcoats had abandoned the chase. He took a deep breath and sat down next to the men in chains. Removing the shackles with no tools would be impossible and twilight was approaching. Better to look for shelter and deal with the chains later. After a long exhausted sigh, he got to his feet, turned and found himself staring into the face of woman standing in front of a group of armed men. He'd never even heard their approach.

Her skin was dark, matching the ebony color of her eyes, her head covered with a tightly wrapped cloth, much like a turban. The men carried long knives, not cutlasses, shorter, similar to a machete. All of them were barefoot and their clothes were a mix of the color brown and green. An early version of camouflage Kai decided.

The woman moved closer and the men behind her fanned out, encircling Kai and the four newly freed slaves. She spoke to one of the men trembling on the ground in a language Kai didn't understand. The first chained man answered the woman, shaking his head and gesturing animatedly toward Kai. The woman nodded and spoke to Kai in her own language.

"Sorry but I don't understand what you're sayin'. We'll hurry up and get off your property. Okay?"

The woman smiled. "You have a friendly voice. You speak the language of the Redcoat devils but 'tis not the same. I am Nanny of the Maroons. We will not harm you or your men."

"These aren't my men. I was tryin' to help 'em get away . . . "

"From the soldiers, yes I watched them chase you across the bay. We will remove their chains and feed them. Make them healthy again." The woman spoke kindly, in an accent that most in Kai's time would not recognize.

"What about the Redcoats, Nanny? They're probably gettin' more men and they'll be back to search these hills. I don't want to make trouble for you," he explained.

"Do not fear. The Redcoats search but never find us. These men will join us and be taken care of and protected. What do I call you?"

"Kai."

"You are full of the magic, Kai."

Kai laughed. "Yeah, my friend Jack tells me I'm full of somethin' all the time. Look, I don't want to be rude but it's gettin' dark and I need to get back to my friends. I've got a lot of rowin' and walkin' ahead of me yet."

"I will help you reach your friends."

Jack and Rachel stood at the end of the wharf looking southwest across the deep water inlet to the hills behind Half Moon Bay. They had left Bennett in town near his home, not wanting to put him in any danger. Q was, once again perched on Jack's shoulder. "So the last time you saw him he was rowing toward those hills," said Jack.

"Yes and there were two boats loaded with the Redcoats giving chase and firing their weapons. He had four men in the boat with him."

"I don't see any sign of a boat onshore."

"The Redcoats, no doubt, retrieved it," said Q.

"Do you think they captured him?"

"Who can know? I will fly over and search for him."

"I'm going over there to look instead of waiting around. No offense but maybe he's hurt or shot. Let's borrow a longboat," said Jack.

"You get the boat and a rope. I will tow you over," said Q.

"Huh?"

"Get the rope, I will handle the rest."

Jack found a boat unattended below the dock. He rowed to the end and looked across the horizon before he heard Q's voice. "Throw the rope into the water." Off the bow a dolphin circled. Rachel tossed the rope into the water. The dolphin grabbed it and towed the longboat across Half Moon Bay to the opposite shore.

It didn't take long to find the tracks where several men had run into the thicket toward the hills. "They cut through here," said Jack as he led the way.

They spotted Kai, accompanied by a woman and three escorts, walking toward them. "Heard you had a problem," said Jack with a worried smile.

"You could say that," said Kai.

Jack eyed the entourage warily. "Do you still have a problem?"

"Everything's cool. This is Queen Nanny. She helps escaped slaves by hiding them from the British and the slave traders. Nanny, these are my friends Jack, Rachel and Q."

Nanny stepped forward looking at all three. She stared into Jack's face. "You are a brave and loyal young man, with much wisdom for your years." Standing in front of Q she said, "You are a man of the ages, a man of royalty and great power." Finally, Nanny turned to Rachel. Her eyes filled with tears as her fingers lightly traced the side of Rachel's face. "You have lost so much, child, yet your spirit is kind, gentle and giving."

Rachel swallowed hard. She thought of how she had lost her parents, of being alone, hungry, living on the streets before Jack had rescued her, and how his grandparents had taken her in and treated her as one of their own. "Thank you, Nanny," she managed.

Nanny turned to Kai. "Now that you and your friends are together, you need not rush to Port Royal. We will welcome you all to our village to share our food and hospitality. Rest yourselves until morning. It is not so far from this place."

Rachel spoke up first. "I think that's a fantastic idea."

Kai, Jack and Rachel followed Queen Nanny to the Maroon's hideout. Q changed again and flew off into the jungle. Two of Nanny's men walked to the longboat and tucked it behind the trees.

The village was tiny, the huts nothing more than little boxes made from sticks and dried mud, covered with branches and palms. One large fire pit centered within the cluster and surrounded on three sides by a man-made barricade of stacked logs also covered in branches and palm. Inside a fire blazed, a wild boar suspended on a spit above the flames. Nanny noticed Jack looking at the way the fire pit was made. "We have to conceal our fire. From time to time the Redcoats send patrols looking for us. We burn pimiento wood because it makes very little smoke and the barricades hide the flame."

"Have you ever been caught?" asked Jack.

"No. We have men posted throughout the woods and a warning system of calls that travel through the trees to sentries posted at our perimeter." She motioned toward a large tree with vines covering its trunk. On her signal, a man stepped into the open. He was covered in vines and leaves and had blended in perfectly with the surrounding vegetation, a natural camouflage. This is what we do to keep our freedom and stay alive," Nanny explained.

After eating their fill and listening to Nanny's stories, they crawled into one of the huts to get some sleep. The jungle sounds were loud and threatening, the floor, covered with woven mats, was uncomfortable and damp but it took only minutes for sleep to overtake them.

~X~

By dawn, they were awake and huddled near the fire. "What I wouldn't give for a hot shower," said Kai. "I feel like a total dirtball."

"Best we can do is stand under a chilly waterfall. There are plenty of them here in the hills," said Rachel. "My hair feels so ratty. What do people around here use for shampoo and conditioner."

"I don't think that's high on anyone's priority list," said Kai. "What are you thinkin' about, Jack?"

"I'm thinking about how you're going to have to stay away from the wharf now. Wonder how many people got a clear look at you? You did a great job of stirring things up," said Jack with a smile.

Kai leaned back on his elbows, looking thoughtful before answering. "Hard to say, Jack. Maybe a few . . . dozen. I had to nail five or six Redcoats with an oar when we were in the boat shovin' off, you know, when they were tryin' to stop me. All of those guys are pretty lumped up. That was after I kicked the crap outta that slave trader dude. Had a nasty lookin' hook for a hand and when he swung it at me I ducked, gave him a straight right to his left eye, a chop to his throat and a kick to his left knee, then I dropped-kicked him from the wharf into the bay. His two helpers jumped in and pulled him out so he wouldn't drown. Before that, I was mostly runnin' and shovin' people outta the way 'til I reached the slave-sellin' creep. The worst was gettin' shot at. When those musket balls hit the boat, wood just splintered into small chunks. Felt like bee stings. One just missed my head, felt it whiz by. Good thing those Redcoats were lousy shots."

Jack laughed. "Did you use that spin kick you're always practicing?"

"Yup. Perfect placement too - underside of the chin. If

he'd had his tongue stickin' out, he woulda bit it clean off."

"So you went all crazy on this guy because of the slave trading thing?" asked Jack.

"Yeah, that and the way he was treatin' those four men. You woulda done the same."

"Hey I think what you did was awesome." He paused. "Rachel do you think Bennett would keep an eye and ear out on the wharf for us?" asked Jack. "Q can check in on him from time to time. He wouldn't have to do anything dangerous."

"Oh you never think anything's dangerous," she sighed.

"We need to find out when they plan to move Captain Rackham and his crew from the ship and how many Redcoats they plan to use to guard them. Would help to know where they take them too. I assume Fort Charles but maybe not. There's gallows inside the prison, but our favorite pirate told me they hanged him at Gallows Point. That's outside the fort on the west side, where the island juts out into the sea. Now if Bennett can gather the info and pass it along quickly, we might be able to rescue Rackham and his crew before they're even locked up."

"You're going to try rescuing them before they get hauled to the prison?" asked Rachel.

"That might be easier. If they keep Calico Jack and his men waiting on the ship for a while, that might give us time to snag a boat for our getaway and break them loose before they send a regiment of soldiers from the fort as an escort. I'm thinking that the governor wants to put on a show and plans to march the pirates through the streets with a lot of fanfare," said Jack.

"Sorry, but I don't like it. There's no wiggle room. You're countin' on too much goin' right inside a tight window. I say we break 'em out of the jail," said Kai. "That at least gives us time to fine tune an escape plan, and have a boat ready to go."

"You might be right, but if Bennett learns that the ship is going to be docked for several hours before the prisoners are offloaded, we might get lucky. Getting in and out of the prison is going to be tough."

Rachel spoke up. "Rescuing them from the ship would be best; getting them out of the prison sounds impossible. Where I think you're wrong is trying to escape right from the dock and out to sea. I know you guys can sail, but you don't have experience with ships from these times, at least not enough to make a getaway with the British Navy on your tails."

"Calico Jack and his men would help, they're good sailors," said Jack.

"Maybe, but don't forget, they're probably all chained together like the men Kai rescued. There won't be time to stop and cut them loose if we're all on the run," she said. "And we won't know what kind of shape they're in either. Some of them might be sick, beat up or even shot."

"I'm just thinking that if they get Calico Jack and his crew inside that prison, the odds against us go way up."

"We'll come up with somethin'. You made the guards think you were the governor and Q can change into anything he wants so between the two of you, it'll work," said Kai.

"If we . . . " the sound of a high-pitched wail nearby interrupted Rachel. The three moved toward the noise, now reduced to a steady whimper. They found a man kneeling over a young child holding the girl's hand over a hollowed out gourd as blood drained into the makeshift bowl.

"What are you doing?" yelled Rachel as she ran toward the startled man.

Queen Nanny stepped out from one of the huts and

placed her hands on Rachel's shoulders, stopping her several feet short. "This is our healer Toju. The child has the fever and he is taking it away to make her well."

Rachel pushed her way past the woman and knelt next to the little girl. "He's cut the vein above her thumb. How does this make her better?"

Toju pointed to the blood inside the bowl. "Fever."

Rachel shook her head and turned to Nanny. "This won't make her better. It will only turn into an infection. Please get me some fresh water so we can get her cleaned up and make her more comfortable."

Nanny spoke to Toju. He nodded and walked into the woods. The little girl shivered and pulled her knees up to her stomach while she rocked from side to side. Rachel tore off a strip of cloth from her shirt and wrapped it around the bleeding hand. "When did she get sick?" asked Rachel.

"Two nights ago she found the sickness."

"The sickness?"

Nanny didn't reply.

"What is her name?" asked Rachel.

"Adanna. She is Toju's daughter."

"Do you know if she ate something poisonous?"

"It is the sickness. Many of our children die."

Jack and Kai stood off to the side watching silently while Rachel and Nanny spoke to one another. Toju returned with fresh water and joined Rachel next to his daughter. His eyes darted between the two. He had taken on the look of hopefulness. Rachel tore another piece of her shirt, dipped it in the water, wrung it out lightly and swabbed the child's face. "Jack, I need more cloth and I need to speak with Q right away."

Jack and Kai each removed their shirts and handed them to Rachel. Toju noticed the brand on Jack's arm and his eyes widened. "It's alright; I won't hurt her," said Jack.

"Rachel, to find Q I have to get to the beach. He knows to look for us there, away from the trees."

She nodded and Jack and Kai ran into the woods down the hillside toward the sea. It took ten minutes to reach the sandy cove. Q joined them a few minutes later. They ducked into the trees before Q transformed into his human form.

"Q, Rachel is trying to help a very sick little girl and needs to talk to you. Can you meet her near the campfire?" asked Jack.

"Yes. Will you be waiting here?"

Jack sighed. "What do you think, Kai?"

"Until Q finds out what Rachel needs, I think we should. No sense wasting time climbing through the hills."

"Okay, we'll wait here for half an hour. If you don't return by then, we'll walk back."

Q changed again into the quetzal bird and flew off into the jungle and Kai and Jack moved onto the beach.

～X～

"The waves here kinda suck," said Kai as he stared out at the azure waters of the Caribbean. "We gotta get back home so we can take the boards out. I don't think I've ever gone this long without surfin'. I just keep thinkin' about cruisin' with Val around St. Augustine in my Jeep, havin' our cookouts on Crescent Beach and catchin' some good sets. This rescue stuff and all the walkin' is gettin' on my nerves."

"I'm still worried about Nan and Pop. They must be in a panic by now," said Jack.

"I don't know if I'd say panicked. They seem to roll with the weirdness pretty well." Kai laughed. "But they'd totally freak if they knew we've been shot at a couple of times."

"Let's keep that part to ourselves once we get home," said Jack.

"I'm goin' swimmin' and get some of the crud washed off me," said Kai.

"Good idea."

"I get them once in a while."

❧ 9 ☙
SHAPE SHIFTERS

⟋JACK AND KAI FLOATED on their backs relaxing beyond the breaking surf. Kai noticed the giant gray fin thirty yards away sticking nearly four feet above the water's surface. It was circling them.

"We gotta get to the beach, Jack. There's a monster shark stalkin' us."

Jack flipped over to tread water next to Kai. "Think we can swim hugging the bottom until we get to the shallows?"

"Better than thrashin' around, I guess. Looks like it's zeroing in on us though. How big d'ya think that thing is?"

"Huge. Let's try it. We'll stay together so we look bigger. Maybe that'll make it shy away."

They eased their way below the surface very deliberately, careful to avoid sudden movements that could signal panic. With their hands touching the bottom, they moved toward shore, each keeping watch on the shark's cautious approach. As they neared the shallower water, the predator gained speed taking a direct line toward Jack. When the shark was fifteen feet away, it opened its massive jaws, ready to strike. Jack turned, positioning himself to make an attempt to fight the creature off but the giant shark turned away, to swim parallel with the surf. Kai tugged at Jack's arm and the pair broke through the white water, swimming with abandon into the safety of the shallows. They stood looking out to sea in knee-deep water walking backwards toward the dry sand.

"It had me! I can't believe it swam off," yelled Jack.

"That shark had to be thirty feet long. Did you see that mouthful of teeth?"

"I saw them up close and personal. Each tooth was the size of my hand. That monster could have swallowed me in one bite," said Jack breathlessly as they reached the beach.

"Look there it goes, just past the breakers. I didn't know there was such a thing as a shark that big. It might even be a thirty-five footer. Unbelie . . . what's it doin' now? It's cuttin' through the surf headin' this way. What the . . ." Kai didn't finish as the shark burst through shallows right at them onto the beach. Jack and Kai ran toward the trees. When they reached the edge of the jungle, they stopped and turned in time to see Q walking their way with a sheepish grin on his face.

Both boys leaned over with their hands on their knees laughing. "Punk'd by an Aztec King," said Kai.

After offering his not-so-sincere apology for the shark attack, Q explained that Rachel needed certain roots and berries for medicine and a supply of clean cloth. Q would take Jack to join Bennett so they could spy on the Redcoats. Kai would help Q collect the medical supplies and deliver them to Rachel. The plan left one major wrinkle.

"I'll do whatever, Q, but you're gonna have to show me what to pick or dig up," said Kai.

"I will show you, my friend," said Q. "Wait here while I take Jack to meet Bennett. I will return soon." He turned to Jack. "We will swim across the bay."

"You're not going to change into that shark again, right?"

"Trust me," said Q. He cocked an eyebrow toward Kai and smiled.

Kai laughed as Jack, still looking a bit shaky, disappeared into the surf with Q. A minute later a dolphin circled, paused in front of Jack long enough for him to grab the dorsal fin, and together they were off, plowing through the water toward Port Royal.

Jack climbed out of the water shirtless and dripping wet. Q changed into the quetzal bird and circled overhead until Jack understood that he needed to follow. Finally, they arrived at the shop behind the Devil's Elbow Tavern where they found Bennett stacking goods in the corner of the storage room. Q flew in ahead of Jack and perched on a barrel off to one side.

"Hi, Bennett, remember me? I'm Jack, Rachel's friend." He motioned toward the colorful bird, "You know Q."

Bennett took a deep breath, walked to the doorway and looked around. There was no one within earshot. "I told Rachel I would help if I could, but I don't want any trouble."

"I understand." Jack turned toward the bird. "I think we're okay here, Q. Better help Kai and Rachel now." With that, Q nodded and flew out through the doorway.

"You're soaked. And where's your shirt?" asked Bennett.

"Right now it's being chopped up into rags and bandages. Rachel is trying to help a little girl who is very sick on the other side of the bay. Q is helping my other friend Kai to collect stuff to use for medicine."

"Are they up in the hills over there?"

"Yes."

"With Queen Nanny and the Maroons?"

"You know about Queen Nanny?"

"Of course, but what does she have to do with Captain Rackham?"

"Kai was at the wharf trying to find out about the pirates. Some slave trader came ashore with four slaves to sell and was getting ready to lash them when Kai, uh . . ."

"He's the one that broke those men loose?"

"You heard about that?" asked Jack.

"Everybody heard about it. People said he was like a one-man army. They even shot at him and couldn't stop him. Is he bigger than you?"

Jack smiled. "Not quite."

"That man he beat up is Marcus Hook. He won't stop until he and his men find your friend and kill him."

"They won't find him."

Bennett walked over to the barrel where Q had perched and sat down. "So what do you want to talk to me about?"

Jack paused. "I'm glad you heard about Kai's fight at the wharf. He went there to spy on the Redcoats so we could find out about their plans for Calico Jack. Now the British are on the lookout for him so obviously he can't go anywhere near the town or the docks. With my three friends busy with other important stuff, that leaves me to watch the prison, the wharf and the troops by myself."

"And you want my help?"

"I'm hoping, since your shop is so close to the wharf, that you could watch and listen to what goes on over there so we can find out what the Redcoats intend to do with Captain Rackham and his crew."

"You already told me they plan on hanging him. That's why you're here to rescue them."

"But we need to know when they plan to take them off the ship and if they plan to parade the pirates through the streets with a regiment or just a handful of guards. I think they'll go to Fort Charles, but I don't know if maybe they use another prison. The one inside the fort only has six cells and one way in and out."

"You went inside the prison?" asked Bennett.

"Yesterday."

"How?"

"Let's just say I managed."

Bennett stared ahead, thinking. "Is everyone from your time a lunatic? Do you know what they would do to you if you were caught?"

"Throw me in a cell 'til they got around to hanging me?"

"If you were lucky. They would probably give you twenty lashes, put you in the rack to stretch your joints for an hour and then lock you in the stocks for the rest of the day before sending you back in chains to your cell. They would do that every day for a week and THEN they would hang you and shove your body in a metal cage so the birds could peck at you until all that was left were your bones."

"Hmmm . . . nice people. Guess I'd better not get caught. Calico Jack told me about the floggings and the guy with the whip. Said avoid him at all cost," said Jack.

"I know about the man you're talking about. His name is Schaeffer Tolliver and he really is a mean one. They say he once sailed as Blackbeard's Quartermaster."

"That explains a lot. Edward Teach, also known as Blackbeard, might have been the cruelest of all pirate captains. He died in battle in 1718 off the coast of North Carolina. After the British sailors shot him several times, they chopped off his head and tossed his body overboard. Once his headless body hit the water, they claim it swam around the ship three times before sinking out of sight."

"I don't know about that but you can see why I don't

want to get caught," said Bennett.

"I don't intend for anyone to get caught and if you want no part of this, that's your choice. No one will try to make you do something you don't want to do."

"I'll watch the docks and pass along whatever information I can."

"That's great," said Jack as he shook Bennett's hand. "I need one more favor."

"I knew it."

"Think you could find me a shirt?"

Bennett laughed. "Yes and I'll get some wintergreen powders for Rachel to use. They relieve pain. And we might have some leeches too."

"Thanks, Bennett, but let's skip the leeches. Now let me tell you something else, about how you can talk to me when I'm not around. It's almost as strange as Q changing into birds and stuff."

Jack explained the Rackham Curse to Bennett, describing how he could control minds and communicate mentally. They practiced by holding a short mental conversation until Jack was sure Bennett felt comfortable. Finally, Jack pulled on the borrowed shirt and left through the back door.

X

Kai sat on a rock looking out into the Caribbean wondering if he would ever see home again. It had been ten days since leaving the pier in Key West aboard Calico Jack's ghost ship. Now as the days passed, returning home safely seemed unlikely.

The dolphin swam through the surf on a direct line to where Kai sat. As it reached the beach, it transformed seamlessly into King Quetzalcoatl. The Aztec never broke stride as he moved to join Kai. "You are troubled, my friend," said Q.

"I'm okay."

"You think you will die here and never return to your time or home."

Kai looked up at Q perplexed. "Can you read minds too?"

"No, but it is obvious that you are in a melancholy state of mind. Someone of reasonable intelligence would notice and understand the reason for your deep concern."

"Q, I don't want to sound like a quitter, but the more I think about it the less sure I am that this rescue is gonna work, even with your magic and Jack's ability to control minds," said Kai, his head hanging slightly.

"I had no idea that Jack could control minds. I've not seen him attempt to use it."

"It's some curse that Calico Jack put on him. There's a brand on his forearm with the Rackham symbol. He tries to hide it. Jack didn't want any part of it."

Q cradled his chin between his thumb and forefinger. "This is interesting. So Jack could have used his special power to force that young Tinnermon fellow to help, but left it open as a request rather than a demand. That is truly remarkable."

"Well think about it. If the kid was controlled to follow an order, no matter how crazy it might be, he could get himself seriously hurt or maybe killed because all sense of risk would be gone. Jack wouldn't do that to someone."

"I had intended only to follow along until you met Captain Rackham and return to my people before you crossed into the past, but there was something about all of you that I didn't understand and I desperately needed to satisfy my curiosity. The simple fact is you are taking these risks upon yourselves in order to do something that you believe is good and right and not at the expense of someone's well-being," said Q.

"The bottom line is, Calico Jack kidnapped Rachel and we had to rescue her."

"But I heard the captain offer you the chance to abandon this quest and return to your homes without traveling in time to save him, yet you decided to see it through. Does a great fortune await at the conclusion of this venture?"

"None that I know of. Besides, we're already loaded."

"Loaded?"

"Already have a great fortune, as you would say. We found lots of gold and treasure on two separate treasure hunts. Of course, we probably won't live to spend it," said Kai.

"I believe you will be successful. What was it that you called me when I changed into another creature?"

"A shape-shifter. I said being a shape-shifter must be a really cool gig."

"That seems an accurate name for my ability. I now suggest we get to the mountains to retrieve the roots and berries that Rachel requires."

Kai turned around facing the jungle and the climb ahead. "I guess I'll gather the stuff and you can shuttle it to her."

"What we need is not on this side of the island." Q pointed northwest. "The roots will be found near the summit of the Blue Mountains."

"Well, Q, you're going to have to change into something that can carry me over there. Rachel needs the stuff right away. It'll take me all day to walk and climb that far," said Kai.

"Maybe a flying horse?"

"Whatever gets us back and forth the fastest works

for me. Besides, you're the shape- shifter, you choose."

"Very well." Q opened one of his bracelets and removed a small pouch. "Hold out your hand"

Kai reached out with his palm turned upward and Q dumped a small amount of a dark grainy substance into Kai's hand. "Swallow this potion."

"Are you serious?"

"I believe that if you also have this shape-shifting ability it will prove invaluable toward the success of this most difficult quest. I do ask, however, that you not change into a quetzal bird for reasons that I am sure you understand."

"Are there side effects? Do I get sick or crazy or anything like that?" asked Kai.

"Of course not. Changing into another form is not painful or uncomfortable. You simply have to will yourself to change into whatever you decide and it occurs instantly."

"Do I have to chant something?"

"There are no incantations. When you want to revert, picture your human form and will yourself to change. You are limited to changing into creatures that walk, swim, fly, crawl or slither and as you learn, you may enjoy variations, as I do. You have seen me already as half man and half snake," explained Q.

"Wow. This is gonna be incredible." Kai swallowed the mixture with some difficulty. "Don't feel any different."

"As I promised you wouldn't. Now decide what form you want to take, I suggest a bird for now, and let us begin our search for Rachel's medicines."

The quetzal bird lifted off across the treetops toward the mountains. A majestic eagle followed close behind.

Adanna's fever broke and her energy and appetite returned, but now Rachel stared at six more suffering children. Toju and Nanny pitched in trying to make the children comfortable. Scared and overwhelmed, Rachel knew she needed help soon or some of the kids might die.

Q and Kai arrived late in the afternoon with a second batch of berries and roots. Followings Q's instructions, Kai smashed the berries, heated them over hot coals and strained them through a cloth into two wooden bowls. Twenty pounds of berries produced only a gallon of the desired purple liquid. Q and Rachel cleaned and peeled the roots, separating them by type and size into different pots filled with water. These were hung over a continuously stoked fire. They boiled the roots for more than an hour until they were soft enough to mash. Once they cooled, Q and Kai crushed them into fine pulp, spreading it over the flat surface of a ramshackle tabletop so that the pulp could dry before grinding it into a fine powder. Rachel complained that the conditions for preparation were not sanitary but it was the best they could manage.

While they prepared the medicines, Rachel helped Toju and Nanny erect a tent-like covering for the children. They laid out palm fronds covered in cloth to keep the children from lying on the bare dirt. Now she had seven patients, some crying softly, others shaking and staring listlessly into space with enough medicine to last only two days. With all of the kids washed up and bedded down, Rachel began the task of gently helping each child sip the bitter concoction.

Kai knelt next to Rachel and placed his arm around her shoulder. "We need to take some of Queen Nanny's men to the Blue Mountains to show them which roots and berries to collect. It will take a whole day for them to get there, a day to collect and another to get back. They have to hide from the Redcoats and bounty hunters when they travel so that might slow them down even more – maybe it ends up being four days altogether."

"Kai, we don't have that much time. These little ones will die. There must be a closer source. We have to find it," said Rachel.

"I'll make another trip with Q so we can collect more. In the meantime, Queen Nanny needs to send at least six men to the Blue Mountains right now. I can meet them there to show them what to do. Her men will have to keep shuttling back and forth to keep the supply chain going. After that, when the kids feel better, maybe the Maroons will move to that part of the island. It looked like there was plenty of fresh water, wildlife and fruit over there."

"How are you getting back and forth so fast?" Rachel giggled. "Does Q change into a giant pelican and carry you in his pouch?"

Kai stood and walked around to face Rachel. After checking for prying eyes he said, "Watch this." He changed from his human form into a fuzzy gray koala. He waddled over, and reached his stubby little arms into the air. Rachel, too stunned to speak, picked him up, holding him like a toddler. From the koala came Kai's voice in sync with the movement of the little bear-like creature's mouth. "Pretty cute, huh? I'm KoalaKai. Hey that sounds kinda Hawaiian. Q decided to make me a shape-shifter so now . . . Rachel? Rachel?"

X

Bennett walked casually among the dockworkers, sailors and merchants, pleasantly nodding hello and addressing strangers and acquaintances alike while he made his way toward a British Brigantine as it tied up at the south side pier. Since he frequently delivered goods to the merchant ships, no one gave it any thought when the friendly boy with the familiar face stopped and leaned against a piling close to the gangplank of the arriving naval vessel.

It took only minutes before Bennett heard the name Calico Jack Rackham mentioned by an officer with a booming voice. "Expect to see that scoundrel Rackham dragged through Port Royal by noon tomorrow, along with his thievin' crew. Serves him right, stealin' a ship in plain sight of the Royal Navy. When the governor sets that monster Schaeffer Tolliver loose on him, Calico Jack will beg for the noose."

"They're bringing him here then? Thought maybe the lot of them would be executed and dumped at sea," said a scrawny man in a blue waistcoat.

"A guest at Fort Charles he'll be, at least until the trial ends or 'til he dies from the brutal floggings. No the governor won't be made to look the fool without exacting his bloody revenge. Rackham will be made an example and you won't likely see pirates sailing these waters for a generation. It will be a grand spectacle indeed."

Bennett heard enough and ambled away unnoticed from the brigantine and her crew across the wharf and into town. After he arrived at the little storage building behind the sundry shop, he let Jack know what he had learned, through a mental conversation; no one actually saying a word. They agreed that Jack, Kai, Q and Bennett would meet that night in the storage shed behind the Tinnermon's shop around midnight.

The last to arrive was Bennett. While trying to get through the creaky door of his house without waking his parents his father had stirred leaving Bennett trapped halfway out the door for several minutes petrified to make the slightest move. He finally joined Jack and the others as Kai finished explaining to Jack how he could now change into the form of other creatures.

"Great job today, Bennett. With Rachel up in the hills helping Queen Nanny and the Maroons we're going to have to rescue Calico Jack from the fort. Rachel needs more time with those kids."

"Can't we rescue the captain and crew and hide out on land for a few days?" asked Kai.

"Too risky, especially for the Maroons hiding in the hills. The governor would put a few hundred soldiers on the hunt for the pirates. With that kind of manpower, the Redcoats would be bound to stumble on Queen Nanny and her people and that could lead to a slaughter on both sides," said Jack

"I agree with Jack. As Mr. Tinnermon here has advised, the governor plans to make this a spectacle. That, it seems, means we have some time to accomplish this rescue," said Q.

"You're right, but I'm thinking about that guy at the prison, the one that whips the prisoners 'til they almost die."

"Schaeffer Tolliver," reminded Bennett.

"Right. The guy with the scar."

"When you went inside to see the prison, you used mind control on the guards and made them believe you were the governor. Why not try that again," said Kai.

"I was only controlling two minds and wasn't walking out with a bunch of pirates trailing behind. Besides, I think I can only do that with a few people around, not a crowd. Sounds like they're going to have half a battalion assigned to guard Rackham and his crew," answered Jack. He paused and looked off into the distance before clearing his throat. "I think we're going to have to fight our way out, no matter how I get in."

The shipload of pirate prisoners did not arrive the next day as expected. Unfavorable winds had slowed the British sloop's progress. Bennett stayed close to the wharf listening for further news. Kai and Q shuttled between the Blue Mountains and the Maroon camp gathering and stockpiling more roots and berries for the homemade tonics. Jack stayed with Rachel, helping her prepare the medicinal concoctions. He checked in periodically with Bennett and Kai through mental conversations for updates. The day ended with no important news or activity as Jack, Kai and Rachel relaxed around the campfire.

"All of the kids will make it, a couple of them even complained they were hungry and managed to eat a few bites of mango," said Rachel as she rubbed the back of her neck.

"That's awesome. Figure out what made 'em sick?" asked Kai.

"Not yet, but I think I'll hang out here for one more day and help Nanny and Toju. There's a lot going on now that they're getting ready to move to the Blue Mountain."

"Guess we just chill until Captain Barnet arrives with our pirate friend," said Jack.

"So we'll wait here and rescue 'em when they get to the fort?" asked Kai.

"Not sure there's another option."

"Yeah, well I'm beat. We need to get some rest in case we get our chance sooner than later," said Kai as he stood to walk into the hut.

~10~
WELCOMING COMMITTEE

GOVERNOR WOODES ROGERS stood behind his massive desk looking toward the sea through a floor-to-ceiling sized window. "I want one hundred men guarding Rackham and his crew the instant Barnet's sloop arrives in port. No one gets near that vessel. Is that understood, major?"

"Yes, your lordship." The major bowed, turned and left the room. To him, using a hundred men to watch a dozen pirates seemed excessive, but the governor had ordered it, and he would carry out the pompous little man's instructions to the letter.

It was nearly two in the afternoon when Captain Barnet's sloop approached the wharf. Redcoats swarmed onto the dock, muskets at the ready forcing all merchants and sailors to clear out, leaving their ships and goods unattended. Those objecting too loudly found themselves rounded up, bound in chains and dragged off to receive five vicious lashes from Port Royal's sadistic executioner Schaeffer Tolliver.

Rackham and his crew listened to the commotion from the deck above the sloop's brig. "Sounds like they be preparin' the welcomin' committee, lads," said Calico Jack.

"Aye, welcome us they will with a twist of hemp about our necks," answered Tucker Gunn Calico Jack's Quartermaster.

Anne Bonny, still dressed as a man, spoke up. "Had

you louts put up a fight 'stead of fallin' down drunk in your own vomit, might all of us escaped to a life of plenty."

"Calm yourself, Anne. 'Tis not a worry now, lass," said her friend Mary Read.

Captain Rackham looked across at his two female crewmembers. Pirates held to many superstitions, one being to never allow a woman aboard ship, yet here were two, posing as men, fighting, swearing and carrying out their duties as part of one of the most notorious crews in all of the Caribbean. "Expect a tough time of it for sure, but I feel it in me bones, mates, escape we will. Straighten yerselves, chins high, an' look smart when they march us through Port Royal. Tuck, see to it now."

"Aye, captain."

Calico Jack looked up as the brig's hatchway slammed back against the deck. "Bless all here, lads. It be time to greet the locals."

They dragged the pirates from the brig, chained them in groups of four and offloaded them onto the dock where armed Redcoats surrounded them. Calico Jack and his men marched through Port Royal toward Fort Charles while the townspeople gathered along the route jeering and hurling insults and threats at the military escorts while shouting out words of encouragement for the doomed buccaneers. When they arrived inside the fortress, Schaeffer Tolliver met them at the center of the courtyard. He had a sneer on his face and a whip in his hand.

Bennett followed the procession, communicating mentally with Jack along the way. He didn't understand how this bit of magic worked but it did. Jack's voice had a slight echo to it, he wondered if his sounded the same to Jack. Q swooped down, his tail feathers grazing the top of Bennett's head. "*Q is here,*" said Bennett without actually speaking.

"*Good. I asked Q to do what he could to keep*

Tolliver from beating Calico Jack and his crew half to death."

"He's already waiting with a brand new lash in his hand," reported Bennett.

"Let's hope Q can stop him. You, on the other hand, need to stay back. If you can see Tolliver, you're too close. Don't take any chances. Got that?"

"I'll be careful."

"Wrong answer, Bennett. Stay away from the prison. Don't even go into the courtyard," said Jack.

"Whatever you say, Jack. Don't worry."

"I'll check back with you later."

This was worse than expected. Calico Jack and his crew found themselves surrounded by Redcoats and townspeople with Schaeffer Tolliver standing at the ready rhythmically waving his new bone-tipped cat-o-nine tail waiting for the order to put it to use. The governor, a short little man with a hooked nose and wearing a powdered wig, stood facing the pirates, his tiny hands clasped behind his back. He cleared his throat before addressing Calico Jack. "I do suppose, Rackham, that you found great satisfaction attacking a ship sailing under His Majesty's colors, within plain sight of the harbor." His voice was high-pitched and whiney.

"Aye, 'twas ripe fer the takin', Excellency," replied Calico Jack with a smirk and a nod.

"We shall make sure that you lose that arrogance before you lose your life. I decree that you and your crew shall receive twenty lashes each day until the start of your trial, though I suspect, after a time, the beatings themselves shall claim at least some from your crew of thieves and cutthroats." Governor Rogers turned to face the executioner.

"See to it, Tolly that these men suffer like no one before them. Inflict such pain that they beg for death. If one of these men should lose consciousness during a lashing, revive him and resume your work from the beginning of the count. Am I understood?"

"Yes, m'lord," answered Tolliver as he suppressed a smile.

"Surely ye don't intend to beat the women in me crew, gov'nor," said Rackham as he pointed at Anne and Mary.

"What the devil are you talking about, Rackham?"

"Ladies please, ye must now end yer clever ruse," shouted the pirate captain.

Tolliver stood shocked, lost as to what to do next and looked toward the governor for instruction.

"Take these women to a cell and chain them together," ordered Governor Rogers.

Four guards carried out the order, roughly dragging the protesting women across the courtyard and through the double doors of the prison.

"Proceed immediately with the floggings, Tolliver. Begin with the biggest man and save Rackham for last so that he can see the misery he has brought upon his crewmembers." With a backward wave of his hand, the governor and his escort walked across the square to the waiting carriage. He did not linger to watch his orders carried out.

Schaeffer Tolliver nodded toward two stout Redcoats. They unchained Tucker Gunn and strapped his hands together before ripping the back of his shirt open. Gunn, a tall muscular man walked without prodding to the whipping post and raised his bound hands for the guards to secure them through the iron loop holding a thick black chain. Turning his head to face Calico Jack he said in a booming voice "Could do with a wee dram of rum, Cap'n Rackham," and then threw back his head and laughed.

Rackham smiled and nodded proudly toward his second in command. "Aye, 'twill be plenty, Tuck where we be headin,' mate!"

At this display of fearlessness and disrespect Schaeffer Tolliver swept his lash across the pirate's back, swinging so hard that he lost his balance, toppling off the edge of the flogging platform. This caused Gunn to laugh even louder before addressing the executioner who now sat awkwardly in the dirt, the crowd enjoying his embarrassment as they howled and jeered the man known for his cruelty.

The pirate spat on the ground, inches from Tolliver's leg. "Pray fer yer sake I never break loose. I daresay killin' ye would require but a paltry effort."

Tolliver scrambled to his feet, slipping in the process to fall flat on his face. The crowd roared again with delight as he staggered comically onto the platform. Gunn laughed again and with a backward heave, ripped the iron loop from the center of the timber post and turned to face his would-be torturer. "Now let's have a go, Mr. Tolliver."

The Redcoats swarmed over Gunn. The big man put up a ferocious fight swinging two-handed blows with his bound hands and cracking the short length of chain against the heads of several British soldiers. He took out more than a dozen men before they finally overwhelmed him, pinning him to the ground.

Schaeffer Tolliver, his face contorted in fury, screamed at the soldiers to secure Gunn to the post. The crowd laughed and taunted, while pelting the executioner and Redcoats with garbage and small stones. Rackham and his men watched as the hysteria mounted hoping that a full-scale riot might lead to an escape opportunity.

The Redcoats, having lost control of the situation

ignored Tolliver's demands, formed a barrier around Rackham and his men and dragged them through the crowd and into the jail, leaving the enraged executioner behind searching for his lost whip.

Satisfied that Schaeffer Tolliver's opportunity to lash Rackham and his crew had passed, Q flew off toward the jungle, the whip hanging from his golden beak.

They sat around the fire at daybreak outside their jungle lean-to. Rachel walked off to check on the recovering children. "Guess I'll go to the prison this morning to meet Calico Jack and let him know we're breaking him loose," announced Jack.

"The sooner we get things rollin' the faster we get home," said Kai. "I assume you have a plan."

"Not exactly."

Q rolled his eyes. "He plans to get himself arrested and join the imprisoned pirates. In the meantime, Kai, you and I will make the escape arrangements outside the prison while Jack works out the details inside."

"How do you know that?" asked Kai.

"Because it is the only way to succeed, my friend," said Q.

Kai turned toward Jack. "Is that really what you're thinkin'?"

"Well . . . yes. I have four of you on the outside to help, and I need to convince Calico Jack and his crew to work with me from inside," said Jack.

"What about the guy with the whip?" asked Kai.

"Let's hope Calico Jack's luck holds."

"What are you gonna do to get arrested? Pick a fight

with a Redcoat?"

"No they would just shoot me," said Jack.

"What if you were caught stealin' from the Tinnermons? They could turn you in without you gettin' shot," said Kai.

"Bennett and his family can't be seen with us. There can be no association at all. We're going to pull off a huge jailbreak, rescuing a pirate that the governor hates. Once we escape, the Redcoats will arrest anyone suspected of having contact with us," said Jack. "I'm going to work my way close to the jail cells and try using mind control on the men closest to the door."

"Queen Nanny and the Maroons should move their village before the pirates are rescued," said Rachel as she returned.

"You think so?" asked Jack.

"The Redcoats chased Kai to this side of the bay. They'll assume the Maroons helped in some way."

"How do you get them to move so fast without tellin' them our plans?" asked Kai.

"Nanny will keep our secret. I'll just need to push her to move sooner."

Jack stood and moved next to Rachel. "We're getting started today. I'm going to . . ."

"Get thrown in the prison with Calico Jack," interrupted Rachel.

"Uh, yeah. How did you know that?"

"It's the only way you can get inside," she said.

Jack smiled and hugged her tight. "We'll be home soon, Rachel." He kissed her and stepped away. "I have to go."

"I know. Be careful," she said, trying to sound brave.

~X~

They were less than a mile from Fort Charles when Jack, Kai and Q split up. Kai changed into a Seagull while Q reverted to his favorite Quetzal bird. Jack trudged alone into the courtyard of the fortress. He walked up to the guards at the prison's entrance and reached across to touch the Rackham brand. As it glowed, Jack spoke to the two Redcoats without uttering a word. *"You will give me your keys and put me in the same cell with Calico Jack Rackham and you will not remember doing it."*

"Right this way, m' lord," answered the shorter of the two guards as he unlocked the steel door and swung it open for Jack to enter.

Kai watched from the parapet of the watchtower as the guards ushered his best friend into the jail below. Satisfied that all had gone smoothly, he flew off toward the wharf in search of a suitable ship to steal.

~X~

Q landed on the railing at the back entrance of the Tinnermon's shop. Bennett looked around; made sure no one was nearby and motioned that it was safe to enter.

"Hello, Q."

"Bennett," said Q as he reverted to his human form.

"What do you need?"

"Nothing. Jack wanted me to give you something for your troubles as well as a message."

"Is he alright?"

Q hesitated. "I suppose, but I'm not to discuss his . . . quest. You see, he does not want you to know anything from this point forward as a means of keeping you and your family safe."

"Where is he?"

"Don't pry, Bennett. You know too much now and that could be dangerous."

"He sent you here to tell me . . .?"

"First he wanted you to have this." Q handed Bennett several gold coins along with Jack's *Freestyle* dive watch. "I must say, this timepiece should be destroyed. His gesture is generous and heartfelt but I should think he would see the danger in leaving behind an object from the twenty first century here in the eighteenth. How could you ever explain having this in your possession should someone discover it?"

Bennett looked down at the watch and the gold.

Q continued. "Jack said he wished he could be here himself but that's not possible. He also wished he could give you part of his great fortune but this bit of gold is all that he carried."

"There is enough gold here for my family to live for a year, maybe two, without ever opening the store. I can hide the watch. What did he want to tell me?"

Q frowned as he looked again at the watch in Bennett's hand. "He said he appreciates your help but now you need to forget all about the four of us. Stay close to the shop for the next day or two. He doesn't want anyone to associate you with us, for your own safety. He also said to tell you that when you get older, go to America. He suggests settling in a place called Philadelphia."

"So that means he is ready to rescue the pirates."

"I did not say that, Bennett."

"But it is starting."

"Be well, my young friend. Please do as Jack has asked."

Bennett watched Q fly away before grabbing his hat and walking out the door toward Fort Charles.

~X~

The guard led Jack down the steps into the dank prison. It was cleaner than his last visit, the corridor now brightly lit with torches. He was relieved to see that the shackles and chains that had hung from the walls were gone, removed as Jack had ordered while pretending to be the governor. So far, the pirates had been spared most of the pain and cruelty that the dead Calico Jack had described so fearfully several days earlier.

The door swung open to the second cell and Jack entered. As the jailor locked the door, Jack held out his hand. "The keys please."

The guard complied then turned and walked away, oblivious to his blunder.

Jack nodded toward the three pirates occupying the cell. They were chained together at the wrist and two of them carried the defeated look of men who had given up hope, preparing to meet death. "I'm looking for Calico Jack," said Jack.

"Well he ain't here so leave us be," said one of the cellmates.

The pirate in the corner that had kept his head down finally looked up. "Who be askin' 'bout the captain?" asked Calico Jack.

"Hello, Captain Rackham. We need to talk privately. Your life, and the lives of your crewmembers depend on how our conversation goes," said Jack.

"Well I ain't the captain," announced the pirate.

"In that case I'll leave and you can go about the business of having your neck stretched at the end of a rope," said Jack as he removed the cell keys from his pocket.

"How'd ye get them keys?"

"Does it matter? Do you want to get out of here alive or not?"

"I be John Rackham, known in these parts as Calico Jack. Now state yer name n' business, lad an' be quick about it."

"I'm Jack Rackham, your descendant and I've traveled back in time three hundred years to rescue you, Miss Bonny and the rest of your crew."

The pirate sneered. "Aye, 'tis a good tale ye tell, lad. In but a fortnight we shall all meet our doom at *Gallows Point*. That rogue gov'ner sent ye here to learn me secrets an' find me treasure. There be but one Jack Rackham and that be me and I'll be tellin' no tales. Now use yer keys an' leave us be."

Jack sat down on the floor across from the captain. "I'll tell you how it turns out. They do hang you and your crew, except for Anne and Mary, since they're both going to have babies."

"How d'ye be knowin' such things?"

"You told me everything when you gave me this." Jack pulled the *Serpent Dagger* from inside his waistband and handed it to the pirate. "You kidnapped my friend Rachel to force me to rescue you. I didn't volunteer."

Calico Jack laughed. "So ye think a far-fetched tale such as this'll make me tell ye where me treasure be!"

'Your treasure is in my … ship. We collected your gold from the tunnel that your men, the ones you called the rat eaters, dug on Fishtail Cay. We found it using your copper plates with the numbered codes," explained Jack.

"Impossible. No one knows 'bout them plates but me n' … "

"Anne Bonny? Her father rescued her from Port Royal and she returned to his plantation in North Carolina where she raised your son Jacob. In the twenty first century, my grandfather, also your descendant, bought those plates and used the codes for his search. A few weeks ago, in our time, your ghost visited us aboard our boat. That's where I ended up with the *Serpent Dagger.*"

"So, we just march from this prison an' through the gates to freedom eh, lad?"

"Something like that," said Jack.

The pirate laughed. "Ye got a spine but no sense. Think ye can make Captain Calico Jack look the fool?" He tossed the dagger hilt-first to Tucker Gunn. "Cut his throat an' be quick about it."

"But cap . . .'

"Ye heard me, Tuck. Now get the deed done."

Jack reached down and touched the scar on his forearm. "Hand me that dagger, Mr. Gunn. I'll let myself out and all of you can go ahead and hang." He reached his hand out and Tucker Gunn, staring ahead trance-like, placed it gently in the palm of Jack's hand.

"What the devil did ye do to him?"

Jack rolled up his sleeve exposing his forearm scarred with the still-glowing Rackham insignia, a skull over crossed cutlasses. "You cursed me with this brand on Fishtail Cay. I have the ability, thanks to you, to control minds. Haven't used it much because I think it's pretty creepy, but it got me in here. You just saw how Mr. Gunn defied your order to kill me and handed me the dagger."

"Aye, it be nothin' more n' trickery, sleight of hand, or p'raps island magic."

"Captain, I have nothing to prove. I came here with my friends, all of us risking our lives, to keep a promise that I made to the dead Calico Jack but since you're determined to die on the gallows with your eyeball popped out, hanging in a bloody mess against your cheek, that's fine, I'll be on my way."

Mary Read stood in the adjoining cell leaning with her face against the bars. "Captain, methinks it high time to listen to this lad. Leastways we've the chance to die fightin' 'stead of cowerin' in this filth awaitin' our fate. If ye prefer dancin' from the hemp, stay behind but don't ye be standin' in our way."

The pirate sighed and hauled himself upright. "Aye. It be a chance against mighty odds but a chance it be," said Calico Jack. "Unlock hell's gates, lad. Today we make war with the King's devils."

"Maybe we should get some weapons and wait until dark to escape?" asked Jack.

"What sport would there be in that?" shouted Anne Bonny. "I say we go now, catch them Redcoats off guard."

Jack walked to the cell's gate. "Is that you Miss Bonny?"

"Aye."

"There's one condition that everyone must agree to before I unlock anything," said Jack. "No matter what happens, Anne Bonny must be kept safe. As I explained to Captain Rackham, I traveled here from the future. If Anne dies and doesn't have her baby, the Rackham family dies with her and I won't be born three hundred years from now. If I'm not born, this rescue never happens and everyone here dies. Does everyone understand and agree to that?"

Everyone grunted their acceptance of his terms. Whether they believed Jack's story or not, they all wanted to protect Anne. Jack removed the shackles from Calico Jack, Tucker Gunn and a smallish pirate named Carty. He opened the cell door, stepped into the hallway and repeated the process at each of the next three cells. With everyone freed, they lined up single file behind Jack at the bottom of the stairway, waiting for instructions. Calico Jack, not content to allow young Jack to lead his crew, stepped forward to take the point.

"Wait while I go out there to dismiss the sentries and collect some weapons. I'll be back in a few minutes," said Jack.

The pirate reached out to stop Jack from opening the door. His hand landed on top of the brand and Jack fell down onto the steps in agony as steam billowed from his forearm. Several seconds passed before Jack caught his breath and stood. He looked at his arm. The Rackham brand was gone. He looked at Calico Jack and grinned. "You just removed the Rackham Curse."

"Aye, seems me timin' ain't so good. Now ye can step aside an' let me lead me men since ye won't be controllin' any minds now, lad," said the captain with a smirk. "Now pay heed ye lubbers. Rush the guards and then scatter. Steal whatever weapons ye can lay hands on but don't stop to fight if ye can help it. We meet on the main island near the top of Blue Mountain."

"That's it? That's your plan?" asked Jack.

"Aye. Better'n yers. Leastways mine gets us past the door."

Jack unlocked the prison gate and stepped aside, allowing the pirate captain to lead his crew into the courtyard. In seconds, the two guards were subdued and their weapons confiscated. As ordered, the pirates fanned out, sprinting through the courtyard ambushing unsuspecting soldiers, stealing weapons and rushing out of the fortress from different exits. Jack paused to watch Anne Bonny escape through the east gate accompanied by Calico Jack and Tucker Gunn. Satisfied that Anne was safe, Jack sprinted through the confused crowd toward the main gate. As he turned the corner a Redcoat met him outside the entryway, the butt of his musket already halfway through its swing. Jack had no chance to react as the gun's stock caught him flush on the side of his head. He was unconscious before he hit the ground.

Bennett stooped behind the parapet smiling and silently cheering as he watched the pirates escape. As he turned to leave he saw two Redcoats dragging Jack through the square toward the stocks. What could he do to help his new friend? It wouldn't take long for Schaeffer Tolliver to arrive. The sentence for aiding pirates was death and Tolliver would make sure that Jack would endure great pain before his execution.

When Jack regained consciousness he found his head, arms and legs locked between great slabs of wood. The left side of his throbbing head was caked in dried blood and his left eye was swollen and sticky. From his good eye he could see a few dozen people milling around staring at him. The stocks were clamped down in a choke hold around his neck preventing him from turning to see to his left. His wrists were shackled, which seemed unnecessary considering how tightly the stocks compressed his arms. Obviously they were not built to accommodate someone his size. He wondered how long he had been unconscious but seconds later everything went dark again.

Bennett kept looking to the sky, hoping to see Q. He had never felt so helpless. If he could somehow get word to Jack's friends, maybe they could save him before the executioner arrived. His thoughts were interrupted by the sound of beating hoofs as Schaeffer Tolliver and his entourage arrived.

Bennett moved closer, hiding behind a stack of barrels near the edge of the parapet to watch the scene unfold below.

Tolliver ordered one of his men to revive Jack with a splash of dirty water from an animal trough. When Jack regained consciousness, they dragged him from the stocks and threw him to the ground before grabbing the chain at his wrists and pulling him through the dirt to the whipping platform. Once there, they stood him up and slammed him face-first against the post, securing his chain to the steel loop at the top. Another of Tolliver's men stepped forward and ripped the shirt open, exposing Jack's back.

The executioner walked up to the post and looked up to face Jack. "We've witnesses that say it was you what helped Calico Jack and his cutthroats escape. Now you'll see how we deal with the likes of you. Fifty lashes! You'll get twenty-five across your back, another twenty-five on your chest. I'll be seeing your guts fall out before I'm through and there won't be much of you left to hang."

Jack looked Tolliver in the eye, his bloody mouth set in a mocking grin. "You should get off this island while you can. One lash across my back and my friends will hunt you down and tear you to pieces. You'll find out what real pain is all about."

Tolliver stepped back; a look of cold terror crossed his face. After a few seconds he composed himself, knowing he couldn't take back his bellicose pronouncement in front of the gathering crowd. "We shall see about that," he announced not so confidently before turning to retrieve his whip.

Jack laughed. "So you've just proven to everyone here that you really are a coward."

"I would gag you this instant, lad but prefer to hear your bloody screams," said Tolliver as he readied his whip.

Bennett looked around one more time with a final

glance into the blue sky. There was no sign of help coming from Q or Kai. He ran to the munitions supplies stacked next to one of the cannons, grabbed a two-inch ball from a grapeshot charge and ran back to slide behind the parapet, to a spot in line with whipping platform. He stood, checked the position of Schaeffer Tolliver, took two steps back, hefted the heavy ball as far back as he could and took a leaping giant step toward the edge of the low wall, launching it with every ounce of strength toward the executioner just as Tolliver reared back to deliver the first strike. Bennett didn't see where the ball landed as he lost his balance with the heave. As the small iron ball left his hand, his momentum caused him to slam into the parapet wall, his body doubling over at the waist his eyes focused on the stone courtyard thirty feet below. Reaching to clutch at anything, his fingernails seemed to dig into the brick slowing him just enough to keep him from catapulting over the edge.

He gained his balance and stood upright. That's when he saw Tolliver lying on the ground in a heap, face in the dirt, his whip curled harmlessly beneath his upper body. The ball resting conspicuously a few feet away. Redcoats rushed in to disperse the crowd. One of them pointed up at Bennett and yelled out orders. At least twenty soldiers ran to the stairways leading to the parapet. He was trapped and his only escape would require a long drop, no matter which direction he chose. Bennett ran east toward the bay. He stopped and peered over the edge. There was water below, but it was one hundred yards from the fortress wall. The Redcoats had him surrounded and closing fast, some raising their rifles taking aim. He ran fifteen feet to his left, and lunged for a rope that swung from a little-used hoist, hoping the frayed rope and rusted wheel would hold long enough for him to reach the bottom in one piece. As he leaped, the first shots rang out and chunks of brick flew from the parapet over his head as he descended hand-over-hand, banging hard against the fortress walls with each motion. Fifteen feet from the bottom, the muskets erupted again, one ball barely missing his head. With a deep breath, he let himself slide the next ten feet, his hands burning and blistering with every inch of progress. Nearing the bottom, he let go, rolling hard onto his left shoulder as he hit the ground before popping up and running toward the water, head down and heart pounding as the musket fire continued from behind.

Bennett's distraction worked. With most of the Redcoats chasing Bennett along the parapet, Calico Jack and Tucker Gunn rushed into the fortress, easily wiping out the remaining guard detail. Gunn ran to the whipping post, ripped Jack's irons loose and twisted the wrist chains apart while the outnumbered pirate captain continued attacking Redcoats, slashing through their ranks with a pair of cutlasses, ignoring the smoking muskets aimed in his direction. Once Jack and Gunn joined the fight, using the broken chain and timber as weapons, the Redcoats bolted for cover, leaving the gates unattended for an easy escape.

The trio ran into the wooded area north of the fortress. When certain they had lost the Redcoats, they paused among the trees to get their bearings.

"So what happened back there? I thought you guys were long gone," said Jack.

"We doubled back lookin' for a way to get ye out. 'Twas the lad on the parapet what gave us the chance to storm the gates," said Gunn.

"But you were free, why take the risk? Is Anne alright?"

"Scoundrels we be but leavin' our rescuer behind to

die would go against …"

"Wait. What lad on the parapet? What did he do? What did he look like?"

"Aye a young lad he was. Light hair, not big like yerself but not small. The boy lobbed somethin' toward yer executioner and that evil devil dropped like a stone."

"I didn't see him get hit with anything. I did know the Redcoats were chasing someone but couldn't see from where I stood," said Jack.

"They set upon that lad with half the battalion an' that be when we made our grand entrance," said Calico Jack. "I daresay, young Rackham, ye be bloody an' terrible swollen 'bout yer face n' head."

Jack looked at the pirate, "I have to find Bennett, that's the boy they were chasing. I just hope he's not dead or captured. Captain, you need to get your crew together up to the mountains. Hide out there until I come find you. Keep an eye out for a very colorful bird with a long tail. He's one of my friends and he can help. By the time I get back we should have a plan and a way to get off this island. If you don't see me by dawn, don't wait. Get away when you can. And thanks for coming back for me, but you do know it wasn't the pirate-thing to do."

Jack clapped the pirate on the shoulder before climbing through the bush and running in the direction of the fort.

❦11❦
SCATTERED AND BATTERED

BENNET HAD TO WARN HIS PARENTS but the town was swarming with soldiers. Once the Redcoats discovered his identity a regiment would surround the Tinnermon's shop with their muskets at the ready. His parents would be arrested and shackled as accomplices for a crime they knew nothing about and the whole family would be hanged together, thanks to him. Jack wasn't answering his mental communication, which could only mean one thing, Jack was dead. He dragged his water-logged body to shore, walked a short distance onto the sand and passed out lying flat on his back on the beach on the wrong side of Half-Moon Bay.

❦X❦

Q had collected enough roots and berries for Rachel to use as medicine to treat the sick kids while the Maroons prepared for their move to the Blue Mountains. This was his last trip and Q was grateful for that. A king flying as a Quetzal bird or eagle was perfectly acceptable, traveling as a pelican with a stuffed pouch, on the other hand, was quite embarrassing, not to mention uncomfortable.

Something big must have happened in Port Royal. Redcoats were everywhere. Q wondered if Jack and the pirates had already escaped, but since Kai was still looking for the right ship to steal, and the opportunity to steal it, an early escape seemed unlikely. He swooped down for a closer look. Seeing the prison still under guard, he continued his flight across the bay to make his final delivery. As he approached the shoreline he noticed a shape lying in the sand at the water's edge.

Kai had always been afraid of heights, until now. Disguised as a common seagull he scouted the ships moored in the harbor below. It made the job safe and easy. The ship with the most promise was a single-mast sloop moored at the outside edge of the dock that had been offloaded only hours before. He chanced a closer look and landed on the spar. The sloop carried four cannons, the decks were in good condition, the rigging was tight with few signs of fraying, a fair indication that the sails were probably in top shape. This would be their target. Now it was time to eavesdrop and see when the crew planned to set sail. Kai scurried down the rigging toward the deck, this time in the form of a rat.

Jack rubbed his forearm sorry, for the moment, that the curse had been lifted. His ability to communicate mentally was gone. Three times, since leaving Captain Rackham and Tucker Gunn he had barely managed to duck for cover from the patrolling Redcoats but his luck couldn't hold much longer. Finding Bennett's parents and convincing them to leave their home and shop to escape the island was crucial. If he could get everyone together, and that included Bennett, they could hide in the mountains until they found a suitable ship.

Rachel lowered the pot of boiling water and ran to meet Q. He walked toward her carrying Bennett in his arms. The boy's skin was cold. Rachel assumed he was dead.

"He is alive, Rachel. I found him lying on the beach. It appears that the young man swam across the bay. He is no doubt exhausted. Something must have happened in Port Royal that made him act so drastically," said Q.

"Let's get him some water and move him next to the fire. He's probably dehydrated."

Rachel mopped Bennett's face with cool fresh water. His lips were cracked from the exposure to the salt and sun. After a few minutes he stirred.

"Rachel? Q? How did I get here?" asked Bennett.

"Q found you on the beach. It looked like you swam across the bay. What happened?"

Bennett suddenly sat upright. "Jack! They caught Jack. Schaffer Tolliver, the executioner, had him tied to the post to beat him. I tried to stop it and then the Redcoats chased me. They were shooting at me. We have to go find Jack. He might be dead by now."

Rachel looked at Q. "Do you think he's dead?"

"I noticed many Redcoats in the streets and wondered if Jack and the pirates had escaped."

"That's not what I asked, Q," said Rachel.

"The pirates *DID* escape but the Redcoats caught Jack," said Bennett.

"Think any Redcoats recognized you?"

"I don't think so. I was running and had my back to

them."

"But they will eventually figure out who you are and how to find you."

Q interrupted. "Rachel I think you and Bennett should go to the Blue Mountains with Queen Nanny and her people. I will go look for Jack and Bennett's parents."

"No. I'm going, and so is Bennett."

"But the Redcoats are looking for Bennett ..."

"I'm going too, Q. They need our help and we're wasting time arguing," said Bennett.

Q looked at the pair and smiled. "As you wish." He extracted a small cloth from his belt. "Would you please assist me with this?"

"What is it?" asked Rachel.

"Hold the corners and walk backwards keep tension on the cloth."

Bennett and Rachel followed Q's instructions. The fabric stretched into a blanket and they laid it out on the ground. Queen Nanny approached as they finished smoothing out the edges.

"You are leaving us?" the old woman asked, her eyes filling with tears.

Rachel hugged her tightly, tears coming to her own eyes. "We have to hurry and find Jack and Kai and return to our own time. I left you plenty of medicine for the children and you know what to do now."

"Thank you, child. You have our love and gratitude forever. You should know your friends are well. I have conjured their images and have seen this for myself." She looked at the fabric lying on the ground. "I always believed the traveling cloth to be nothing more than a legend." She patted Q on the hand. "Please take care of my friends, Q." She looked at Bennett. "You will find your family. You have a most remarkable future ahead, young man."

Queen Nanny stepped aside and nodded toward Q who smiled and pointed to the blanket. "Please stand in the center for me."

Rachel and Bennett moved to the center, holding hands as they did. Q gathered the corners pulling them to a point above their heads and secured it with a golden cord. Once done, he pulled the cord tight and the newly made bag shrank until it was no bigger than a small pouch. Queen Nanny watched as Q, now a Quetzal bird flew off toward Port Royal with the tiny bundle suspended from his golden beak.

X

Jack crept into the storeroom behind the Tinnermon's shop. It had been ransacked. He wondered if the Redcoats had trashed it looking for him or for Bennett. He turned and stared down the barrel of a musket, a tall bearded man held it steady, daring him to move.

"Mr. Tinnermon?"

"You must be one of the pirates that the Redcoats are looking for."

"Yes, they're looking for me, but I'm not a pirate. The pirates are hiding in the mountains waiting for me to help them escape from the island."

"So you thought you would hide where they already searched."

"No, I came to warn you and your wife that they will be here soon trying to find your son Bennett."

"Bennett? What would they want with Bennett?" Tinnermon relaxed his grip slightly.

"I helped the pirates escape but they caught me. Bennett rescued me from Schaeffer Tolliver and his whip.

When the Redcoats figure out who Bennett is, they'll come back here to arrest him and the chances are they'll hang him for helping me."

"I don't believe you. Bennett is a good boy, not one to get involved with the likes of you."

"You're right, he's a good boy. He's very responsible and has a good sense of right and wrong. You and your wife should be very proud. I told him I was here to help Calico Jack and his crew escape and to stay away from the fort, but I guess he was too curious. We've become friends these past few days. Guess he couldn't stand the idea of Tolliver beating me to a bloody pulp and felt like he had to help," explained Jack.

"I should shoot you where you stand for getting my boy in trouble."

"I don't blame you for feeling that way but right now you and your wife need to leave this place before the Redcoats return. I'll help you."

"I should take a stranger's word for this?"

"You don't have a choice, Mr. Tinnermon. You have to leave now."

"We'll see about that." Mr. Tinnermon grabbed the end of the gun barrel, switching the musket around to use the stock as a club.

Jack stood up straight putting his hands behind his back. "I've already been hit like that once today." He turned slightly. "Look you can see all the dried blood and the swelling but I'm ready to get hit again if that helps prove that I'm here to help."

"Bloody Redcoats. They're no better than pirates, if you ask me." Mr. Tinnermon leaned his weapon against the wall. "I'll send the missus to hide while I look for Bennett. Would appreciate any help you can lend."

"Well, some help just arrived," said Jack as Q flew

inside the storeroom.

"What the devil is this?" asked Tinnermon.

Q placed the tiny bundle on the floor, stepped away and changed into his human form causing Mr. Tinnermon to reach for his musket again.

"It's alright, give me a minute to explain," said Jack.

Q ignored Jack and Mr. Tinnermon while he bent down and untied the tiny pouch, pulled the corners open and stepped back allowing Bennett and Rachel to appear in their normal size in the center of the room. Bennett rushed to his dad both hugging one another like they would never let go. Rachel took one look at Jack and covered her mouth with her hand before moving over to wrap her arms around him.

"What did they do to you?" asked Rachel, tears streaming down her cheeks.

Jack smiled, "Guess this is where I'm supposed to say 'you should see the other guy'. Right now we have to get Bennett's mom and get out of here before the Redcoats come back.

Mr. Tinnermon moved to the open doorway. "It's too late, they're here. Bennett, you know what to do," he said.

The boy ran across the room, moved a barrel toward the wall and lifted a trap door. He motioned for everyone to follow.

They were inside a tiny tunnel that connected the storeroom to the shop. Bennett pushed the floorboard up a few inches to make sure all was clear. His mother was behind the counting table by herself. "Ma! Hurry, we have to go," was all he said. She moved across the room and crawled into the tiny tunnel as Bennett pulled the hatch closed. Mr. Tinnermon was now at the opposite end of the crawlspace sliding a bolt through the underside of the trap door. From below they could hear the Redcoats stomping around overhead.

"They must have seen us coming and run out the back door, men. Put a torch to the place. Half of you move to the shop, the other half, go to the house. Burn it all. Your orders are to shoot on sight, all of them."

They were caught below the wood floor with only scattered dusty rays of light squeezing down between the floorboards. Bennett tugged on Jack's arm and whispered, "Follow my Pa. We have one more tunnel."

Crawling on their hands and knees for several yards, they could smell the smoke as it filtered into the passageway. Finally, they reached the end where there was enough room to stand. "We need to pull these planks off. Behind the planks are a few large rocks that look overgrown with grass and palm scrub but they are actually planted that way. I'm going to shove the rocks aside carefully so they won't roll and make noise. Once we get outside we need to hug the hillside and go west into the woods. Everyone has to remain quiet; we are still not very far from the storeroom."

It took five minutes to clear the opening as the thick smoke enveloped them. One by one they exited the tunnel and moved into the wooded hillside. Q changed into a gull and flew away, circling above to monitor the Redcoat's search.

They assembled below a ridge a mile from town where they watched the smoke from the burning home and business. Mr. Tinnermon sat with an arm around his wife and son. "I guess you're wondering why I built those tunnels," he said to Jack.

"I'm glad you did and yes, the question crossed my mind."

Mr. Tinnermon chuckled. "Pirates! The town's full of them and you could never tell when they might want to make mischief."

Rachel smiled. "And now you and your family are on the way to join up with a crew of pirates and sail away from here."

"True, Missy." He looked at his wife and squeezed her around the shoulders. "You're so quiet. Suppose you're thinkin' about how we have to start all over?"

Mrs. Tinnermon looked at her husband and smiled. "No, Brian I was thinking how happy I will be to move away from this place." She looked at Jack. "Do you suppose we could we go to America?"

Bennett answered. "Jack said we should go to a place called Philadelphia. And look what he gave me," he said as he held the pocketful of gold. "There should be enough here to help us start over." He looked up in time to see Q land a few feet away and change into his human form.

"I despise flying as a gull. They're so dreadfully common."

"Then why did you change into a gull instead of the usual?" asked Bennett.

Q gave Bennett the look. "So that I *could* be dreadfully common, and blend in while spying on the Redcoats. Do you have any idea what seagulls consume? They're very much like rats, with wings."

Bennett introduced his friends to his parents. He told them the story of how they met and the rescue of Calico Jack. Q gave Jack directions on where to find the pirates, changed, this time into a quetzal bird, and flew off to find Kai. Jack, Rachel and the Tinnermons resumed their climb into the woods toward the pirate hideout.

Kai discovered that the ship he hoped to commandeer would

be in port for three days. They would take on provisions and cargo tomorrow, their second day. That meant most of the crew would be ashore the following night, and that's when Kai and Rackham's men would strike. As he climbed the ratlines, still in the form of a rat, he noticed the quetzal bird circling overhead. He changed into a seabird flapping into the trade winds to join Q.

"We'll be seein' Rackham's Cay here shortly," said Pop.

"Are we going to dock in Port Royal?" asked Val.

"No I think we'll anchor off the cay for a day or two and see what, if anything happens."

"You think when Jack and Kai return to the present they'll show up here?"

"I don't know what to think, Val. My gut's tellin' me that if somethin' is gonna happen, it'll happen here, not in St. Augustine. Being here works with the timeline that Jack mentioned in his note. That's why I didn't rush to get here. I'm guessin' that by now they've made it to Port Royal and are in the process of rescuing Calico Jack, but it's all still a guess."

"What if we dock in Port Royal first, visit the museum and see what the historians say about Calico Jack and his crew. If Jack and Kai were successful, I'd assume there might be something describing the escape rather than documents and stories of the hanging. Rackham's Cay might even be known by a different name," suggested Nan.

Pop looked at Nan and smiled. "You're on to something there but we can't dock in Port Royal. The last thing we need is to be boarded by Customs agents."

"We aren't transporting anything illegal," said Nan.

"No but how would we explain havin' a ton of gold stowed below?"

"It wasn't stolen."

"True, but how did we get it? We have no documents for it. There would be no way to stop a government official from detaining us for as long as they wanted while we tried to prove something that couldn't be proven."

"Okay so we go online and see what history says about Captain Rackham," said Nan.

"That's what we'll do once we anchor," said Pop.

～12～
RENDEZVOUS

⌒**AS TWILIGHT ARRIVED,** Kai and Q landed at a small clearing near the top of Blue Mountain and reverted to their human forms.

"Was that the vessel you intend to steal?" asked Q.

"Yeah, it's perfect. They're taking on provisions tomorrow and the crew will be ashore once they get loaded," said Kai. "Should be pretty easy."

"We shall see. Jack and the Tinnermons will arrive soon and we can then join Captain Rackham and his crew," said Q.

"The Tinnermons? You mean Bennett AND his family?"

"Yes. The Redcoats burned down their home and business."

"No way!"

Q explained as much as he knew about Bennett, Tucker Gunn and Calico Jack rescuing Jack from Schaeffer Tolliver and the Redcoats. He also told Kai about their narrow escape through the tunnels as the buildings burned over top of them.

"Wow. What are they going to do now?" asked Kai.

"Escape to America on that ship you found. They have nothing left here."

Kai thought about that for a minute. "Bennett could

have gotten himself killed. Why'd he go n' stick his neck out like that? It's not like he n' Jack have been best buds forever."

"Obviously he felt a duty to stop a cruel injustice. I find it very commendable, showing such bravery in the face of great odds."

"Doesn't make sense."

"And you don't feel that you and Jack and Rachel are taking a great risk for the sake of someone else? Calico Jack released you all from this quest before you crossed through time. I found that quite curious, as I mentioned before."

"Well, you've got me there, I guess."

"But the outcome does not affect the three of you. If Calico Jack lives or dies, the Rackham lineage continues as long as Anne Bonny survives. The fact that your friend Jack and his family live in the new times is proof enough of that," said Q.

"I dunno. Don't get me all confused with this time stuff. Captain Rackham's no choirboy, that's for sure, but he wanted a chance at turnin' things around to be a good guy and a good dad. How d'ya say no to that?"

"What is a choirboy?"

"It's, uh, . . . just an expression," said Kai.

"I see. Well . . . I believe I hear your friends approaching."

"'Bout time you got here. Geez, you guys sure took your sweet time," said Kai as Jack, Rachel and the Tinnermons walked into the clearing. "Jack, you look like crap by the way. What happened?"

"Good to see you too, moron. What've you been up to all day?" asked Jack with a laugh.

"Nothin'. I hung out at the beach all day daydreamin' about home, surfin', jet skis, Val, you know, normal life kinda stuff. Heard you were partyin' with the boys in the red coats."

Jack sighed. "Yeah, you could say that. Any luck finding us a ship? Oh, sorry. These are Bennett's parents. They're joining us." He faced the Tinnermons but pointed toward Kai. "This is my friend Kai and you've already met Q."

"Hi. Nice to meet you. Sorry about your house n' stuff, Q told me about it," said Kai.

"So the ship? Any luck?" asked Jack.

"Oh that. Yep. Got our cruise ship lined up and it sails tomorrow night, assumin' our pirates can help us."

"Calico Jack and his crew are over that way on the back side of the ridge. Hopefully they scrounged up some food. I'm starving," said Jack.

Q nodded toward Jack and Rachel. "I think I'll go hunting." Out of sight from the Tinnermons he changed into a puma, let out a fierce growl and stalked into the jungle.

They resumed their uphill hike. Bennett's mom fell in step next to her son. "How on earth did you involve yourself with people such as these?" she asked.

Bennett smiled. "They are from the future, Ma! Except for the pirates, Calico Jack is from our time. Well, Q is from the past, he is an Aztec king and can change into birds and animals whenever he pleases."

"Don't give me that foolishness. Mrs. Tinnermon put her hand on her son's forehead. "You have no fever but you must be suffering some form of delirium. Did you say pirates?"

"Yes but they won't hurt us. That's who we are sailing with to America," said Bennett matter-of-factly.

"No we most certainly are not."

"We have no choice. The Redcoats are trying to find us. You wouldn't want to have to hide in the mountains and eat berries for the rest of your life."

"I cannot believe this is happening."

"Everything will be fine, Ma. My friends will help us."

"Yes and the thought of such strange people helping us frightens me."

"But we will be living in America, Ma."

"So you say, Bennett. So you say." She leaned over and kissed him on the cheek and sighed.

Captain Rackham and his crew sat huddled around a small fire. Tucker Gunn stood guard, the musket, stolen from a Redcoat during Jack's rescue, was primed, ready to fire. He raised the weapon toward the jungle as Jack, Kai and the Tinnermons approached. Gunn spread his feet slightly before moving his finger to the trigger. Unfortunately for the near-sighted Mr. Gunn, Q had silently inched his way to within a few feet and was not about to wait to see if the trigger would be squeezed. Still in the form of the large puma, he leaped from the brush with a vicious roar, knocking the big man to the ground. The musket fell harmlessly out of reach as the big cat pinned Gunn against the base of a tree, his bared fangs inches from the pirate's face.

Kai jumped through the thicket as the pirates scrambled for their weapons. "It's okay! Q let him up. Captain, tell your men to stand down."

With a final snarl, Q pushed away from Gunn, collected the musket between his teeth and walked past the wide-eyed pirates to join Kai and Jack.

Jack chuckled as the big cat approached. "Here, kitty,

kitty," he said in a mocking high pitched voice.

"Don't go makin' him mad now," said Kai. He looked at the petrified pirates. "He's liable to tear everyone to pieces unless I tell him to stay."

"Aye, then please tell him to stay, lad. Gunn din' mean ye no 'arm," pleaded Carty, the smallest pirate in the Rackham crew.

Kai took the musket from Q, winking as he did. "Good boy. Now check those scalawags out and tell me which one's the troublemaker in this bunch."

The big cat moved in a menacing circle around the huddled group, his fangs exposed, making eye contact whenever possible. He inched his way toward Mary Read who held her ground, though she trembled slightly. Q relaxed, hiding his fangs and nuzzled gently against Mary's shoulder.

Mary laughed. "He be just a big kitten, this'n!"

Kai smiled. "Usually he's a bird. Everybody relax, no one's gonna get hurt. Okay Q, that's enough flirtin', let 'em see the real you. Rackham – you wanna introduce everyone?"

Q reverted to his human form in front of everyone causing both Mrs. Tinnermon and Carty to faint. Jack and Captain Rackham shook hands and went about the introductions.

Nan and Val scanned the internet for stories of Calico Jack and Port Royal but history still showed that the pirate and his crew had met their end at Gallows Point.

～13～
SITTIN' DUCKS

～THEY ATE FIRE-ROASTED IGUANA
and fresh ackee as they planned their escape.

"Like I said, the sloop's bein' loaded tomorrow and the crew's goin' ashore once the heavy liftin' is done. They plan to sail the next day on the morning tide. The ship's not big, but it's got plenty of room, and carries ten cannons. I don't know what kinda shape the sails are in, but the rigging looked good and tight so that makes me think the sails have been maintained," explained Kai.

"The trick of it be boardin' under the gov'nor's hooked nose," said Anne Bonny.

"Another be gettin' under sail from the wharf widdout bein' seen," added Tucker Gunn.

Calico Jack was quiet, deep in thought. "Ye say there be a brigantine at the dock, Kai?"

"Yep. Close by too. They docked the day before you and your crew arrived."

"Bloody Redcoats could row that brigantine alongside an' blast us with cannon fire whilst we still be stackin' sail, Captain Jack," said John Howell the master gunner.

"Aye, Howell. 'Twas jus' what I were thinkin'," said Calico Jack. "May be a trap."

"Could we board at night, hide below decks and take over the ship once it's under sail?" asked Rachel.

Anne Bonny smiled. "Ye should've been a pirate, lass."

"Works for boarding but if one of us is seen or caught, we're all trapped. Pretty tough to hide nineteen people. They wouldn't bother capturing us to march ashore for a trial and hanging; they'd just block our exit and shoot us as soon as we tried to move. We'd be defenseless," said Jack.

"Sittin' ducks," said Kai.

"What does that mean - sittin' ducks?" asked Mary Read.

"Just an expression. It means the same thing Jack said. We'd have no way to escape or defend ourselves," answered Kai.

"Steal some small boats," said Q. "Let me and Kai handle the rest."

Calico Jack perked up. "What do ye be suggestin', sir?"

"Steal the boats. We," he said pointing to Kai and himself, "will get you in position. You will board the ship and cut the ropes loose. While the crew readies the sails, we will tow the ship from the harbor into open water under cover of darkness. I should think the ship would be well away from Port Royal long before it was discovered missing."

"An' how d'ye propose towin' a sloop to sea?" asked Captain Rackham as he stroked his pointed chin whiskers.

Kai smiled and answered the captain. "We can change into sea creatures, maybe whale sharks, something big enough to haul a heavy ship. It's a brilliant plan, Q."

Bennett looked at Kai. "You can change into animals too?"

"Uh huh. Q taught me. I'll teach you later," said Kai with a smirk.

"You will do no such thing," said Mrs. Tinnermon as she wagged her finger in Kai's direction.

"Awww chill. I was just kiddin'," said Kai.

"I have no idea what that expression means but you keep your distance, young man."

"Let it go, Kai. Two shape shifters in the bunch is enough," said Jack with a laugh.

"I daresay we should sleep. 'Twill be a difficult slog gettin' all of us rogues into Port Royal whilst the Redcoats be searchin' for us," said Anne Bonny as she stifled a yawn.

"Agreed," grunted Tucker Gunn. "An' no big cats t'night," he added as he pointed toward Q, the slightest sign of a grin peeking from below his thick bushy mustache.

"Take the first watch, Carty," ordered Calico Jack.

"Aye, Cap'n," he answered with a sigh.

~X~

They woke the next morning with their stomachs growling again. A few men marched off into the jungle looking for food. Kai stoked the fire while entertaining Bennett and his dad with stories about the future. Rachel and Mrs. Tinnermon chatted while Jack huddled off to the side with Calico Jack, Anne Bonny and Mary Read.

"So yer tellin' me ye be my nephew three hundred years hence," scoffed Anne.

Jack smiled. "That's right. You're going to have a baby boy and name him Jacob and three hundred years from now there's going to be another Jacob Rackham, he's my cousin. So you see we, especially you, have to make it out of here alive."

"'Tis a fine strong name that," said Mary.

"Aye, an' a strong lad he'll be," added Captain Rackham. "An' devil a doubt, 'twill be a lubber, ne'er to go on the account."

"No worries. You and Anne are the last of the pirates in the Rackham family," said Jack.

"No more blasted tales, lads, we be needin' to find boats fer t'night," said Anne.

"There's no rush. We can't wander off too early. It's best to lay low, get some food, relax and wait until it starts getting dark," said Jack. "We'll get Q and Kai to scout the area for a few longboats to borrow and they can keep an eye on the ship that we're going to commandeer."

"Them rogue friends o' yers bein' able to change into birds an' such, we might join t'gether an' rule the seas," said Anne, her eyes flashing.

"Once we get you and the rest of the crew to safety, we're going home to our own time. Hopefully you'll all give up the pirate business for good," said Jack.

"So 'tis true ye met me ghost?"

"It's true," said Kai as he walked over to join Jack. "And believe me, you looked awful. Your neck was all raw n' bloody, your eyeball popped out of the socket a few times, and your skin kept fallin' off the bones, just a big nasty lookin' mess."

Calico Jack looked horrified.

"And you were wearing the same clothes that you have on now," said Jack.

To their left came the sound of men tramping through the brush causing everyone to take cover. It was Gunn, Carty and Howell all carrying more fruit and iguanas, enough to feed everyone.

Rachel sighed. "I can't wait to get home so I can get a shower, fresh clothes and some decent food, and it won't include iguana. Speaking of clothes, I wish we could go to the shanty and get our real clothes. This shirt is rough and scratchy, like burlap."

"Kind of risky getting that close to town." Jack

smiled. "Let's go."

After finishing their meal, Kai flew off with Q. Tucker Gunn and two men marched off to acquire weapons. The plan was set. They would leave the jungle hideout at dusk, and if all went well, they would find themselves sailing the open sea well before dawn.

◦—X—◦

Jack and Rachel reached the clearing behind the shanty. After making sure all was clear, they hurried to the door and squeezed inside. They found their things just as they had left them and bundled everything together to make it easier to carry on their uphill hike. Within a few minutes, they were on their way back to the camp.

"What do you think Pop and Nan are doing? Do you think they're okay?" asked Rachel.

"I think they're worried and probably trying to figure out where they need to be in case we need help," said Jack.

"But they *DO* know about the time travel part, right?"

"Yes."

"Well, you sorta think like Pop. What would you do?"

"Actually, I've thought about that a lot."

"So?"

"Pop would put all of the info together. I told him we had thirteen days to rescue Calico Jack and the crew. Tomorrow is day thirteen. He knows we had to go to Port Royal."

"But we traveled back in time. How does that help?"

"Maybe it doesn't but you asked what I would do if I was thinking like Pop."

"Okay," said Rachel with a sigh. "What . . ."

"I would sail to Port Royal and hang around for the thirteenth day. If nothing happened, I would sail north to St. Augustine to see if we were there. After that, I'm not sure."

Rachel spread her hands making a point. "He could be standing right here, on this very spot, three hundred years in the future, it wouldn't matter, he wouldn't see us."

"You're right. Everything about this . . . trip, defies logic. And if we go back to our time stuck with a boatload of pirates from the eighteenth century? *THAT'S* another thing to worry about," said Jack.

"That *would* be a disaster." Rachel laughed. "Nan would freak out." Rachel paused, her smile faltered. "Think Nan, Pop and Val are okay?" she asked again. "Maybe they think we're all dead."

"They've been through plenty of crazy scary stuff. All of them have come face to face with ghosts. Nan took on three of them all by herself when she rescued me at the lighthouse last year. No worries. This is all just another Rackham adventure."

"I hope you're right and, for everyone's sake, that this latest Rackham adventure ends soon," said Rachel.

⌒X⌒

Nan scanned the internet again. "So far there's no change in any historical records about Calico Jack."

"Tomorrow is day thirteen. We probably won't see the change until then," said Pop.

"You both seem pretty confident that Jack, Kai and Rachel are going be successful," said Val. "They still have to get back to the present."

Nan reached her arm around Val's shoulder and

hugged her tight. "I'm sure they have everything under control. They figured out how to travel back in time and they'll figure out how to get home. Don't get me wrong, I'm still furious that Jack and Kai went off on this excursion without asking for help. Might wish they'd stayed in 1720 by the time I get done with them."

"Well, they went back there to rescue Rachel, not the pirate. It's kind of tough to get mad at them for doing what they did."

"They should have . . . well, I guess you're right. Pop would never have let them go alone and it doesn't seem like Calico Jack wanted anyone but Jack and Kai to do this. And let's face it we wouldn't turn our backs on Rachel."

"I can't get . . . well, you should have seen the look on Rachel's face when she was, you know, being controlled. She was absolutely terrified. I just couldn't get to her in time to stop her," explained Val.

"This is no one's fault. There's nothing any of us could have done. She's okay, I'm sure of it, and it won't be long until all three of them are home safe and sound," said Nan.

Rachel and Jack were the last to return to camp. Tucker Gunn and his men had collected several cutlasses and flintlocks along with a few muskets, axes and a worn-looking blunderbuss – a short musket with a flared muzzle. It was an impressive collection of weaponry considering it had all been stolen over the course of only a few hours. The pirates busied themselves cleaning, loading and sharpening their newly acquired cache of weapons while Kai and Q chatted animatedly with Calico Jack.

"Looks like Tuck made out pretty good. How about

boats, do we have anything lined up?" asked Jack.

Kai looked up at Jack and nodded. "We have three. Pulled them ashore and hid them under a bunch of brush and limbs. We were just talkin' with the captain here about the best way to approach the ship since it's tied up at the wharf. He said it would have been easier to steal a sloop anchored at the edge of the harbor."

"We'll be splittin' into three groups, lad an' approach from the port side an' her stern. Bennett an' his family'll board with ye, Rachel, Mary an' Anne once me n' me crew have taken over the ship," announced Calico Jack.

"You sound like you've appointed yourself captain already," said Jack with a smirk.

"Aye, an' Cap'n I'll be, ye lubber," answered the pirate with a chuckle. "Yer not puttin' yerself in harms way on my account again. 'Tis likely thar be bloodshed to reckon with in this reckless endeavor."

"Let's hope not," said Jack. "I don't suppose you've told Anne and Mary that they're sitting this fight out."

"No, an' ye best keep that to yerself."

"My lips are sealed."

Tucker Gunn walked over and handed cutlasses to Jack and Rachel. "Ye might still be needin' these in case it all goes bad. Ere's a dagger as well."

"No guns?" asked Rachel.

"Ye know how to be usin' 'em?"

"Not really."

"Then we shan't be wastin' 'em on the likes of ye. Don't tell Cap'n Rackham but Anne n' Mary'll have 'em though. They be better shots than any of us," said Gunn.

"Sundown's only an hour away." Jack rummaged through one of the bundles. "Here's some salt-pork and smoked something-or-other that we had tucked away. Better grab something to eat and rest up before we leave. By the way, were they loading the ship?"

"Yep. Looked like they were almost done when we flew away. Crew's probably headin' ashore by now," said Kai.

Tucker Gunn spoke up. "Nah. It'll take them lads time to get everythin' stowed properlike an' their cap'n will be wantin' the ship made ready to sail b'fore they go off to drinkin'. Some of them blokes'll be havin' a wee bit too much rum in 'em an' some'll miss the ship altogether."

"'Tis never happened to any of us, has it Tuck?" scoffed Calico Jack.

"Aye, never!" laughed Gunn. "An' I hope they loaded plenty o' rum. I'm parched."

Rachel smiled and whispered to Jack. "They're just a bunch of big kids."

"Don't underestimate them, they're still pirates," said Jack.

⌒X⌒

Everyone watched the sun sink slowly on the horizon while waiting for Calico Jack to give the order to go. They assembled at the beach, three boats positioned at the edge of the surf.

"Lads, ye know what to do. 'Tis our last sail together. Me piratin' days be over an' suggest the same for the lot o' ye standin' here. Thanks to me new friends, we've been saved from our dance with the devil. It be time to leave the sweet trade. Man the boats an' let's be off."

They divided into three groups as previously decided. Anne Bonny argued that she should be part of the initial boarding party but Rachel reminded her that too many risks had been taken by others for Anne to chance getting killed stealing a ship. After some prolonged pouting, Anne agreed with Rachel and grabbed a pair of oars.

Q and Kai transformed into large bats and flew off toward the wharf. They landed on the uppermost spar of the targeted sloop and watched the deckhands clear off toward town. Only the captain and one mate remained aboard.

"Seems pretty quiet," said Kai.

"I expected to see a bigger crew left behind since there is a band of pirates on the loose," answered Q.

"Think we should go back and tow the boats, you know, save them from having to row six miles?"

"No. Jack and Captain Rackham agreed that we need to keep watch and prepare to warn them if anything peculiar happens."

"I only saw maybe a dozen Redcoats gathered at the end of the dock. I guess that's how they plan to protect the ships from Calico Jack and his crew. They probably wouldn't expect them to come in from the sea."

Q's tongue did a quick flick and he shook his bat-head. "Ugh! I'd forgotten how bitter mosquitoes tasted."

"Why'd you eat it then?"

"Well right now I am a bat and I am hungry."

"Gross. I think we should do another flyover of the town and docks, make sure everything is cool. We haven't looked around since late afternoon."

"I'll fly over the town, you should stay up here and watch," said Q.

"I kinda like flyin'. Why don't you stay and I'll check things out?"

Q bared his fangs. "I'm in the mood for a quick bite. Something other than mosquitoes."

"So you're gonna go bite someone's neck 'cause you're a vampire bat?"

"Did you know that most vampires detest changing into bats? They hate the smell."

"Oh, like there's such a thing as vampires," said Kai with a bat-squeak.

"It would be better that you keep believing that, I suppose. I won't be long," said Q as he flew off toward town.

Kai remained hanging upside down from the spar and squeak-muttered to himself, "I hope this is all just a bad dream. I'm too young to be crazy."

He adjusted his wings, tucking them in tight against his body to warm himself against the cool ocean breeze and watched. The captain seemed nervous, looking down the wharf, out into the harbor, up into the rigging and down the wharf again. Something was wrong. The captain walked toward the cabin door turned his back and spoke, but the mate was several feet away closer to the bow coiling ropes. Kai flapped away from the spar flying in a circular direction behind the sloop. As he crossed beyond the stern he saw a Redcoat hiding inside the doorway, musket in hand. An ambush had been set up and the ship was pirate bait.

X

Calico Jack and his crew reached the mouth of the harbor as dawn approached. The pirate held up his hand for the rowing to stop, then motioned to pull the boats together for last minute instructions. He raised a finger to his lips for quiet.

"Do ye see those brigantines, mates? They be positioned on opposite sides of the harbor so's we cross between their guns."

"You think the Redcoats have set a trap for us,"

whispered Jack.

"Aye an' 'spect they be waitin' for us near or aboard the sloop we be plannin' to steal, lad."

"So what do ye have a mind to do, cap'n?" asked Tuck.

Calico Jack snickered. "Bless all here. We steal the brigantine closest to the edge of the harbor, of course."

The low rumble of complaint passed through the three small boats. Clearly the pirates had no desire to assault a warship loaded with Redcoats.

"We ought'n to go back to the camp, sir," suggested Carty.

"Where's yer spirit, Carty? It be only a matter of days 'til they find our hideout," replied Calico Jack.

"We could cross the island, leastways go deeper'n the jungle," suggested Howell.

Jack stood up partway, waving to get everyone's attention. "Quiet down or we won't be going anywhere. I agree with Captain Rackham. Our time is running out, we have to capture that ship tonight," he said pointing at the brigantine anchored on the easterly side of the harbor entrance. He sat down as Q and Kai flew over, both transforming into their human forms as they landed inside the boat on either side of Jack.

"It's a trap," blurted Kai breathlessly. "We gotta go back."

"We figured that out already so we're going to steal a different ship," said Jack.

"Maybe we should try again in a couple of days," suggested Kai.

"Tomorrow is the thirteenth day. If we don't do it by then, we might not make it at all," reminded Jack.

"Forgot about that," admitted Kai. "What do you think, Q?"

The Aztec thought it over for a minute and nodded at Calico Jack who appeared put out that plans were being made as if he weren't there. "Captain Rackham, could your men man the cannons on that ship?"

"Aye. Tuck and Howell be ..."

"Sorry, don't mean to interrupt but we're drifting closer and need to decide fast," said Jack.

"Jack, since you're probably the best swimmer, maybe you could swim into the harbor and disable a few of their ships while Kai goes with me to help Captain Rackham secure our ship," said Q.

"Wait a minute," hissed Rachel. "Jack's not going anywhere."

"Q, I think you've got a screw loose," said Kai. "We stick together. Period."

"We cannot outrun all of the ships in port, Kai. We need to take away their ability to give chase. The ship that we are about to commandeer is bigger . . . and slower. And while there are several weapons aboard, we have only a handful of men able to put them to use."

Calico Jack spoke up. "Yer help be most appreciated, Q but none of me crew's to be left behind. A good fight's what them bilge rats want and so they be gettin' it so we may's well be underway an' the devil may care."

Q nodded. "As you say, captain." He turned to Kai. "Are you ready?"

"I guess so but what're we doin'?"

"Trust me."

"Well your last idea sucked," said Kai before he eased into the water, changed into a sea creature and swam toward the brigantine.

"Man the oars, mates, we be losin' the tide," said Calico Jack in a loud whisper.

~X~

Two sea snakes slithered up the anchor line of the brigantine named *The Isabel*. Once on deck they changed into monitor lizards, their jaws filled with razor sharp teeth. Smoke escaped through their flaring nostrils. The lookout at the bow was the first to spot them and as he yelled out a warning Q breathed an intense blast of yellow flames in his direction, enough to blister the Redcoat's hands before dropping his musket and diving overboard. In minutes the panicked crew abandoned ship amid the fire and smoke without firing a shot.

Calico Jack and his crew boarded the ship as the last Redcoat plunged into the water. He looked around as the flames died out. "'Twas beginnin' to think ye might burn the blasted ship down to her keel, Q."

"Nothing is damaged," answered Q.

Rackham turned his attention to his crew and shouted out orders. "Man the guns, Tuck and aim fer that brigantine. Avast, yer first volley must be fair n' true, lads! Unfurl her sails n' be quick about it, cut loose the anchor upon the sail, we need be underway!"

The cannons roared to life, the first blast hitting the brigantine amidships. The second caught the forward hull at the waterline. Redcoats scurried across the docks firing their muskets across the harbor.

Jack worked furiously up in the rigging dropping sail. Rachel and the Tinnermons tucked in behind the main cabin away from the guns. Four pirates worked with Gunn and Howell loading and wadding the cannons. On the back side of the harbor, away from the wharf, Redcoats on horseback and on foot raced toward the slow-moving ship. Rachel spotted them first and yelled out to Kai over the thundering cannon fire, "They're going to be on top of us before we're underway!" Kai ran across the deck to Q.

"Can't shoot our way outta here, we gotta pull this ship out to sea."

Q nodded and dove overboard.

Kai herded Rachel and the Tinnermon's up to the bow. The Redcoats were now close enough that the ship was within musket range. The brigantine across the harbor had recovered and returned fire. The well trained British sailors had dropped sails and the brigantine moved off from the dock. "I need some help. Me n' Q are gonna pull us out of here. Finish tying off these ropes and throw us the looped ends as soon as we surface but keep your heads down."

Kai jumped overboard and Rachel and Mr. Tinnermon went to work on the ropes. The pirates not manning the cannons now concentrated musket fire on the approaching Redcoats on their starboard side. Rachel tossed the first line overboard just as the boat shuddered violently before listing hard to starboard. The port gunwale and a section of decking toward the stern disintegrated into a mass of flying splinters. Gunn and Howell were blown backwards from their stations at the cannons with Howell plummeting into the gaping hole of the deck. Jack lost his grip in the rigging falling several feet before looping his arm through the ratlines, barely holding on just ten feet above the ruptured deck. Rachel and Mr. Tinnermon were slammed against the portside gunwale. Mr. Tinnermon zig-zagged his way forward beneath a withering hail of musket fire, grabbed the second rope and threw the looped end into the water before diving behind the riddled wood.

Jack dropped from the ratlines onto a sliver of buckled deck and ran to the bow in time to see a pair of whale sharks grab the looped ropes and pull the slack out of them. Within seconds, the ship moved at speed toward the harbor entrance, the sailcloth whipping uselessly from the masts. Another cannon blast caused Jack to duck. The heavy projectile barely missed the stern where Calico Jack stood on the remnants of the shattered rail, his cutlass raised, oblivious to the musket balls tearing into the ship all around him as he rallied his crew, barking orders above the explosions, smoke and fire.

"Tuck, man that cannon. Get out of it, man and return fire! Where be Howell? Carty, take up that cannon and make haste. All hands cover our flanks. Tuck, make them cannons thunder. Thar brigantine be catchin' the wind. Use the grapeshot n' aim fer her sails, mates. C'mon, lads yella's not a pirate's color!"

Jack turned checking to see that Rachel was safe. The ship moved quickly out to sea, thanks to Kai and Q while Anne and Mary fired their muskets at the Redcoats on shore. Tucker Gunn and the undersized Carty struggled to reposition one of the cannons. Jack ran to help. It took another full minute before the Rackham crew returned cannon fire, but they made the most of it as the grapeshot ripped through the forward sail of the chasing brigantine.

"Thar ye be, lads! Another like that n' they'll nowise trouble us again. Hurry now, give 'em a taste of hellfire."

Tuck realigned the cannon a second time and Jack loaded a six-pound ball. "We'll make a pretty death of her this time," yelled Gunn as he fired. It was a direct hit that wiped out at least two of the British cannons and shattered a section of the second mast causing it to lean precariously, ready to snap. Fire broke out on the starboard side. The brigantine gave up the chase and turned to port as Calico Jack Rackham and his crew of pirates cheered and crossed into the open sea with the sunrise.

"Aye, lads drop all sail. Jack, take the helm. Tuck, account fer the crew an' report what our damage be. Carty! The rum if ye please."

They had won a brief but hard-fought battle. The ship and its crew had paid a heavy price. Two of Rackham's crewmembers were missing and Howell was confirmed dead. There was a gaping crater in the deck and the block for the second mast had been blown to bits along with a good portion of the rigging. It would make sailing at speed impossible. And there was no rum. In fact, there were very few supplies. Kai and Q climbed aboard as soon as the remaining sails filled and Jack turned the helm over to Captain Rackham as the crew gathered around.

Kai, Rachel and the Tinnermons collected at the bow. Jack and Q paused near the helm, where they held a hushed conversation before Q changed into the quetzal bird and flew off toward Port Royal.`

Kai poked Bennett and smiled. "What'd you think of your first sea battle, kid?"

Bennett, his ears still ringing, managed a smile. "I won't say it was fun but somehow I knew all along that we would get away."

Jack joined them at the bow and draped his arm over Rachel's shoulder. She had cracked her head hard below the gunwale's edge when the ship had been hit and it still throbbed. Mr. Tinnermon held his aching ribs, thinking he must have broken a few. "Don't think we could survive another battle like that, so let's hope that was it. All of you did a great job," said Jack.

"You know the governor will chase us down," said Rachel. "They're probably leaving port already. I heard Calico Jack say we won't be able to sail fast because we have a lot of damage."

"You're probably right about the governor," said Jack. He looked over at Kai. "How far and fast do you think you could tow us, assuming we have to outrun the Redcoats?"

"I don't know. Thought it would be easy but this boat

is heavy. Could probably manage for a little while, I guess," said Kai.

Calico Jack and Anne joined them. "Ye did a fine job've it. Fine pirates ye woulda made. If ye ever want to . . ."

Anne interrupted. "Not to worry, we be out've it, surely. I don't fancy the sweet trade n'more. Time to try bein' a proper mama."

"Aye, we be keepin' our oath to ye s'long as we keep us ahead of the gov'nor ships," said the pirate.

"How bad is it?" asked Jack.

Calico Jack sighed. "'Fraid we be takin' on the briney deep, lad."

"You mean we're sinking?" asked Bennett.

"Aye, but we won't be visitin' Davey Jones' Locker jus' yet. Leastways she won't be sinkin' straightaway, young Bennett."

"Well if we can stay afloat under sail for a few days, maybe reach Tortuga . . ."

"A few days ye say?" Calico Jack laughed. "'Twas hopin' fer a few hours, lad."

"That bad, huh? So we need to find an island," said Jack.

"Aye, the trick bein' to find one soon, an' careen the ship on the lee side of the island out of sight from the British to make repairs."

"Sail ho!" came the cry from the lookout.

Calico Jack turned and shook his head. "Avast, seems our luck's gone run aground an' we bein' only a few hours at sea!"

Kai climbed the rigging and looked across the crystalline sea toward the white sails on the horizon. "It's not flying a British flag," he yelled down. "Looks like a sloop."

"She might be a merchant ship. 'Spect she'll stay well

clear of us then," said Anne.

"Nope. She's changed course and headin' this way," reported Kai.

Mary Read joined them, checking one of her flintlocks as she leaned against the gunwale. "Might be the Redcoats commandeered the sloop to chase us down or p'raps the governor put a bounty on our heads an' it be a merchant or slaver's joined the chase thinkin' we be the helpless lot."

Kai, out of the rigging and back on deck, nodded in agreement. "That makes sense. Put all the ships in port out to sea and on our tail. One of 'em was bound to get lucky and find us right away. Do you have a . . . aww whaddya call it, a spyglass?"

"Carty!"

"Aye, sir?"

"Fetch the spyglass for master Kai, will ye?"

"Tuck!"

"Aye, Cap'n."

"Make the cannons ready, Mr. Gunn an' put Anne and Mary on one this time 'round."

"Thar ain't much powder, Cap'n."

Calico Jack sighed as he watched the sloop approach. "Kai, that expression ye used . . . remind me, lad."

"Sittin' ducks?"

"That be the one. Aye, we be sittin' ducks."

"What's the big deal? We're sinkin' and there's a sloop on the way to try to capture us and take us back to Port Royal to be hanged," said Kai with a smirk.

The pirate spared Kai an odd look. "Ye be tetched in the head, lad."

Jack laughed. "He's right. It's actually a good thing. They have to board our ship to capture us and collect a bounty. When they do, we take over theirs. We're on the same page, right, Kai?"

"Exactly what I was thinkin', Jack," said Kai as Carty handed him the spyglass. "Thanks, Carty." He climbed into the lower rigging to check out the approaching sloop. "Uh oh," said Kai.

"What now?" asked Jack.

"Well guys, I know who's chasin' us."

"So do you want to tell us or is it supposed to be a surprise?"

"It's that slave trader with the hook for a hand. The one I got into that little scrape with."

"Great. The same guy you kicked in the chops."

"Yep. Same dude, dude."

"His name is Marcus Hook," said Bennett. "I heard people talking about him and how mean he is."

"He's going to be even meaner once he sees who's on this boat," said Jack.

"I could fly over there and do the fire breathin' thing on 'em," offered Kai.

"That would be great if we weren't sinking. We need that sloop," said Jack.

"Tacks and braces, mates. We ain't waitin' fer that devil to arrive. Make speed there an' we'll cut to his bowsprit an' heave at 'im all we got!"

"What's that supposed to mean?" asked Kai as he watched the pirates scurry across the deck.

"It means we're going to attack Marcus Hook," said Jack.

Kai climbed higher into the rigging with the spyglass in hand. "I'm gonna get a headcount for the party. Be nice to see how many men he's got."

As Kai put the glass to his eye there was a loud blast

from the direction of the sloop. The cannonball landed harmlessly into the sea several yards off the stern. "Okay. He's got at least one cannon, and I count seven . . . no eight on deck plus Hook," reported Kai.

"Put yer backs to it ye louts! We needs to run straight fer 'is bow, so's he can't use the cannons!"

Rackham's crew brought the ship about in a tight sweep; Hook's men couldn't find the range and lost their chance to get off another shot. The two ships were on a collision course.

~14~
MARCUS HOOK

"SEE ANYTHING YET?" asked Nan.

"No. Still says Calico Jack and his crew were hanged," said Val from her seat in front of the computer. "You're sure this is the thirteenth day?"

Nan sighed. "It's day thirteen and Pop's ready to weigh anchor and get underway. He's really fidgety. I've never seen him so wired up."

"It's understan . . . wait, look at this. The part about Calico Jack's hanging is blank."

"Click over to another site, Val. Let's see what it says."

Val pulled up another website. "It says Rackham and his crew were captured and taken to Port Royal where they were . . . and then it goes blank like the other site."

Let's see what Pop thinks," said Nan as she walked to the cabin's hatchway.

Pop bounded down the stairs two at a time. Val moved over so he could sit in front of the screen. He stared as he clicked from one site to another. "I'm not sure what this means. They must be . . . Rackham and his crew must be off the island."

"Move with the sloop, Mr. Fetherston. Don't let 'er get us lined up with 'er cannons."

"Aye, Cap'n."

"Tuck! Ye be ready to fire on me command. Scatter the deck an' mind the riggin'."

"Aye." Tucker Gunn blew out a deep breath. "How's he expectin' us to scatter the deck an' not be damagin' the sloop," he said to Mary Read as she shrugged and wadded the third cannon.

Jack moved toward the bow to join Rachel. You, Anne and the Tinnermon's need to hide up in the . . ."

Anne Bonny interrupted. "If ye think I'll be runnin' from this fight yer mad."

"But you have . . ."

"I 'ave to survive at all costs. 'Tis why I be joinin' the fight, lad. Now be off with ye."

"I'll have a cutlass and musket if you please," said Mr. Tinnermon. "I can protect my family. We need everyone for this battle, Jack."

"Okay, but keep your heads down as long as you can." Jack kissed Rachel, handed Mr. Tinnermon a cutlass, dagger and a flintlock and moved to the stern in search of more weapons.

George Fetherston kept one eye on Calico Jack, the other on the sloop bearing down on them. He didn't hear the shot and barely felt the musket ball that entered his chest ending his life. With a dead man at the wheel the brigantine drifted hard to starboard giving Hook's crew the opening they needed. Three cannons fired in unison, taking out one mast, another section of the port gunwale, and the entire helm of Rackham's brigantine. Carty, Dobbin and Harwood were all lost in the blasts. Calico Jack rallied what was left of his crew. Mary Read and Tucker Gunn, bloodied and dazed, crawled back to the cannon as the first of the grappling lines cinched into the oak gunwales of their stolen ship. Gunn lit the fuse and moved away. Mary did the same at the second cannon. A few seconds passed. The explosions were furious and the damage to Hook's sloop, devastating.

Kai found himself bleeding and pinned beneath the spar and rigging from the collapsed mast. Everything around him sounded distant, all moving in slow motion. He could see Jack and Anne. They were fighting with cutlasses, two against three and Jack's face was a bloody mess. Calico Jack sat propped against the starboard gunwale, his left side covered in blood, his head hanging down resting on his chest, not moving. He caught a glimpse of Mary Read struggling as she crawled across the deck, reaching for a cutlass. Rachel. Where was Rachel? He pushed against the wood spar working furiously to lift the heavy timber and escape the tangled mass of wood, rope and sailcloth.

Rachel didn't know what to do. Both ships were sinking and the deck was awash with seawater and blood. Mr. Tinnermon had joined the fight while Bennett argued with his mother to let him go to help his father. Rachel spotted the longboat lashed to the deck at the bow. "Bennett, forget the fight, I need you and your mom to help me get that boat in the water. We'll tie it off until we're ready to abandon ship. We're all going to die otherwise."

Jack knew he couldn't hold out much longer. He had a gash on his left arm and a large chunk of splintered wood impaled in his side courtesy of a shattered section of gunwale from a cannon blast. He swung a series of three heavy blows, all blocked before rushing at the man and shoving him backwards over the side of the ship. He turned in time to see Mr. Tinnermon on top of one of Hook's men trying to wrestle a dagger from the bounty hunter's grip. To his left he watched as Anne ducked beneath a sweeping blade before landing a vicious chopping blow of her own onto the top of her opponent's head. As he scanned the bloody deck looking for Rachel he felt an agonizing stabbing sensation at the top of his shoulder. He fell hard against the stump of the center mast. Jack reached up fighting desperately to free himself. From the corner of his eye he caught sight of Anne charging in his direction, sliding across the blood-soaked deck, her cutlass raised. She was yelling, but all sound had faded.

Marcus Hook sneered as he ripped his hook from Jack's shoulder and with the shriek of a madman he swung his cutlass upward, preparing to deliver the mortal blow. As his arm started its downward motion he felt a terrible burning sensation and saw that his good hand was now falling into the frothing gore still clutching the sword, leaving behind a useless blood-pumping stump. As he reached for his mangled forearm with his hook, Anne grabbed the sharpened steel just below the point and pulled with all her might, swinging the slave trader toward the starboard gunwale. The strap holding the hook snapped and he flipped backwards over the side into the crimson patch of sea lapping against the hull of the sinking brigantine and into the waiting jaws of frenzied sharks below. Within seconds the brutal man known as Marcus Hook was dragged below the surface.

Kai dropped the cutlass as he stared at the severed hand lying on the deck next to Jack. His whole body trembled and his breath came in short catches. Anne Bonny moved over and knelt next to Calico Jack, checking his condition. Mr. Tinnermon, himself exhausted and bloodied from the ferocious battle, limped to the bow to join his family.

Rachel crept slowly toward Jack and Kai. "Is he . . . ?"

"I . . . I don't think so," said Kai, "but I'm too scared to check."

Rachel kicked the severed hand away and knelt down beside Jack. His shoulder was soaked with blood and still bleeding. Gently she turned Jack over on his side and pushed his long blonde hair out of his face. She breathed a deep sigh and smiled through her tears. He was breathing and looking at her. "We beat them," he said hoarsely as he tried to return her smile.

Mr. Tinnermon joined Jack and Rachel. "I hate having to state the obvious but both ships are sinking fast and the surrounding sea is teeming with sharks. We need to get everyone into that longboat. There's no time to spare."

Kai snapped out of his fog. "You're right. We won't be afloat much longer; the water's almost up to the gunwale. This ship could break apart or capsize at any minute." He looked at Mr. Tinnermon. "Brian, you'll have to help me get Jack and the captain to the boat. We'll get Bennett and your wife aboard first, then round up the survivors. That work for you?"

"We need to hurry," answered Mr. Tinnermon as he helped Kai lift Jack from the deck.

Calico Jack was smiling at Anne. "We thrashed them scalawags we did," he said.

"Aye, now get yerself standin' an' make way to the bow. The ship be sinkin' from under us an' we run outta time."

"Move yerself, lass," ordered Tucker Gunn as he grabbed the captain and hoisted him roughly over his shoulder.

"Blast it, Tuck! Me guts be pourin' out on ter the deck an ye be haulin' me like a sack."

"Sorry, Cap'n. No time to be gentle. Davey Jones' Locker be callin' fer us. Anne, fetch Mary will ye? She been seein' to the lads to find who be still among the livin'," said Tuck.

"Avast, Mr. Gunn there be but four of us left, the others 'ave drawn their last," reported Mary as she sloshed toward the bow behind Calico Jack and Anne.

"Aye, the lads put up a good fight they did."

"Sharks are circlin' for their next meal," said Kai as he watched them thrashing near the longboat which was now almost level with the gunwale of the sinking brigantine. "Okay hurry up. Me n' Tuck will hold the boat tight to the ship while y'all climb aboard. Just don't tip it over. We're only gonna get one shot at this."

It took a few minutes to get everyone loaded. By the time Kai was ready to board, he was knee-deep in bloody seawater on what remained of the brigantine's deck. "Wait! I forgot something," he yelled and splashed toward the stern.

"What are you doing, Kai? The ship is breaking apart and sinking. There are sharks out here," screamed Rachel. "C'mon. Hurry!"

Kai ran through the water back to the longboat and in one swift move climbed aboard and pushed the smaller boat away from the sinking brigantine. "Made it," he announced.

"Why did you go back?" asked Bennett.

"To grab this for Jack," said Kai holding up Marcus Hook's once-deadly hook.

Rachel shook her head. "I don't think he'll ever want to see that thing again." She hugged Jack tightly, but he had passed out before they shoved off.

They drifted east watching the two ships sink below the waves. The sharks ignored the longboat, continuing their bloody feast as the two ships plunged to the sea bottom. The gulls swooped in scavenging the leftovers that floated to the surface.

An hour passed, then two. All traces of the ferocious sea battle were now gone as they drifted on the tide. Anne and Rachel managed to patch Jack and Captain Rackham enough to stop the bleeding. Rachel, with Kai's help holding Jack down, removed the large splinter from Jack's side and stuffed the deep wound from the hook with the cleanest bit of cloth she could find. Anne, sitting toward the bow of the small boat, had expertly removed two musket balls from Calico Jack's shoulder and bandaged his head where a cutlass had sliced his forehead above his left eyebrow. Most everyone had their share of cuts, bumps and bruises but nothing approaching the severity of the injuries suffered by Jack or Captain Rackham.

"The lad put up a heroic battle, he did," said Mary Read glancing at Jack before nodding at Rachel. "He were fightin' two an' three at a go. Been a fine pirate, that one."

"Aye," added Tucker Gunn. "Was doin' fine, he was, 'til that hooked devil come up on him attackin' from behind like he did."

"Bloke paid fer it, din' he," laughed Anne as she smiled at Kai. "Went to Davey Jones Locker with no hands left to him. Ye nicked him just in time, lad."

"Yeah, guess so," answered Kai without enthusiasm. "I never killed anyone before."

"Naw, ye helped him along but 'twas the sharks what put an end to him," said Tuck.

"You okay, Kai?" asked Rachel.

"I dunno."

"Hey, you did what you had to do to save Jack," she said.

"I know. I get it. Marcus Hook got what he deserved. I don't wanna talk about it. Think Jack's gonna be alright?"

"He will as long as we don't drift out here too long. I'm worried about infection setting in," said Rachel.

"What happened to Q? Why would he disappear like that right before the fightin' started and why did he take the *Wind Jewel?*"

"Wind Jewel?"

"Remember that emerald we used in the jungle at the big stone time-wheel thing? Jack always kept it hanging around his neck inside a pouch," said Kai.

"Okay, I remember. What about it?"

"It's gone. Might be wrong, but I'm pretty sure we need it to get home to our own time," said Kai.

"And you think Q has it?" asked Rachel.

"Well the *Serpent Dagger*, including the stone, is really his. It's not like he stole it."

"Maybe Jack gave it to him. I saw them talking right before Q flew away. Maybe Jack sent Q off to find another ship since ours was taking on water. You know him better than anyone. He was probably setting up a back-up plan. What do you think?"

"Yeah, you're probably right. He's always thinkin' about Plan B."

⚬—X—⚬

"Here it is. It says that Calico Jack Rackham and his crew escaped Port Royal and were never heard from again," reported Pop as he stared at the computer screen.

That means they made it!" cried Val.

"So it seems. Says here that '*Rackham commandeered a heavily guarded British Navy brigantine and with cannons blasting, he and his crew fought through a fortified harbor blockade before moving out to sea and escaping all pursuers while running at great speed under minimal sail, putting on a remarkable display of seamanship.*' Wonder what that last part means?"

"The part about seamanship?" asked Nan.

"I don't know why the mention of 'at great speed under minimal sail' is included."

"You think it's important?"

"I don't know. Can't see how it could be."

"Are we leaving now for home?"

"Might as well. We're no help here. Looks like my instincts were way off," said Pop.

"Your gut feelings have been right more often than wrong," said Nan.

"Yeah, I suppose," he sighed. "Okay, let's get *Reckless* underway. Hopefully the kids will be home waitin' for us."

X

Jack felt weak and his wounds screamed with the slightest movement. He struggled to an upright position to take in his surroundings. There were ten of them drifting at sea in the longboat with no provisions and no water under a hot cloudless sky.

"You feeling okay?" asked Rachel quietly.

"I'm alright. Hurts like crazy, but I'll live," answered Jack. "How about you?"

"I'm fine but Calico Jack is in pretty bad shape. He was shot a couple times. Like I told Kai, I'm mostly worried about infection."

"Is there another boatload of Rackham's crew?"

Rachel shook her head. "They were all lost. We're the only survivors."

"The guy with the hook?"

"Dead. And both ships sank. We're all that's left."

"So we lost eight men."

"And the other ship probably lost ten or twelve," said Rachel.

"Wow, twenty or more men altogether. Dead. We knew it would be a fight to the death. How long was I out of it? I don't remember climbing into the longboat."

"Kai and Mr. Tinnermon carried you aboard. That

was about two hours ago. You had a sharp chunk of wood stuck in your side. Mrs. Tinnermon helped me remove it and clean the wound. You passed out when we stuffed that cloth in the gash from that nasty hook. Had to do it to stop the bleeding. It's lucky you didn't go into shock."

Kai joined Jack and Rachel, taking care not to rock the small boat. He slid across from them and smiled. "You look like crap, Jack."

"Thanks. Think you told me that once before, fairly recently if I recall. You okay?"

"Guess so. I was going to fly around to see if there was an island nearby so I could push the boat to shore but I guess the stuff Q gave me wore off."

"Timing is everything," said Jack.

"Yeah, always. Glad to see you're okay," said Kai.

"Thanks to you," added Rachel.

"What happened? Why thanks to Kai?" asked Jack.

"Look, never mind that stuff. I have to know. Q flew away just before Marcus Hook and his guys boarded our ship. Did you give him the *Serpent Dagger* and *Wind Jewel*?"

"Yes."

"That's it? Yes?"

"I sent him on a mission. There's no sense explaining it now because it will just get everyone's hopes up for nothing," said Jack.

"We're bobbin' like a cork in the middle of the ocean, go ahead and say somethin' that'll get my hopes up, moron."

"I sent him to find help."

"He could've helped us fight Hook and his crew, maybe breathed fire at 'em or somethin'," said Kai.

"Maybe, but I figured we were evenly matched since it was a merchant ship."

"Hook is a slave trader, or I should say, was. That

probably wasn't even his crew. He got a chance to make a small fortune as a bounty hunter, hired a bunch of criminals and chased us down," said Kai.

"That fits. And when you looked in the spyglass you only saw a small crew, maybe eight or ten guys. Right?"

"Some must have been hiding below decks," said Kai.

"I wasn't sure how the battle would go and since we were already sinking, I sent Q off to find help."

"So you gave him the *Serpent Dagger* and *Wind Jewel* in case, you know, we didn't make it."

Jack smiled. "Not exactly."

Kai rubbed his forehead. "Not exactly. Do I have to pull everything out of you?"

"Makes the story more dramatic," said Jack through a weak grin.

"Doesn't get much more dramatic than being adrift at sea in another time with a bunch of pirates now does it? Stop playin' games and tell me what Q's up to?" said Kai.

"Jack sighed. "Doesn't matter now. Look over your shoulder, there must be five or six British ships sailing our way."

⟁15⟁
RECKLESS ENDEAVOR

⌒POP STOOD AT THE HELM puffing on a Cohiba cigar and keeping an eye on the radar and GPS as *Reckless Endeavor* cut through the calm azure waters at a comfortable twelve knots. Nan joined him at the control panel carrying a steaming cup of strong Italian coffee.

"Val keeps checking websites about Calico Jack Rackham to see if the story changes," said Nan as she placed the mug to the left of the control console.

"Thanks, sweets. She ought to get topside and enjoy this fresh salt air and nice warm breeze," said Pop.

"I hope we're not disappointed when we get home. I keep waiting for Jack's voice to come over the radio saying he's at the house waiting for us to get back."

"Well I have a better feelin' about all this knowin' Calico Jack escaped. Means they finished what they started and they're headin' back to their own time. I'd guess they have that time travel part all figured . . ."

"Look at that bird! Have you ever seen anything like it? I have to go below and get my camera. Oh I hope it doesn't fly away," said Nan as she ran toward the cabin stairway.

Pop watched as the brightly colored bird with the long tail continued circling. It drew closer with each turn. Nan and Val charged onto the deck across to the stern as Nan fumbled with her camera trying to change lenses. By the time she had it twisted into place, the beautiful bird was gone. She sank into one of the deck chairs.

"Missed it. That's why I should bring all my stuff on these trips so I don't have to change lenses," said Nan. "I wonder what kind of bird that was."

"I think it was a Quetzal but they're from South America somewhere," said Pop.

"Are they bright green, red and turquoise with really long colorful tails and gold beaks?" asked Val.

"The one circling us was," said Nan still upset about her missed shot.

"Well that bird is perched on the spar at the forward mast," said Val.

Nan stood from her seat and crept forward toward the bow, her camera raised level with her chin. She had a clear view and, adjusting the zoom manually, zeroed in for a half dozen photos. It was as if the bird knew what she was doing and spread his wings, posing before leaving the spar to resume flying in tight circles around the boat.

"That bird is . . . so gorgeous . . . I swear it was posing,"

"Must be tired 'cause he's so far from home. Look, he's going to land again," said Val.

The Quetzal bird landed ten feet away next to the starboard gunwale near the stern. Within a few seconds the bird transformed into King Quetzalcoatl, his muscular gold covered arms crossed over his chest. Pop reached for his shotgun.

"There is no need for that, Mr. Rackham. I am sorry to have startled all of you. I am here on behalf of your grandson Jack and his friends.

Pop abandoned the shotgun and took a few steps toward the visitor. "Are they alright?"

"They were well when last I saw them."

"Where are they?" asked Nan.

"They are close by but three centuries removed. We need to go get them," said Q.

"Okay, but who are you?" asked Pop.

"I am King Quetzalcoatl, your grandson and his friends call me Q. It was my pleasure to have met Jack and Kai near the Valley of the Kings. I accompanied them on their journey in time to assist in their quest to rescue Captain Rackham, an ancestor of yours, I believe."

Val spoke up. "You say we're close by but they're three hundred years behind us. How do we get there to help them?"

"You must be Valerie."

"Yes, but everyone calls me Val."

"Kai has spoken of you often," said Q offering a brief smile.

"Really?" Val felt herself blush.

"Yes. Kai, Jack and Rachel will have many stories to share, but there is no time," said Q as he held out the *Serpent Dagger* and *Wind Jewel* in his opened palm for all to see. "We need to leave now."

"Captain, the lookout reports the sighting of a longboat at twelve degrees to port, sir."

"Thank you, Jennings. Maintain present course. We shall confirm that it is indeed that rogue Rackham and by your mark as witness report accordingly to the governor," replied Barnet.

"Are we not to take him aboard, Captain?"

"I did indeed discuss Rackham's fate with our despicable sniveling governor. Woodes Rogers is a most repugnant little man."

"Captain, please don't speak such treason. The men might overhear."

"Blast the men and the filthy governor. Are you aware that the entire contingent of guards assigned at the time of Rackham's escape, twelve men in all, were put in prison, given sentences of five years each with no chance to plead their case? Had you heard that Schaeffer Tolliver, the executioner, has been ordered hanged from his own gallows on the next full moon, again with no trial? Don't speak to me of treason, Jennings. Woodes Rogers is an evil contemptible devil and were it possible, I myself would give the man over to Rackham and his band of cutthroats to deal with in whatever manner they determined. I'd wager the pirates would be more decent and humane than our disgusting excuse of a governor."

"Sir, with all respect, we must fulfill our duty. Agree or not, we still serve the King."

"Aye, Jennings. And so we shall. Send four of our ships back to Port Royal. This fool's errand has left our harbor woefully vulnerable to attack. Notify Captain Miller to join us at the point. Alter course and bring us close enough to verify that it is Rackham and his crew. As our governor requires only confirmation of Rackham's death, we shall take the opportunity to sharpen our cannon skills and take turns firing upon the longboat until one of us finds the mark and Calico Jack Rackham is, for once and for all, dead. Suspect Miller might fancy a wager, at least make it a sporting go."

"Aye, sir. At once, sir," replied Jennings as he scurried from the helm.

"Looks like four ships are leavin'" said Kai.

"And two of them are heading this way," replied Jack.

"Aye be figgerin' they ain't be needin' the lot of 'em to chain up the likes of us," added Tucker Gunn.

Calico Jack, wincing with every move, sat up straighter and motioned to Kai. "Pass me the spyglass, if ye please, lad." The pirate stared through the glass for a few minutes before collapsing it and taking a deep breath. "Avast. Bless all here. 'Tis Captain Barnet 'imself an' he be givin' us the broadside. He ain't plannin' on takin' us to Port Royal in chains, he be fixin' his guns on us to blow us all to kingdom come," he said matter-of-factly.

"Well 'tis the end of it then," announced Anne Bonny. "Sad that ye lot'll perish with the likes of us," she said as she offered a sad smile toward the Tinnermons and Rachel.

Mary Read laughed. "That bloke thinks to hit this wee boat from such a range. Might be we all die of old age first," she quipped.

As the words left her mouth they saw the first flash of cannon fire followed by the sound of the explosion. Three seconds later the water erupted fifteen feet to their starboard side.

"Seems we could meet our bleedin' end a might sooner'n expected," said Mary.

Kai looked across at Jack. "We really coulda used a plan B this time."

"Plan B is running late," said Jack with a deep sigh. "We can't abandon the boat because we're all either bleeding or bloody. Better to take our chances with cannonballs than sharks."

Another explosion sounded and the water gushed upward ten feet off of their port side.

"Must be the gunny's an Irishman," bellowed Tuck.

"What d'ye be meanin' by that?" fumed Anne, she

having been born in Ireland.

Captain Rackham stepped in. "Don't the two of ye be goin' to the depths of Davey's Locker fightin' 'mongst yerselves. Anne, dear girl, Tuck's payin' a compliment. Their gunny must be Irish. Devil a doubt an Englishman might require a week to find the range."

"Great, we're about to get blown to bits and they're arguin' about the Irish and the Brits," said Kai. "So what *was* Plan B? Just curious."

"Q went to see if he could find Pop," answered Jack.

"Bit of a stretch, don't you think?"

"Probably."

Q held the dagger out and addressed Pop, Nan and Val. "Please gather around."

As they assembled, Q plunged the dagger into the wooden trim across the top of the instrument panel and in that instant, there was a loud crack followed by the sound of howling wind. "It is now 1720," announced Q as he pointed northeast in the direction of six wooden sailing vessels all flying the British flag. Four of them were sailing south, two were stationed a mile beyond, firing cannons toward a small object to the west.

Pop squinted through his binoculars in the direction of the small target. "They're trying to blast that small boat to bits and there are people on it."

"Yes. Jack, Kai and Rachel are in that small boat along with the pirates and some others. They are quite defenseless and time is running out," replied Q. "I will try to gain you some time," he said as he jumped overboard.

Pop fired up the twin CAT engines on the schooner

and altered course toward the bobbing longboat. "Deb, you're gonna have to take *Reckless* to the west side of the life boat, but don't get too close and give the British a better target. You'll be safe running at one-third throttle, no need fighting the sails."

"Why am I running the boat?" asked Nan.

"You'll see in a minute. Val I need you to help me lower Jack's boat from the davit. I'll pick them up in that while you and Nan keep running north. Slow the schooner when I give the signal and then speed up as soon as I'm loose."

Pop swung Jack's twenty-two-foot center console *Bad Latitude* into position behind the transom of *Reckless* and lowered it enough to climb aboard. He gave the thumbs up. Without hesitating, Nan slowed to a near-stop as Val pressed the controller. The small boat hit the water a few seconds later and Pop unhooked the hoisting straps. Nan hit the throttles as soon as Pop yelled out the all clear. The 250 horsepower engine roared to life as Pop spun the wheel hard to port aiming *Bad Latitude* toward the stranded longboat.

The lookout hollered, warning Captain Barnet that a small ship now approached from the southeast.

"What the devil is that?" asked Barnet.

"I've no idea," blurted Jennings. "Seems they've launched a small vessel from the stern and . . . and it has no sail nor oarsmen, yet it travels at great speed."

"Man all cannons and fire at will before they escape," ordered Captain Barnet. "Signal the others to return and join the fight!"

The British sailors swarmed across the decks cursing

as they loaded the cannons, preparing to unleash a barrage against the longboat and the fast moving schooner. The four ships sailing toward Port Royal changed course to take a direct line on the longboat and the odd-looking white vessel speeding in the same direction.

"Hurry men," bellowed Barnet an instant before the ship shuddered and listed hard to port. Crewmembers were knocked off their feet and cannons rolled from their stations some crushing sailors beneath them with the violent crash, others lost overboard amid the chaos and screams. Seconds later Miller's ship was rocked ferociously in the same way with similar results.

Barnet struggled to his feet amid the carnage in time to see a large whale surface and circle across the bow, preparing, it seemed, to ram the two ships a second time. "Brace yourselves for another strike, mates" he yelled above the panic and confusion.

The whale swam past Barnet's ship, its head breaking the surface through the swells as if to confirm that the ship had been suitably disabled to stop the cannon-fire. With a great heave, the whale rose up from the water crashing into the sea with a massive splash, its tale waving as it submerged, swimming in the direction of the longboat.

Jennings joined Captain Barnet at the gunwale to watch the whale as it swam on a collision course with the longboat. "That beast will crush Rackham and his lot," said Jennings.

"Perhaps, but I want another try, surely there would be one cannon that could be positioned with haste," replied Barnet.

The small boat rocked, nearly capsizing as Rachel jumped

from her seat. "Look! There's *Reckless*! It's Pop and Nan. They found us."

"No way," shouted Kai as he twisted around.

Everyone turned to get a better view of a schooner sailing in their direction.

"Hope this be a friendlier lot headin' toward our wee boat," said Calico Jack. "How d'ye suppose they be sailin' so blasted . . . now they be stoppin'. How'd they stop their ship in the middle of a sail?"

"No worries, they're friendly . . . what are they doin'?" asked Kai.

"Probably dropping *Bad Latitude* to pick us up so they don't give the navy guys a bigger target," answered Jack.

Jack had just finished explaining to Kai what he thought was happening when *Reckless* sped up revealing the white fiberglass boat reaching plane from behind the schooner's stern. At the same time there was a loud crack and everyone turned in time to see Captain Barnet's ship list hard to port before righting itself then watched in shock as a whale slammed into the escort ship.

Reckless Endeavor sailed past, horns blasting, as two women smiled and waved enthusiastically from the deck. The smaller white boat closed the gap quickly. The pirates and the Tinnermons stared awestruck by the scene unfolding before them.

Bennett turned, sneaking a peak toward the two British ships. "That . . . thing is swimming this way to ram us like the others," he yelled.

"No it's okay, Bennett. It's just Q. He changed so he could knock the ships out of commission so they couldn't fire at us with their cannons," yelled a grinning Kai.

A minute later Q, still in the form of a whale moved alongside the longboat while Pop piloted *Bad Latitude* up to the opposite side and tossed a rope across to pull the two boats together. Tucker Gunn tugged the rope until the slack was gone and the two boats bumped against one another.

"C'mon. Let's go. Let's go. They're probably tryin' to line up another cannon volley," barked Pop as he reached out to help Anne Bonny board.

Calico Jack complained that as captain he should be the last to leave the longboat as Tucker Gunn and Kai hoisted the injured pirate over the gunwale into the waiting boat. Gunn was the last to board the overloaded boat from the future.

"Everyone hang on," yelled Pop as he pushed the throttle forward. A few seconds after they were underway, they heard a lone explosion from the direction of the two British ships and turned in time to see the longboat obliterated.

Kai elbowed Jack who winced in pain. "Sorry, forgot you were banged up. Was just gonna tell you your Plan B cut it a little close."

Jack smiled, "Yep. Pop will have to work on his timing for future adventures but considering he had to travel three hundred years on short notice, we'll cut him some slack."

Kai laughed. "Yeah, we can let him off easy this time. Look at him, he's itchin' to either yell at us or give us giant bear hugs."

"We'll probably get both. Right now he's focused on getting all of us out of cannon range and climbing aboard *Reckless*."

Nan watched *Bad Latitude* approach from the stern of the schooner, her heart pounding with anticipation. They were well ahead of the British ships now and in a few minutes she would be reunited with her grandson. Val draped her arm over Nan's shoulder as she tried to contain her excitement.

Pop pulled alongside the magnificent schooner as Val dropped a rope ladder over the gunwale. Kai tied off a line to *Reckless*. Within a few minutes everyone climbed from *Bad Latitude* to *Reckless*, except for Pop and Jack. They stood a few feet apart. Jack was smiling, Pop stared at Jack's battered face and the bloody mess on his side and shoulder.

"You're sure a sight. You okay?" asked Pop.

"Yeah, I'm fine. Rough couple of weeks," said Jack. "Sorry we ran off on our own like that but I was pretty sure you wouldn't let us go." He smiled. "You probably would have gone to rescue Rachel by yourself."

"I'm pretty sure you're right. Only an idiot would allow their grandson and his friends go to do what you guys did. We've been pretty upset, especially Nan and Val."

"But we didn't have a choice. We wouldn't have put any of you through this if Calico Jack hadn't kidnapped Rachel. Couldn't pretend . . ."

"I know. Look, you better get your butt on deck and see Nan. We'll catch up in a little bit. Think I'll tow your boat along for a little while; set it in the cradle once things calm down."

"Okay, Pop. See you topside," said Jack as he gave Pop a quick hug using his good arm before reaching for the ladder.

Nan was waiting. "Look at you! You're hurt."

"I'm okay, just a couple scratches," replied Jack as he stooped down to hug her.

"Rachel told me already, sliced by a cutlass, big splinter in your side from an explosion and stabbed with a hook. We need to get those wounds taken care of now."

"Alright. Let me check on everyone first."

"That can wait, this can't. Let's go. I'll get Rachel to help me," said Nan.

"Okay. Better check Calico Jack too. He was shot a couple of times."

"Thanks to *HIM* my grandson and two others that I love were nearly killed. He can wait."

Calico Jack's eyebrows rose in surprise but he chose to let the statement go unchallenged.

X

Kai and Val both grinned as they spoke with a wide-eyed open-mouthed Bennett. The Tinnermons and the Rackham crew stared at the bottles of spring water as Pop handed one out to each person. "Sorry ya'll, forgot you've never seen plastic bottles before. Look, you hold it here in the middle, grab the cap on top like this, and twist it to your left," said Pop as he demonstrated.

"Well Captain Rackham, guess I'm supposed to say welcome aboard but there's still the problem of you kidnappin' Rachel," said Pop with a not so friendly look.

"Beg pardon, sir, 'ave we met b'fore?" asked a puzzled Calico Jack.

Kai laughed. "Pop! The Calico Jack that you met was dead. This one never kidnapped anyone. He's okay."

"Oh yeah, guess you're right, Kai. Forgot about that. My apologies, sir."

Kai stepped in. "Captain Rackham, this is Jack's grandfather . . . another Captain Rackham."

"That's okay," said Pop. "You can call me . . ."

Nan interrupted as she, Rachel and Jack returned topside. Jack had showered and changed into a Billabong T-shirt, cargo shorts and flip flops and had tied his wet blonde hair into a pony tail. His shoulder and side had been disinfected and bandaged. "Captain Rackham, I think you need to come below so I can get a look at those gunshot wounds," said Nan.

"Would ye mind me helpin'?" asked Anne Bonny rather timidly.

"Of course not. Both of you can follow me. Once we get you patched up, we'll all sit down and have something to eat. Shouldn't take too long," said Nan as she managed a smile and patted Anne on the arm.

Bennett walked over to Jack. "Are they the kind of clothes people wear, uh, in the future?"

"Sometimes. Depends on the weather, or where I'm going, things like that. Hey maybe a little later I'll show you some pictures of what things look like three hundred years from now," said Jack as he clapped Bennett on the shoulder.

"I would like that. Can my parents see too?"

"Sure. Why not?"

Pop joined Jack and Bennett. "Pop, this is our friend Bennett Tinnermon," said Jack. "Be extra nice to him, he saved my life back in Port Royal."

Pop smiled and shook hands. "Good to meet you, Bennett. Appreciate you lookin' out for my wayward grandson and his friends."

"It's nice to meet you, sir. Jack and his friends helped us get away from the Redcoats."

"You wouldn't have had to escape if you hadn't rescued me," said Jack. He turned to face Pop. "Bennett kept the executioner from beating me. They chased him while Calico Jack and Tuck broke me loose from the whipping post. They never caught up with Bennett but someone recognized him and the Redcoats went to his home and burned it and his family's business to the ground. We managed to get to the Tinnermons just as the Redcoats arrived. I promised that I would help them get to America."

"Jack suggested we go to a place called Philadelphia," said Bennett.

"Philadelphia was quite the American hub back in, I mean *is* quite a hub these days." A look of profound sadness crossed Pop's face. "Bennett are you tellin' me that you and your family have lost everything?"

"Not exactly, sir. Jack gave me a bag of gold that should be enough to help us get started again," said Bennett.

"But I didn't give you enough to build a house and set up another business, Bennett," answered Jack.

"But it is enough to get us to America, maybe even Philadelphia."

"No worries there, Bennett. Somehow I'm gonna see to it that you and your family not only get to Philly, I mean Philadelphia, but that you'll have enough start-up capital to set up a business that's bigger and better than before," said Pop.

"Are we going to sail all the way to Philadelphia?" asked Jack.

"I'm not sure but now that you mention sailin', we'd better raise more sail, shut down the engines and conserve our fuel. It's not like we can pull *Reckless* into a marina along the way for a tank of diesel, besides, there's no chance of the British Navy catchin' us now."

"I'll get Kai and Tuck to give me a hand," said Jack.

"Let them do the climbin'. You're too banged up to go up top," said Pop.

"You want topsails too?"

"Topsails, jib sails, and staysails. We managed the mainsail and inner jib but that's when your friend King what's-his-name flew aboard and told us y'all needed rescuin'. Where'd he go, by the way?"

"He changed into a whale and attacked those two

British ships that were firing on us. He bought us time while you maneuvered around to pick us up. I have no idea where he is now but expect he'll show up sooner or later," said Jack. "C'mon Bennett, we'll teach you something about sailing."

Twenty minutes later *Reckless* moved through the light swells under sail as Pop shut down the CAT engines.

~198~

～16～
CHEESEBURGERS IN PARADISE

CALICO JACK RACKHAM shuffled onto the deck, his arm in a sling, wearing a pair of Pop's shorts, a Guy Harvey fishing shirt, a Phillies ball cap and a pair of *Dockside* boat shoes. He didn't look happy. Anne Bonny did her best to keep from laughing out loud while Mary Read made no effort to contain herself as she cackled until her sides ached.

"I see you're stylin' there Cap'n," said Kai with a smirk. "Look at those chicken legs."

"How d'ye get aroun' wearin' breeches the likes of these?" thundered the pirate.

"Guess he's got his panties in a bunch," laughed Pop.

"Should have given him a pair of whitey tightees," answered Nan with a wink. "Well it's just too bad, Captain Rackham. You needed to get cleaned up and there's no way you were traipsing around this boat in those filthy bloody clothes."

"'Twasn't me to blame fer bein' locked away!"

Jack laughed. "You were in jail for one day."

"Aye an' in the hold of a British ship a'fore that, lad."

"All of you go ahead and laugh," said Nan. "I'll explain to all of you how the, uh, plumbing works. Every one of you is going to get a hot shower and changed into clean clothes before dinner."

Tucker Gunn's eyes widened in horror. "Ye be meanin' fer all of us to be dressed like 'im? I had me a bath in Tortuga."

"Tuck, the bath ain't such a hardship, mate. The water be hot an' . . ."

"While you guys argue, I'm jumpin' in the shower and into some clean clothes," announced Kai as he walked to the cabin door. "See y'all in a few minutes."

"Jackson you'll need to find something for Mr. Gunn and Mr. Tinnermon to wear. Kai will have to loan something to Bennett. Val maybe you can help me get some clothes together for the ladies."

"No problem, Nan," said Val.

"Honey, can you fire up the grill? I think we'll cook outside. It'll be too crowded downstairs and it's nice and cool out now," said Nan to Pop.

"What're we makin'?"

Nan smiled. "Something easy. How about hot dogs and cheeseburgers?"

"Aww, Nan that sounds fantastic," said Jack.

"Better than fire-roasted iguana," added a grinning Rachel.

⌒X⌒

Ninety minutes later, with everyone cleaned up, changed, refreshed and in a general good mood, Pop announced that the burgers were ready for the cheese and that it was time to grab some plates. Pop was no cook, but could do a passable job on the grill.

Val and Kai stood on either side of Pop as he dished burgers onto oversized platters. The pirates and the Tinnermons looked on with obvious curiosity. Jack and

Rachel watched them, chuckling to themselves.

Jack took one of the burgers and demonstrated to everyone the best way to eat one was to apply ketchup, relish and mustard first. Rachel being a New Englander, suggested over Jack's mild objections, that mayonnaise be substituted for mustard, but both agreed that hot dogs only required mustard and relish, adding that the use of onions caused bad breath. Nan delivered a heaping batch of French fries to the table next to the condiments.

Calico Jack and the others listened intently to the advice, some following Rachel's suggestions, others Jack's.

Mary Read stared at the burger, its cheese clinging and melting down the edge of the meat, the ketchup and mayonnaise running together creating a pink colored sauce. She took a tentative bite and chewed slowly, surprisingly so for someone who hadn't eaten much in a couple of days. Anne stared, waiting to see if Mary would get sick or spit it out. Mary smiled and took another bite, this time putting away a full third of the burger. Anne and Tuck laughed and did the same. They gave Nan an odd look when she passed out napkins to wipe off their sopping chins.

In the end all agreed that they liked the food of the future, though the pirates would have preferred rum over Coke Zero and sweet tea. As everyone finished their meal, Q landed on the starboard gunwale and immediately changed from the Quetzal bird into his human form.

"Q! Where have you been?" asked Kai.

"I wanted to see if any other ships had taken up the chase."

"And?"

"Four are returning to Port Royal, two are off course and three new ships are sailing too far east to intercept you," answered Q.

"Well that's good news. By the way, I can't shape-shift anymore," announced Kai.

"The potion has worn off. It is most fortunate that you weren't several hundred feet in the sky when that occurred."

"Really? You mean I coulda dropped like a rock and been killed?"

"No. I was making what you call a joke. Are they hot dogs?" asked Q.

"Yep. Hold on, Q, I'll hook you up," said Kai.

Pop whispered to Jack, "How does he know about hot dogs?"

"Probably gets them when he goes to the Dodger's games."

"Huh? Uh . . . never mind," said Pop shaking his head.

⤳ X ⤲

Pop and Nan relaxed on deck at the helm chatting with Q and Rachel as Q and Pop each puffed lazily on Gloria Cubana cigars. Nan resisted the urge to complain. Everyone else had crashed for the night.

"I'm havin' a hard time wrappin' my brain around the fact that we're sailin' right now in the year 1720," said Pop.

Q turned to Rachel, a quizzical look on his face. "Wrappin' my brain means trying to understand," explained Rachel.

"That makes perfect sense given the circumstances," said Q as he blew out a long plume of blue gray smoke.

"We have a problem and a decision to make, Q," said Pop.

"Yes you do. I assumed you might wish to discuss it."

"What's wrong, Mr. Rackham?" asked Rachel.

Pop stared over at her.

"I meant Pop. Sorry. What's wrong, Pop?" she asked again.

"Well, we have a boat that'll stand out like a sore thumb in 1720, and a bunch of passengers that'll draw all sorts of attention in the twenty first century. I'm not sure which way to go on this. I want to get the Tinnermons to Philadelphia and Rackham and his crew to South Carolina but we can't sail to either place aboard *Reckless*. Besides, there's no way to get fuel or use our GPS and radar back in time. On top of that, Calico Jack needs better medical attention than he can get now. Let's face it, you n' Nan are good at doctorin' but all you have to work with is a first aid kit. He needs some good stiff antibiotics," explained Pop.

"What if we go to St. Augustine, in our, you know, normal time. We'll get Calico Jack checked out by Dr. Butcher and get them all outfitted with decent clothes from their own time at that little costume shop in town. Then we sail during the present day and only travel back to 1720 when we deliver the pirates and the Tinnermons to their final destination," suggested Nan.

"Uh, Q would we be able to time travel back and forth like that?" asked Pop.

"Yes, as long as you have the *Wind Jewel*," said Q as he reached into his waistband. "Here you are Mr. Rackham. I had forgotten. This belongs to you now." He handed Pop the *Serpent Dagger* with the jewel already embedded in the hilt.

"Actually it's yours, Q."

"I am making it a gift to you."

"Thank you. I shouldn't accept but it's such a beautiful relic I can't stand the thought of refusing it." Pop paused and cleared his throat. "Okay, so that's what we'll do. We'll spend a few days at home, get everyone checked out and patched up, then go to Sally Theriault's pirate shop downtown and get everyone outfitted so they look normal when they return to their own time. I'll buy a couple of old wooden longboats, mount them on the deck at the stern and our guests can row to shore. That way no one from the past will get a clear look at *Reckless* when we're back in time," said Pop.

"It will also be my pleasure to show you how the great stone works," said Q.

"Uh, well, some secrets are better left as secrets, Q," said Pop.

~X~

"This be a wonder of a ship, captain," said Calico Jack as he joined Pop at the helm.

"Yes it is, Captain Rackham and don't you be gettin' any piratey ideas either," said Pop.

"Givin' it up, sir. On that ye have me oath."

"What about your friends? They onboard? I mean, they're givin' up the trade as well?"

"Aye. Me n' Anne be startin' anew in Carolina. Got a baby on the way y' know. Tuck be swearin' for a time to be returnin' to Ireland to join up with his own lot. With Mary, 'tis hard to say, she be a might fonder of the fightin' an' plunderin' an' she confided, she did, to Anne that she be wantin' her own ship one day."

Q passed by and nodded to Pop, silently letting him know that they had returned to the present day. This time there was no sensation, big bang or whirlwind, time just changed. Pop reached down and pressed a button on the left side of the helm. There was a slight whirring sound as a new control panel rose up from below the deck and slid into place covering the authentic-looking polished wooden helm. Calico Jack stood back, the shock clearly evident on his face.

Once in place Pop flipped a few switches and the screens lit up.

"*NOW* it be a wonder of a ship. Welcome to the twenty first century, Captain Rackham. These screens show our exact location not only here on the ocean but on the entire planet. See those numbers? And this screen over here shows what's called radar. These blips here are other boats; this one's a ship, all of 'em in our vicinity but not close enough for us to see them with our eyes. This," he said as he turned a small controller, "is what we call a radio. If I want to speak with anyone on any one of those boats that we can't see, I just have to talk into this microphone." Pop removed the mic from the holder and clicked the send button a couple of times."

"I must tell ye, I be findin' meself at a loss fer words."

"Well keep it that way. I don't want to have to deal with a mutiny."

"Avast, captain, ye don't . . . "

"Something wrong?" asked Pop. He was smiling as he watched the wide-eyed Captain Rackham struggle to inspect his battle wounds.

"Me shoulder stopped painin' me." He pulled his shirt up over his head and ripped away the gauze and tape and stared.

"There's no wound, captain. It's healed. Thanks to our friend Q, we have travelled forward into my time. Welcome, sir, to the twenty first century."

DAVID EBRIGHT

PRESENT DAY
ST. AUGUSTINE, FLORIDA

17
THE RACKHAM ESTATE

THEY ARRIVED OFF THE INLET of St. Augustine at mid-afternoon on the third day. Pop fired up the engines. The crew furled the sails and *Reckless Endeavor* motored through the narrow inlet on the north side toward Vilano Beach, opposite a large curling sandbar. The pirates lined up along the gunwale on the starboard side while the Tinnermons moved to their favorite spot at the bow, staring in awe at the dozens of swift moving power boats zipping through the small bay.

Bennett pointed ahead toward the Bridge of Lions. It was the biggest structure he had ever seen. "What is that?"

"That is a bridge, son for people to . . . what are those . . . carriages without horses?"

Val joined the Tinnermons as they stared around at the odd surroundings. "Guess you guys will see some really weird-looking stuff during the next few days. Hey, what's wrong, Bennett? You seem nervous."

Bennett pointed again at the bridge. "Our masts are too tall to get under that."

"Don't worry, Pop blasts the horn three times and they'll . . ." The horn sounded, cutting off her sentence. "Okay now watch the center of the bridge. See the barriers are flashing red and lowering down to block the road and stop the cars. Oh geez, you don't know what a car is. There it goes, see the bridge separating? That opening is wide and high enough for us to sail right through it."

"Astounding," exclaimed Mr. Tinnermon.

"Horseless carriages," said Mrs. Tinnermon breathlessly.

Bennett and his parents continued staring upward as *Reckless* crossed through the opened drawbridge, the rhythmic clanging of a bell kept time with their progress. Several people stepped out of their cars to watch and wave as *Reckless* passed below. Others blew their horns and waved from their car windows. "If you think *this* is a big deal, your heads are going to spin all week. Wait 'til Jack and Kai take you for a ride in one of their Jeeps or maybe a cruise on a JetSki." Val smiled. "You'll have to give surfing a try too. Bennett I think you're gonna have a total blast while you're here."

It took nearly an hour for *Reckless* to navigate the Intracoastal Waterway, known as the Matanzas River among the locals, to reach the waterside Rackham estate. Normally Pop would moor the schooner at the edge of the channel and use Jack's boat or a smaller Zodiac to reach the dock following a day or two of sailing. For longer trips, Pop would tie up at the St. Augustine marina and load provisions and equipment from the city pier. Today the incoming tide made it possible for Pop to edge *Reckless* up to his own shorter dock, though it didn't accommodate the entire boat. "We can tie her up here for an hour or two before we have to move to the channel. By the way, I don't want anyone mentioning 1720. People will think we're nuts," explained Pop.

"Nuts? What does that mean?" asked Calico Jack.

"Didn't we already cover that once?" asked Pop.

Kai laughed. "Pop that was the other Calico Jack, the

dead one."

"Oh, yeah. Right. The, uh, . . . dead one." Pop rolled his eyes and shook his head.

"I'll explain it to you later, Captain Rackham," said Kai.

They tied *Reckless* off using a pair of doubled lines. The stern drifted slightly toward the river, enough to annoy Pop, but he left it alone. "Careful now climbing onto the dock, it wasn't built for a boat this size," warned Pop as he and Kai adjusted an aluminum gangplank hooking it over the gunwale from the walkway.

"We should extend it one of these days," said Kai.

"Gets too shallow here at low tide, Kai and I'm not gonna waste time and money on a dredge. The permit alone would cost a fortune, not to mention I'd be too old by the time I got the permit signed off. Besides, we plan to keep *Reckless* at our new house in the Bahamas, once it's finished."

"Forgot all about that place. Val said it looked awesome from the air. We never got the chance to see it 'cause we were kinda busy with you-know-who," said Kai.

The pirates and the Tinnermons stared at the white two story structure next to the dock. Underneath, supported on a hydraulic lift they saw a sleek thirty eight foot Donzi with the name Laffin' Gaff stenciled on its sides. The adjoining space was empty but on the opposite side sat a Hurricane deck boat, also suspended from a lift. In the last slip a platform supported two small water crafts. As they rounded the corner they noticed a set of steps leading toward a door which was flanked by tall windows beneath a tiled awning.

"Is this where you live?" Bennett asked Jack in a half-whisper.

"No. This is the boathouse. When I visit Pop and Nan

during the summer, I stay upstairs. The main house is over there behind the gardens."

"Is it bigger than the . . . boathouse?"

Jack smiled. "Um, yeah. Now relax and stop whispering. Pop and Nan are nice people."

"Oh, I can tell. I like them and my parents like them too."

"Hey, maybe we'll get you standing on a surfboard by the end of the week," said Jack.

"Val said you might take me for a ride in something called Jeep."

"We can do . . ."

"What is that?" asked Bennett pointing excitedly.

"That's a swimming pool inside what's called a lanai and there's a fountain and some waterfalls in there too. Behind all that is the house," said Jack.

"And you live here?"

"Only in the summer. You know, when you go back to your time, you can't tell anyone about anything you've seen or done here. People will think you're crazy."

"Crazy?"

"Out of your mind? Insane?"

"I don't know if I'm going to like all of this," said Bennett.

～X～

They entered a pair of double doors inside the lanai, crossed a large game room decorated in teak and leather with a big screen TV mounted on one wall. They passed through into a larger two story circular white marble foyer where a wide winding stair separated the dining room and living room, with tall arched windows taking up the wall space on either side of a massive double door decorated with intricate etched glass.

Val showed the pirates and the Tinnermons upstairs to their rooms and explained that the bathrooms functioned much like those on *Reckless.* Since her first encounter on the Rackham's schooner, Mary Read had been particularly taken with the function of toilets, referring to them as 'water chairs'.

"Jack, there's no food in the house so while Pop and Kai get *Reckless* moored, I'll need you and Rachel to go see Tony over at South Beach Grill and pick up dinner for everyone. Tell him we need enough to feed thirteen . . . no tell him twenty, and get lots of salad. I'm sure everyone is extra hungry."

"No problem, Nan."

Rachel nudged Jack. "Let's see if Bennett wants to ride with us."

"Val has already filled his head with suggestions, like surfing and riding Jet Skis. I don't know if all of that's such a great idea just yet," said Jack.

"Stop being so serious. As long as his parents give him permission, what could it hurt?" asked Nan. "You ought to take him on one of those helicopter rides," she said with a wink.

"I told him he better not tell anyone when he returns to his own time. People will think he's crazy," said Jack.

"It'll be fine. I'll go ask Missy," said Nan.

A few minutes later Bennett hurried into the kitchen to join Jack and Rachel. He was beaming. "Are we really going to ride in the thing called Jeep?" he asked.

"Yep. My horseless carriage. Let's roll," said Jack.

They walked out to the garage, Jack aimed his keys at one of the doors and it rolled up. A bright red Jeep Wrangler, its top already down, sat gleaming inside. Rachel sat in the back to give Bennett the front seat. "Snap your seatbelt on like this," said Rachel as she demonstrated. Jack drove down the winding driveway, pausing momentarily for the automatic double gates to open at the end of the lane. Turning left they drove along Highway A1A before detouring onto the beach ramp at Dondellon Road and driving south on the beach for a few miles. Jack made a quick right hand turn between the sand dunes that separated at a small colorful building with a sign reading *South Beach Grill*. He pulled around to the front and into the parking lot. Forty five minutes later, loaded with bags and containers of food, they arrived home, leaving the Jeep outside near the walkway at the back of the house. While Rachel and Val helped Nan put the meal out, Bennett rushed upstairs to tell his parents about his latest adventure.

Dinner was served poolside. Calico Jack and his crew had already decided that the strange food of the future was much tastier than what they were used to, though Anne, munching on her salad, wondered aloud why anyone would want to eat bunches of leaves.

"Jack, tomorrow you need to go downtown and visit **Sally Theriault** at the pirate shop and see about gettin' these folks some eighteenth century clothes. I already called her," said Pop.

Mary Read spoke up. "We won't be havin' to wear dresses will we?"

"Not here but once we get you back to your own time, you might need to dress like a woman until you decide what you want to do. Take your old clothes along just in case, you know, you want to be a pirate after all. We'll get them all cleaned up first," said Nan.

"Aye, an' beggin' yer pardon, Mrs. Rackham, I be most anxious to get into me own breeches again."

"Captain Rackham, I'm afraid your shirt and

waistcoat are beyond repair, I can't make bullet holes disappear," said Nan.

"Well, we have to come up with a story. Can't go tellin' Sally these folks need antique clothes right away when there's no event goin' on in town," said Pop.

"There are people dressed up around town all the time, pirates, Spanish soldiers, you name it," said Jack.

"Yeah and she knows everyone that does the re-enactments, even the out-of-towners. Well, we're not lookin' for pirate duds anyway," said Pop.

"Duds?" asked Kai.

"Clothes. It's an old expression."

"Ain't wearin' no dress," said Mary.

"Fine," said Pop, obviously annoyed. "They can hang you in Carolina as easy as they could in Port Royal. Once I deliver the four of you, you're on your own. Go ahead and wear your old clothes, and they'll arrest all of you about the time your feet hit dry land."

"'Tis no hardship, Mary" said Anne. "We be gettin' a new life."

"Aye, an' we be in yer debt," said Mary as she looked over at Jack, Kai and Rachel.

"Why not go to the shop wearin' your old clothes and pretend to be actors lookin' for jobs?" suggested Kai. "Like Jack said, no one in town's gonna look at y'all twice."

"Kai's got a point," said Val with a giggle. "Maybe they'll get jobs working at the *Pirate and Treasure Museum* or maybe as crewmembers on the *Black Raven* over at the marina."

"Okay, I guess you're right. Maybe I'm overthinkin' this. Jack, you and Rachel can take everyone to Sally's place in the morning."

"Sure."

"We'll have to take two cars but I don't have my

driver's license," said Rachel.

"I can go with them," offered Val. "Rachel can ride with me."

"Okay, you'll have to take Nan's Escalade and my truck. Kai, can you give me a hand in the morning unloading *Reckless*?"

"Yeah, no problem."

"I can help if Nan drives downtown," said Jack.

Nan noticed Tucker Gunn picking at his food. "Is everything alright, Mr. Gunn?"

He smiled and cocked his eyebrow before letting out a sigh. "Aye. Bit tired 'tis all." He chuckled, then added, "Been thinkin' on that bed waitin' fer me upstairs n' tryin' to remember when be the last I slept in one."

⟨~18~⟩
BLACKBEARD'S HEAD

CALICO JACK, ANNE, MARY and Tuck climbed into Pop's bright red truck with Jack while the Tinnermons piled into Nan's black Escalade with Val and Rachel. Bennett was quite pleased with himself, already knowing how to snap into the seat belt without instructions. All, other than Calico Jack, were dressed in their tattered, but clean clothes from their real time in history.

They drove down the long driveway, Jack in the lead. As they neared the double wrought iron gates, a sensor picked up their approach and the gates swung inward, allowing them to drive through without stopping. Making a left onto scenic Route A1A, running parallel with the ocean, they headed toward St. Augustine, observing the speed limit, no need to attract attention, Jack decided. Mary Read, for one, was terrified at the speed they were traveling, forty five miles per hour. Calico Jack, sitting in the front seat, squeezed the center arm rest with such force that he twisted the steel pin holding it to the seat's frame. Pop would not be happy.

"Ye be takin' us to meet our maker!" shouted Mary from the back seat.

"It's okay. This is how we travel. I'm not even going fast," said Jack.

Anne, sitting in the back with Mary and Tuck, seemed relaxed. "'Tis a fine way to travel. There be nary a bump or sway," she said.

Ten minutes later they pulled into the parking garage behind St. Augustine's city gates. "We only have to walk a short distance to Cuna Street. Miss Sally is going to get all of you fitted and dressed. Remember the story, you're all actors and need the clothes so you can get jobs in town doing reenactments," Jack reminded all of them.

"Aye, an' we be in desperate straits, our luggers bein' nicked whilst journeyin' from afar," said Tucker Gunn.

"Luggage," corrected Val.

"Aye. That."

Jack looked at the group assembled on the walkway outside the parking garage and sighed. "Let's get this over with. Stay together and don't say anything unless you absolutely have to."

Rachel leaned over toward Val and giggled. "This has disaster written all over it," she whispered.

They walked into the center of town along St. George Street, a narrow avenue lined on both sides by quaint shops and taverns, some housed within buildings dating to the days of the Spaniards. At the midway point they turned left onto Cuna Street stopping in front of a white two story building with porches stretching across the face at both levels. A bell jingled as they entered the shop. They were greeted at the door by a pleasant lady dressed as a pirate from the early eighteenth century.

"Aye, you must be Jackson. I'm Sally Theriault. Your grandfather called and explained that some of his friends needed to be outfitted," she said.

"Hi, Miss Sally. Hopefully he told you that they're looking for stuff from the early 1700s," said Jack.

"He did and I have plenty of stuff here to choose from and what I don't have we can make. Let's start with this handsome young lad here," she said, her hand on Bennett's shoulder, leading him into the shop ahead of the others.

The store was divided into three parts. Through the door all the way to the back was a single narrow room, its walls lined with shelves, glass cases, flags, pictures and book stands. To the right were two rooms, one filled with racks of clothing, and shelves filled with hats, boots and shoes, the other stocked with weaponry and accessories, perfect for pirates.

Calico Jack stared in awe at the handmade cutlasses, daggers and flintlocks, reaching absently to his midsection where he normally carried his brace of pistols. Sally smiled, looking at the four pirates. "Your outfits are a bit battered and worn, but I'll have to compliment you on the authenticity. It's very fine work. What are your names?" she asked.

Captain Rackham bowed slightly, a crooked smile on his face. "These be me mates, Tucker Gunn, Mary Read, Anne Bonny and I be Captain Calico Jack Rackham."

"Of course," laughed Sally. "You all play the part so well, though I must say, the name Tucker Gunn does not ring a bell."

"Most o' the lads was to call me Tuck or Gunny, bless all souls," said Gunn.

"The lads?" asked Sally.

"Aye, they be restin' below 'n Davy Jones' Locker. Bloody Brits …"

"Uh, Tuck takes his role very seriously," interrupted Rachel giving the pirates a brief warning glare.

"So I see. Well, y'all won't have a problem finding work around here. Let's get started."

As Pop requested, each person was outfitted with two complete sets of clothing, including boots, shoes, coats, hats, and accessories. Rackham and his crew each selected a single cutlass, a dagger and a pair of flintlocks. Mr. Tinnermon chose a dagger, a flintlock and a musket. Bennett, with his father's approval, picked out his own musket.

"Are you sure Mr. Rackham won't object to buying all of these cutlasses, scabbards and accessories? You're running up quite a tab."

"He gave me specific instructions to have you outfit them all properly," said Jack. "Send him the bill and he'll stop by with cash right away."

"Well I can tell you, my friend Smithy King is going to be thrilled when I tell him how many pieces of his exquisite handmade weaponry you've purchased. I'm afraid you'll have to buy the powder and shot elsewhere," said Sally. "Now let me look y'all over one more time.."

Their tattered clothes lay bagged up near the back door. Jack wondered what Miss Sally would do if she knew that her trash was actually authentic garb from three centuries before. The Tinnermons, now dressed as a well-to-do pre-Colonial family, stood next to Calico Jack, who wore a long waistcoat over his white ruffled shirt. Next to him Anne Bonny twirled before a mirror. She seemed pleased wearing her puffy royal blue dress. The pair looked like the owners of a splendid plantation. Tuck and Mary, were dressed as if prepared to go on the account once more, which Jack and Kai suspected would be exactly what they would do once they returned to their own time. Of course it was only Calico Jack and Anne Bonny that had promised to give up their pirating ways.

Most of the weapons, along with the new clothes not being worn, were wrapped up in plastic and brown paper and Jack, Bennett and Rachel carried everything to the Escalade. Jack had reluctantly agreed to let Tuck and Mary hold onto their cutlasses and flintlocks. The others walked with Val along the waterfront bordering Castillo Drive toward the Bridge of Lions.

Calico Jack stopped in the middle of the sidewalk

across from the Castillo de San Marcos and pointed to a Jolly Roger hanging from a sign mast. "It be Vane's flag," said Tuck.

Mary Read waved her hand, dismissing Tuck's observation. "Vane's pennant had thicker bones an' they crossed atop the skull."

"Aye, Mary's right," said Anne.

Still curious, Calico Jack asked Val, "What is this place?"

"Um, it's the pirate museum."

"Pirate museum?"

"They have a bunch of cool exhibits, a real treasure chest, gold coins, cannons, journals, artifacts, Blackbeard ..."

Mary was astounded. "Blackbeard be dead! Heard they chopped his head off, they did."

Val tried not to laugh. "That's the part they have, uh, inside . . . Blackbeard's head."

"'Twould be but a stump o' rot," said Anne.

"Don't forget, Blackbeard died three hundred years ago," teased Val.

"Aye, he be no more n' a skull now," said Calico Jack.

"No. His whole head is in there, still has his beard and eyes and he can talk ..."

Tuck drew his cutlass. "We have to rescue him, him bein' our brethren."

"No, Tuck, put that thing away," hissed Val.

Rachel, Bennett and Jack caught up with the others outside the museum entrance. "What's going on here?" asked Rachel.

"We were talking about Blackbeard and some of the stuff that's in the museum," said Val.

Jack looked at Rachel and grinned. "You've never been in the museum, have you?"

"Nope."

"Let's go visit Blackbeard then."

The lady at the cash register eyed up Jack and his group as they approached. She smiled and welcomed them to the museum. "Your outfits are amazing." She looked at the Tinnermons. "We offer a discount for anyone dressed as a pirate. I feel terrible that I can only make that offer to two of you."

"That's okay," said Jack. "I'll take ten tickets and a copy of that pirate handbook."

"That will be one hundred and thirty eight dollars altogether," the lady said pleasantly, as she reached for a copy of the book.

Jack swiped his card, poked at a few buttons below the screen and accepted the tickets and book from the pleasant cashier. "Thank you," he said and turned to face his friends. "Follow me. We'll start with the cannon and main deck."

They walked through the exhibits, inspecting the cannon, the deck and ship's helm, even the Captain's quarters where they viewed an original Jolly Roger. When they moved into the section known as the Execution Dock, the pirates stopped, their mouths agape. Hanging from a simulated bowsprit the head of Blackbeard swayed as he shouted out angry oaths and threats in his deep gravelly voice, his eyes roaming wildly around the room.

Tucker Gunn again reached for his cutlass.

"Whoa! What are you doing?" yelled Jack.

"Can't leave the man in such a state. I be cuttin' 'im down," said Tuck.

"Aye, 'tis cruelty leavin' . . ." said Mary as she withdrew her own cutlass.

"No. Put those weapons away before we all end up in jail. I know it looks real, but it's not. This is just an animated display. A machine made to look like Blackbeard," said Jack.

Anne walked closer to the severed head. "It be Blackbeard. Met him in Carolina once, I did. There be no mistakin' him," she said.

"Trust me. This is not the real Blackbeard," said Jack.

"It's my fault," said Val. "I told them about the Blackbeard display and pretended it was real. Seemed funny at the time."

"It's sorta funny but no one's gonna laugh if Tuck chops through those cables," said Rachel. "Listen, Tuck. You have to put that away. They have cameras . . . uh, ways to watch what goes on without actually being here. Security people are probably on the way already."

Tuck put the cutlass away with one last look at the hanging head. "As ye say, lass. Seems we be too late to help the poor bloke anyway."

Mary whispered to Calico Jack. "Be a fine day were we to grab that treasure chest 'fore we was to leave out of here."

The pirate looked up and caught Jack and Rachel staring at him. He cleared his throat. "Me piratin' days be over, Mary. I gave me oath on it," he said loud enough for all to hear.

They completed their tour without further incident, exited past the lady at the register, said their goodbyes and walked outside south onto Castillo Drive toward the marina. Tourists and passersby took notice of the pirates and the eighteenth-century Tinnermons but continued on their way without pause. It was, after all, a fairly common sight on the streets of America's Oldest City.

They stopped at a restaurant across from the city marina on the corner of Avenida Menendez. It was an old stone building built in 1790 and moved intact to its present location one hundred and seventy years later. Jack explained that in earlier times it had been the home of a sea captain and later, a cigar maker. They gathered at a pair of round decorative concrete tables below a sweet smelling jasmine covered arbor and looked out over the Matanzas.

Mary spied it first. A large black ship, a bright yellow stripe down its side and three masts with no sails visible floated dockside at the end of the marina . . . and there were pirates aboard.

Pop opened both sets of doors to the balcony of his study. *Reckless* had been offloaded with help from Kai and Q. Moving more than a ton of gold ashore had taken some effort and they had rushed through the chore so they could finish while the pirates were in town with Jack. Kai finally went home to his empty house on Porpoise Point at Vilano Beach. His parents were vacationing in Maine for the entire summer to escape the Florida heat.

"Let's move a couple of these chairs outside, Q. There's a perfect breeze and I could go for a nice cigar. Care to join me?"

"I would like that," said Q.

They folded up the chairs on the balcony and moved them to one side to make room. Together they carried two high backed leather wing chairs from the study outside and placed a small glass table between the two. "These will be more comfortable than those deck chairs," said Pop. He checked his watch. "I think the coast will be clear for maybe another hour or so."

Pop stepped into his study, removed an ornate wooden box from the shelf behind his desk, retrieved a gold cigar cutter and fancy lighter from a desk drawer and carried everything outside. He placed them on the table between the two chairs and walked back into the study. He returned with a crystal decanter filled with an amber liquid, a pair of tumblers filled with ice and a heavy crystal ashtray, which he had tucked precariously under his left arm.

He opened the box. It was filled with cigars of various shapes and sizes. Some were dark brown, others a lighter tan. "Take your pick, Q while I pour us a taste of this," he said as he tipped the decanter over the glass closest to Q. "Do you prefer your cigar notched or clipped?" he asked.

"Clipped will be fine," answered Q as he sampled his drink.

"I bounce back and forth," said Pop as he clipped the cigar. Holding the lighter out, Q leaned over, puffing on the cigar until the smoke billowed in a large cloud above his head.

"Better shut these doors and flip the ceiling fan on. Any smoke gets inside, I'm a dead man," quipped Pop as he closed the double doors.

Pop lowered himself into his chair with a contented sigh, lit his cigar and adjusted his cap to block some of the sun. "I know I said this before, but if it weren't for you, my grandson and his friends probably would not have made it back alive."

"Don't underestimate them. They are all quite resourceful and I have to believe they would have survived. I only assisted where I could. The plans and decisions were theirs. I was most impressed with the way they carried out their quest," said Q.

"Why did you get involved?"

"Curiosity, to start. Once underway it seemed I might

provide assistance, using some of my, shall we say, more unique abilities. This cigar has a wonderful flavor as does this beverage."

"I'm glad you're enjoying both. Help yourself anytime, my friend."

Pop blew out a long plume of blue-gray smoke, feeling relaxed for the first time in weeks. His cell phone rang and he reluctantly fished it out of the small pocket at the front of his cargo shorts. The caller ID said it was Jack.

"Pop, we have a problem," said Jack.

"Is this going to ruin my afternoon?" asked Pop with a deep sigh.

"Probably."

"Okay, let's get this over with. What's up?"

"We need a fast boat right away."

"For what?"

"Looks like Mary Read and Tucker Gunn just stole the pirate ship in the marina."

"Do they realize it's only a tourist attraction?"

"I don't know. We were sitting outside ordering some lunch when the two of them got up and walked into the restaurant. I assumed they were looking for the bathrooms; they've got bathrooms figured out now. After a while, when they hadn't come back, we went in to look for them. One of the waiters said he saw them walk out the back door. Anne figured out where they went."

"Did you actually see them on the ship?"

"Yes but the Black Raven was already underway. I saw Tuck on the quarterdeck waving his cutlass around shouting orders and Mary up on the main deck chasing everyone to the bow," said Jack. "I think they plan on going through the inlet and into the ocean."

"Sit tight. I'm leaving now," said Pop. He hit the end button and looked over at Q. "Feel like another boat ride?"

~19~
THE BLACK RAVEN

POP AND Q HURRIED to the boathouse and the outermost hydraulic lift where Pop hit a green button on a small control panel which made the lift mechanism engage automatically, lowering his boat into the water.

The white Donzi center console had a black T-top, three two hundred fifty horsepower Yamaha engines, all the accessories on the market, and was one of the fastest boats on that part of the Matanzas River. The name *Laffin' Gaff* was stenciled on both sides of the hull, the lettering resembling a series of bent and twisted fish hooks. They climbed aboard and Pop fired up all three engines, letting them idle for a minute while Q held onto a spring line. Finally Pop nodded and Q released the black nylon rope, allowing Pop to pull out of the covered shed and into the Intracoastal Waterway. Once away from the structure and into the channel Pop pushed the throttles all the way forward and the boat's bow rose up out of the water. *Laffin' Gaff* reached plane quickly and moved through the channel at sixty five knots in less than twenty seconds. They rode north toward the city at full speed, standing rather than sitting at the helm. Q held onto the T-top frame, a slight smile had replaced his usual stoic look.

~X~

"Avast ye lubbers move forward an' state yer intentions 'fore we leave port," shouted Mary Read while brandishing her cutlass at the terrified tourists. They did as she ordered, climbing the stairs two at a time to the lookout deck at the bow.

A man dressed much like Tuck approached him from the stern. "Who are you, mate?"

"Ain't yer mate. I be Tucker Gunn, Captain Calico Jack Rackham's Quartermaster and at the bow be me friend Mary Read. We be commandeerin' this ship."

"Right. Well, while you take over the ship, we still have a birthday boy onboard and need to give him his treasure chest," said the lead pirate actor who was made up to look like the character Barbarossa from the movies.

"Treasure chest?" asked Gunn.

"Aye. It's hanging from the center mast. You need to lower it so we can make a big deal out of it with hmm . . . let me see what's this kid's name . . . here it is, so Chad, can get his birthday gifts."

Mary herded the passengers together while she watched Tuck speaking with the other pirate. "Hurry along ye scalawags, unfurl the sails and take her east to the briny deep!" she yelled out to the other crewmembers.

"Sails? We have no sails," said a young lady crewmember known as PirateIvey. "They're only for looks."

Tucker Gunn climbed the mast with his dagger clenched between his teeth. He reached the treasure chest and fumbled with the tie off, finally cutting it loose with the dagger. "Where be the lad by name o' Chad on this ship?" Gunn bellowed from atop the spar.

A boy with a black and white pirate tee shirt raised his hand meekly from the deck below.

"Meet me on the main deck ye young lubber so we

can be seein' what be stowed away in this chest o' treasure." Gunn reached past the chest, grabbed the rope coiled above and, gripping it in one hand and brandishing his cutlass in the other, jumped headfirst from the spar toward the deck, his arms spread wide.

There were screams and shrieks from the crowd below. The rope went taut as Tuck let himself twist upright, his feet now facing the passengers before swinging out beyond the ship's gunwales over the choppy bay in a circular motion and descending to the deck one handed with barely a sound. As he touched down, he loosened his grip on the rope and the treasure chest drifted downward landing gently on a box next to a brightly colored wooden stool. The guests clapped and hooted at the spectacle, Chad, staring wide-eyed broke into a wide grin, two front teeth noticeably missing from his smile.

"Now, lad, let's we see what this fuss be about," said Gunn as he pulled his flintlock and aimed at the hasp.

"No need for that, Mr. Gunn," said one of the pirates. "Just pull the latch to the side."

"Ain't much of a lock then is it? You open it, Chad, and then we decide if ye stay aboard or we be tossin' ye to the depths."

Chad opened the chest. He removed a tri-corn hat, a pirate tee shirt, several handfuls of beads and necklaces, imitation doubloons, a kerchief and a full sized flag – one with the pure white Rackham skull and crossed cutlasses on a black background. He beamed with excitement showing his parents his great pile of gifts.

"Not so much as a piece o' eight 'n the whole lot. Away with ye then, lad," roared Gunn as he put his cutlass away.

"He has our flag, Tuck. Leastways, make him give us our flag," complained Mary Read in a half-whisper.

"Mary, once we go on account, we be makin' our own flag, ye have me oath on that, lass." Gunn motioned her to move closer and whispered, "'B'sides, they ain't got no bloody sails on this ship, an' nary one cannon. We needs a fast sloop and a seasoned crew."

"Aye. So we wait 'til we sail for Carolina," said a disappointed Mary.

It took twenty minutes running at full speed to reach the Bridge of Lions. The pirate ship had circled in the bay near the inlet. Pop slowed going under the bridge observing the no wake limit. "Woulda thought they'd be in the ocean by now, wonder what's goin' on," said Pop. He didn't wait for Q's reply as once through the bridge channel, he gunned the engines and aimed for the black ship.

"There's Pop's boat and Q is on board with him," said Val pointing into the harbor as *Laffin' Gaff* passed below the bridge.

"Yeah, he's going to be ticked off. I told him the ship was heading out to sea," said Jack.

"You didn't know they were only going to ride around the bay."

"Maybe I should have waited before calling. Looks like they're going through their usual routine for the tourists."

Rachel spoke up. "I still think it was the right call. Pop's probably going over there now to make sure they don't change their minds and try going through the inlet."

"Maybe Mary and Tuck had second thoughts about pirating," said Val.

"We're going to find out 'cause now they're heading this way," said Rachel as they walked along the dock to where the pirate ship would tie up.

"Uh oh, and here comes Pop," said Jack.

Laffin' Gaff passed the pirate ship and pulled into an empty slip a few spaces from the end. Pop tossed the line to Jack but stayed aboard with the engines running. "Looks to me that if they'd had a mind to steal the ship, somethin' happened to change their plans," said Pop. He looked at Calico Jack, Anne, and the Tinnermons then to the left at Jack and Val. "Anyone not already drivin' one of my vehicles can ride back to the house with me n' Q."

Bennett was the first to jump aboard. His dad followed but his mom opted to return in the Escalade. Calico Jack edged his way forward, taking sideways glances toward Anne and Rachel. "C'mon, captain. Once we get past the marina, I'll let you take the wheel," said Pop. The pirate climbed down, staring at the helm's controls and electronics. Anne shrugged, deciding to wait for Mary and Tuck.

Jack tossed the rope to Q and Pop backed *Laffin' Gaff* out of the slip before winking at his grandson and pointing the boat's bow toward the bay.

"That went better than expected," said Val.

"Told you it was the right thing to do," said Rachel. "How could you have known they wouldn't put to sea? Or like Pop said, maybe something made them change their minds."

"Well, you can tell Pop's itchin' to give Calico Jack a shot at driving the Donzi," said Val. "Do you realize that this will be the fastest that any of them has ever traveled in their lives."

"Or ever will," added Rachel.

"I beg your pardon, but how fast will they be traveling?" asked Mrs. Tinnermon.

Jack gave a subtle shake of the head to Val and Rachel, warning them to downplay it. Val never noticed and plowed ahead. "Do you know how fast we were riding on the way to town in Nan's Escalade?"

"N-no and must admit, I felt most terrified."

"Okay, well they'll be going almost twice that fast," said Val.

"We have to stop them!"

"Too late for that, there they go," said Rachel.

Laffin' Gaff's engines roared to life once away from the dock, leaving a wide churning wake foaming behind as the Donzi sped downriver toward the Rackham Estate.

"Okay, now we get to hear Tuck and Mary tell their story. Can't wait," said Jack.

Anne Bonny laughed. "So ye think 'twill be a tale they be tellin' us."

"We'll see," said Jack.

The Black Raven docked a few minutes later and the tourists poured down the gangway onto the wharf toward the gift shop and ticket window. Everyone laughed and chatted, raving to all within earshot about their experience. "All of the pirates were great but Mary and Tuck were the scariest and most realistic," said the birthday boy to his sister Anza as he carried his treasures bundled up in his brand new Rackham flag.

Finally Mary Read and Tucker Gunn approached. They were surrounded by three crewmates. "You two were incredible. Come on, we'll take you to meet Grace St Clare, our boss. She'll hire you on the spot, even pay you for this last trip," said one of the pirate actors.

"Avast, mate, we be shovin' off 'fore we know it," said Tuck in his booming voice. He slapped one of the young crewmates on the back before he and Mary joined Rachel and Anne waiting near the walkway.

Jack spoke up first. "So, Mr. Gunn, what was all that about?"

"We was goin' to steal that ship an' go on account, but it weren't a good one," said Tuck, slightly embarrassed with his head staring down at his shuffling feet.

"Aye. Din have no cannons nor sails anyway," said Mary.

"So you decided not to steal the ship and return to your own time instead," said Rachel.

"Aye. We thinks that'd be best," replied Mary.

"Glad to hear it," said Jack. He turned to Anne and Rachel. "Well, there's an honest enough answer. Let's go home. Hopefully this insanity will be over soon."

~20~
BACK TO THE PAST

Q AND POP RETURNED to the balcony outside Pop's study to pick up where they had left off. After some important baseball talk, specifically the probability that Pop's Yankees might meet Q's Dodgers in the World Series, Q changed the subject. He had reached the halfway point on his Cohiba. "Returning to our previous conversation, I think you should know that your grandson and his friends acted with great courage," said Q.

"Never woulda doubted it for a minute, Q."

"Did you know they also helped rescue many others, not only the pirates?"

"No. In fact, I know very little. Maybe you can tell me what you observed. I'm sure Jack and Kai will understate everything, they always do," said Pop. "Hold on one second while I grab a pad so I can take some notes. I like to write about Jack's summertime adventures."

Q spent the next hour, and another cigar, telling Pop the story, from the moment that, as a Quetzal bird, he first observed Jack and Kai in the cavern as they approached his forgotten city up until the time when Pop collected all of them aboard *Bad Latitude*, rescuing them from the British warships.

"Interesting. So Jack no longer has the ability to control minds, that's good. Kai could shape-shift like you and Rachel was quite the doctor takin' care of all of those kids.

And then the part about the kids and the pirates fightin' Marcus Hook and his crew while their own ship sank from underneath them, that's pretty incredible. Well, all of that's good storytellin' stuff but I'm not sure it would come across to readers as, you know, believable," said Pop.

"I agree, it is quite a story, but I assure you, all of it is true. I think you should go ahead and write it," said Q with a smile.

"Oh, I will, that's for sure. Just have to call it fiction this time around. But that's gonna wait until we get our guests packed up and back to their own time. A few more days to go and everything will be as it should, and I gotta admit, I can hardly wait for things to get back to normal, as normal as possible in the Rackham sense anyway," said Pop with a sigh.

"Mr. Rackham, there is no need for you to undertake such a long trip and personally escort everyone back in time. This is something I can accomplish on your behalf with little effort. "I could deliver Calico Jack and his crew to Carolina within the hour and the Tinnermons to Philadelphia soon after," said Q.

"Would you do that?"

"Certainly. I simply need to create a portal. There are no transport limitations. As I said, if you wish to know the secret of time travel, I will gladly share it with you."

Pop shook his head. "No, Q I don't think so. This experience has cured me of most of my curiosity on that particular oddity. On one hand, I'd like to escort everyone to their destination, you know, get a chance to see the good old US of A before it was the US of A, but if you can return everyone to their own time and bring this to a more timely end, I'd be crazy not to accept your offer. Yep. It's time for everyone to get back to where we all belong."

"Well, you just need to tell me when and it will be

done," said Q.

"I think Bennett would enjoy a little more time on a surfboard and he's really getting the hang of some of Jack's video games, besides, I know Brian is itchin' to try his hand at driving and I sorta promised to give him a shot at it. That'll also give me some time to put a few things together for all of them, something to give them all a good healthy start," said Pop. "Let's return Rackham and his crew tomorrow and the Tinnermons two days from now.

"It sounds like a most outstanding plan," said Q as he reached for the crystal decanter.

"How did Bennett make out surfing?" asked Nan.

"Great. It took about a dozen tries, but he made it. Val didn't like the way Kai was teaching him so she took over and once she did, everything clicked, just like when she taught me. He's pretty good, to be honest. You know, I don't know about his parents, but I think Bennett would rather stay here in our time than go back to his," said Rachel.

"I'm sure, but Pop's adamant, they have to return. He says there's no way to know the impact that any of these people might have on the world and to let them stay in our time could change history and maybe not for the better."

"I guess that's true but I feel bad for Bennett and his family."

"Trust me; his parents are anxious to make their new start in the year 1720 where things won't be quite so overwhelming. I think horseless carriages, flying machines and computers have them a bit intimidated. Val was showing Bennett her Facebook page this morning and teased Mrs. Tinnermon that maybe Bennett should set one up for himself. *THAT* didn't go over too well, especially when she saw pictures of Bennett behind the wheel of Jack's Jeep."

Rachel laughed at that. "I know they don't like cameras or phones either. Mary and Anne won't let us take their pictures but Calico Jack and Tucker Gunn will pose anytime. They like seeing themselves 'trapped in the tiny little box' they said."

"But you've taken some anyway, I suspect," said Nan.

"No, I haven't but Kai and Jack have."

"No doubt."

"Are you stoked about traveling back in time again, Nan?"

"Not at all and, thankfully, Pop and Q decided it would be better for Q to take them back.

⌒X⌒

Bennett sat on the surfboard, taking a break, watching Rachel and Val ride the waves. Behind him, well beyond the breakers, Jack and Kai were stunt riding, jumping incoming rollers on a pair of Jet Skis. He would miss his friends but looked forward to his new life in his own time. At the sound of the approaching Jet Skis he turned his board, paddling with his hands. Jack and Kai pulled alongside, sandwiching him in between.

"Your turn, Bennett," announced Kai. "Mind if I borrow your board for a little while?"

"Take it. It belongs to you anyway," said Bennett.

"Here, put this on," said Kai as he handed Bennett his flotation vest.

Bennett climbed onto the Jet Ski, pulled the vest on and clipped the fastening snaps into place. He looked over at Jack and grinned. "You're going to let me ride this by myself?"

Kai smiled over at Jack. "Have a good ride, guys," and paddled off toward Val.

"Yep, it's time to solo. We're going to ride down the coast a couple miles south to the inlet, cut through there into the river, go north past Fort Matanzas and then ride from there to the boat house. Kai or Val will drive my Jeep home. We'll meet them there. Sound okay?" asked Jack.

"Yes. I mean, yep."

"Clip that red elastic cord to your PFD and we'll get going,"

Bennett looked at Jack, not understanding.

"PFD is the vest - personal flotation device. The cord is already connected to the ring below the key. If you fall off it will work as a kill switch and cut the engine so the Jet Ski doesn't keep running along without a driver. It's a safety feature. You remember how to start it up?"

Bennett clipped off and started the engine. "I'm ready," he yelled.

"Okay, stay close and watch my signals,"

The pair revved the engines and took off, first heading out to sea for several hundred yards before turning south toward the Matanzas Inlet.

Once through the narrow waterway and into the Intercoastal, Jack and Bennett cruised north a half mile and pulled alongside a dock next to a small fortress that had been built on the western side of the river facing the inlet. The pair shut down the Jet Skis and Jack tied the watercraft together before looping the nylon rope around one of the pilings. Jack pointed across the river at a large pontoon boat offloading people onto a floating platform. "When that boat leaves, so will we. We're not really supposed to tie up here, but I just wanted to show you something."

"What is this place?" asked Bennett.

"This is Fort Matanzas. It was used to protect St.

Augustine from any southerly attack. It was built in 1742, twenty two years after you arrive in Philadelphia. The area around it is called Rattlesnake Island. Pop found a diary written by a survivor of a shipwreck. It described a buried treasure over on the other side of this island. We spent most of last summer trying to find it."

"Did you find it?"

"Sure did and we barely escaped with our lives. Pretty scary," said Jack.

"You and Kai must go on adventures all the time."

"Only during the summer. Nervous about going to Philadelphia?"

"Yes. It sounds so big compared to Port Royal," said Bennett.

"It is, and you'll see, it's going to get a lot bigger."

"We need a place to live."

"That won't be a problem," said Jack.

"What will you do after we leave?" asked Bennett.

"I'll stay with Pop and Nan for a few more weeks get some surfing and fishing in before going back to my real home in time for school. Philadelphia is close to the town where I live. It's . . . what's wrong?"

Bennett sighed. "I will be dead long before you are even born."

"Yes, but you have seen and experienced things that people from your time could never imagine. Think of that as a gift."

"Bennett forced a smile. "I will try. Do you think you and Kai and Rachel would ever travel back in time to visit me?" he asked, his eyes tearing up as he spoke.

Jack cleared his throat, looked at Bennett and shook his head no.

"I didn't think so," he sighed.

The pontoon boat started across the river toward the fort and the boys returned to their Jet Skis to avoid trouble with the park rangers.

"It's time for all of us to live our lives in our own time. You know, I looked up some history stuff last night. There's going to be a guy, I mean a man, arriving in Philadelphia a few years after you. You're basically the same age, within a year of each other anyway. His name is Benjamin Franklin. Keep an eye out for him. You'll find him to be an extremely smart man, a genius maybe, and I think the two of you might get along well. Maybe you can give him some hints about the future that might help him out with some of his experiments," said Jack.

"I will look for him," said Bennett as climbed back onto the Jet Ski.

Rackham's crew had collected around the glass table in the lanai and were in the middle of a deep conversation about their futures when Pop entered and sat down at the far end, an unlit cigar clenched between his teeth. He smiled as he looked at the foursome.

"Aye. Piratin' ain't for me n' Anne no more, we've a wee one to think of an' it be high time to be makin' a new life," said Calico Jack.

Anne Bonny shook her head. "But what if we don't fancy . . ."

"Ye have to put yer mind to it, lass."

"Aye, but don't be thinkin' it to be such an easy matter as ye make it," said Anne.

"Anne's right," added Tuck. "When ye be in the field, the smell of manure fillin' yer nose, bet ye be wishin' fer the smell of salty air an' the sea breezes …"

"Aye and the deep fragrance of the bilge and thick scrapes of mold below decks and the decayin' rats hidden beneath sail and hemp, avast, might be missin' the lot of it," said Calico Jack with a laugh.

Mary Read nudged Anne, "He ain't gonna last on dry ground fer more n' two seasons." She looked over at Pop and smiled, "Beggin' yer pardon, Mr. Rackham, that be me opinion. Calico Jack ain't no lubber."

Pop waved his cigar in the air, as if brushing off her apology, and smiled. "Let's hope you're wrong, Mary but if you're not, and any of you go back to the sweet trade, I daresay there will be no escape. Piracy, according to history, was more or less wiped out in the days immediately following the hangin' of the Rackham crew. Granted y'all were rescued this time but it still comes to an abrupt end for all your brethren out there on the high seas." Pop stood from the table. "We sail for South Carolina tomorrow. We'll have our bon voyage dinner together tonight. I'm sure y'all are lookin' forward to returnin' to your own time and eatin' the kind of food you're used to."

"Aye, salt pork, smoked fish n' briny stew," said Mary Read with a chuckle. "'Fraid we all come to like the victuals from yer time better n' ours."

"Fergive me fer sayin', din' much fancy the spiggy," said Tuck.

"Spiggy?" asked Pop.

"The white worms in a blood broth."

"Huh? You mean spaghetti," laughed Pop. "That wasn't blood and worms, it was . . . ah, never mind."

It was nearly midnight by the time dinner ended and everyone went their separate way to get some much-needed rest. Jack, feeling restless, left his boathouse apartment walked down the dock toward the Matanzas. He climbed on top of one of the dock pilings, using it as a seat, unwinding, enjoying the feel of the warm breeze and staring at the moonlight shimmering off the water's surface. Minutes later he heard footsteps from behind and turned to see Calico Jack approach from the shadows.

"Couldn't sleep?" asked Jack.

The pirate smiled. "S'pose there be a load of worry on me mind."

"Worry? You worried that you can't give up the sweet trade?"

"Only time . . . time will tell, lad. Hope so. Will try me best but I ain't no gentleman, ain't no farmer, not so sure bein' a father is somethin' . . ." He sighed and looked at Jack. "I need ye to answer me. Why rescue the sorry scurvy lot of us?"

"Not sure, Captain. Guess because you asked. Asking for help isn't a sign of weakness, you know."

"I never asked . . . well me dead self asked, s'pose that counts."

"Why did you come back to the fort to rescue me?" asked Jack.

"Seemed the right thing, it did."

"And it seemed right to me, to do what we did. Guess that's the answer."

"Ye have me thanks, and proud I be knowin' the Rackham family continued on these many years and to include the likes of someone who . . . yer a fine man, Jack Rackham."

"And I'm proud to fly the Rackham flag and tell everyone that I'm the descendant of the infamous pirate,

Calico Jack Rackham," said Jack.

Calico Jack nodded, turned and walked into the darkness toward the house.

At noon the next day, Calico Jack Rackham and his crew assembled outside the boathouse as instructed, waiting for Q. Pop handed each a heavy cloth bag containing forty pounds in gold coins to be tucked away inside the folds of their second set of new clothes, explaining that he hoped they would use their small fortunes to make the most of their new start. After a hearty round of goodbyes, Q arrived and guided them inside the boathouse. Jack noticed the hilt of the Serpent Dagger protruding from Q's waist wrap as the Aztec followed the pirates into the two-story structure. Pop and Jack walked toward the main house. Kai, Rachel, Val and Nan lagged behind. There was a brief flash of light from behind causing Jack to turn, trying to catch a glimpse.

"Wonder why Q insisted that we walk away?" asked Jack.

"Probably 'cause that light might've blinded anyone watchin'. He also likes to protect his secrets, though he did say he would teach me the secret of time travel," said Pop. "The light was just for show. Our friend has a flair for the dramatic."

"Well, Pop, do you think you'll ever want to travel in time again?" asked Jack.

"No, this junket was enough for me. How 'bout you?"

"Might be tempted to go back to see how Bennett's doing, or to see if the pirates stay on the straight and narrow, otherwise, I'd prefer to stay in the here and now."

"I think it best to leave things alone. Bennett and his family will thrive in America. Calico Jack and his crew . . . I have my doubts," said Pop.

"You think Tucker Gunn and Mary Read will team up and take up the trade again?"

"Actually I'm more confident that Anne, Tuck and maybe even Mary will settle into a quiet law-abiding life. Captain Rackham's the one that makes me wonder."

"But Calico Jack is the one encouraging the others. I heard him tell Anne Bonny that she needed to put her mind to it, or something like that," said Jack.

"Granted, he was on his best behavior around us, even actin' like a cheerleader for the others, but I get the sense that he feels invincible and his escape from death was a free pass to do whatever he wants," said Pop.

"But you didn't see him, how sad and scared, full of regret . . ."

"You're mixing up the remorseful dead pirate with the one you rescued. Tell me, how did Calico Jack react when you entered the cell, explained who you were, where you were from and why you were there?" asked Pop.

"When I showed him the *Serpent Dagger*, Calico Jack took it, handed it to Tucker Gunn and told him to cut my throat," said Jack.

"Should have left him behind on that longboat to take his chances with cannonballs and sharks."

"But he and Tuck did return to the fort and fought off a dozen Redcoats to rescue me from the executioner. The whole story is bizarre, Pop." Jack leaned back in his chair. "After this is all over, me, Kai and Rachel will sit down and tell you everything that happened from the beginning.

Promise we won't leave anything out."

Pop smoothed his mustache and beard with his thumb and forefinger. "Can't wait."

〜246〜

~21~
GOODBYE, BENNETT

IT WAS EARLY MORNING. Rachel sat with Bennett on a bench next to the boathouse, her arm around his shoulder her cheeks wet with tears. She would miss her young friend.

"Jack really said that we wouldn't visit you?" asked Kai.

Bennett nodded.

"But it makes sense, Kai. Bennett, don't be mad at Jack. He wants you to go on and have a normal life where you belong," said Val.

"Sorry, wasn't trying to eavesdrop," said Jack as he joined his friends. "Bennett, I'm not going to lie to you. We tampered with history once and almost got you and your parents killed. I hope you never forget us or our insane adventure together but try not to live in the past."

"Yeah, and don't live in the future either," said Kai rolling his eyes. "Geez. Talk about confusing."

Bennett smiled. "I thought when you shook your head it meant you didn't want to."

"We all wish we could hang out with you but you need to go back to your time and we need to stay in ours," added Rachel.

Mr. Tinnermon walked over to his son. "Mr. Rackham says we need to go now, Mr. Q is ready. Say good bye and thank your friends."

Bennett stood and looked at everyone. "I'll never forget any of you," he said.

Pop gave the Tinnermons a pair of battered-looking sea bags filled with their new clothes and more than one hundred pounds of gold, a substantial bit of wealth, plenty for the start-up of a new business and purchase of a new home. Following tearful goodbyes, tight hugs and firm handshakes, Bennett and his parents walked toward the boathouse. Q opened the door but Pop stopped him, pulling him off to the side. "We *are* going to see you again," said Pop in a low voice.

"Unless you object, I had hoped to visit periodically and smoke as many of your fine cigars as possible. Besides, I have a certain relic to return to my new friend."

"That would suit me just fine. I'll look forward to your visits."

"Then it's settled, until we meet again," said Q as he shook hands with Pop.

The Tinnermons filed into the boathouse as Calico Jack and his crew had done the previous day. Seconds later a brilliant light flashed from inside and the last of the time travelers vanished.

"That's that I suppose," said Pop as he took a peek at his watch. "Nan's leaving for the airport soon so I'm gonna take a nap."

"All the way to Jacksonville?"

"No. St. Augustine," said Pop.

"Why is she going there?"

"Whaddya writin' a book?"

"Nope, that's your job," answered Jack with a smile.

"You go on about your business. I'm gonna get reacquainted with my hammock."

Jack shrugged and walked across the walkway to the boathouse, taking the stairs to the upper apartment two at a time.

～X～

Kai walked into the lanai muttering something about all the sand inside his Jeep. Pop sat up and swung his legs off the hammock startling Kai. "Sorry, Kai, thought you were Nan."

One of the glass doors at the house swung open and Nan walked through holding the hand of a blue-eyed boy who Kai judged to be four or five years old. Pop smiled and stood with his arms stretched out to meet his newest guest. "Come here big guy," said Pop. The boy broke into a grin and ran across the lanai as Pop knelt down to exchange growling bear hugs.

"Who's this?" asked Kai, smiling at the little guy in the Phillies shirt and Reef flip flops.

"Kai, I'd like you to meet Jacob Rackham," announced Pop.

"Huh? Jacob Rackham?" He looked at Nan. "You went back . . ."

Pop chuckled. "No, nothing like that, Kai. This is my *other* grandson, Jack's cousin, Jacob David Rackham and he's going to spend what's left of this summer with us."

"Awesome," said Kai as he walked over and bent down to shake hands with the boy. He looked at Pop and then Nan and smiled. "So I guess this is the start of a Jacob Rackham Adventure?"

∼1721∼
PORT ROYAL, JAMAICA

~22~
GALLOWS POINT

A THICK ROPE MADE OF HEMP and flax cinched his neck, biting into the skin while a thinner cord bound the gnarled hands behind his back. Calico Jack Rackham, condemned for a second time to suffer a pirate's death, stood weak-kneed on a wooden platform in the blistering heat facing the sea, his weight supported atop a trap door waiting to plummet into the void beneath the gallows. He prayed that his neck would snap with the plunge, rather than strangling in agony with his blood vessels and capillaries bursting and hemorrhaging.

In the sand, twenty yards away, lay the gibbet, an iron cage made from flat bars curved and wrapped to match the physical dimensions of the doomed pirate. It would be suspended from a makeshift yardarm posted at the entry to the wharf encasing Rackham's corpse for two years while scavenging birds fed on his rotting, stench-ridden carcass until only bleached white bones remained. The display of his decomposing corpse would serve as a warning to buccaneers everywhere that the authorities governing eighteenth-century Jamaica punished piracy swiftly and brutally.

A light sea breeze stirred, providing a brief respite from the searing heat. The executioner nodded, acknowledging the order to carry out his duties. Rackham lifted his head high, taking in the sweet smell of salt air, knowing there would be no rescue. Alone, but determined to die bravely, he forced one final tear-filled smile as he thought of Anne and their baby Jacob. He had left them in South Carolina, unable to resist the temptation of chasing one final prize, the richest ever, only to realize too late that he had fallen for a trap. Governor Woodes Rogers had won.

The sand-filled bags dropped and the hatch cover fell away. Jack, still smiling, plunged a full body length through the opening. As the rope went taut, his neck snapped with a loud crack, sending an excruciating, but short-lived pain throughout his body. The last sensation was the pressure behind the eyes, relieved when his left eye exploded outward to land blindly against his cheek. The corpse swayed and twitched the dance of the hempen jig. Captain Calico Jack Rackham was dead.

~1759~
NEAR THE COAST OF SOUTH CAROLINA

~23~
MEMORIES OF THE SWEET TRADE

ANNE BONNY SQUEEZED a large gold coin between her thumb and index finger, her auburn hair flowing in the warm breeze, sea spray erupting over the bow splashing the deck, washing across her bare feet as she enjoyed the prettiest sunset she had ever seen. The tangerine-colored ball sinking in the west seemed close enough to kiss the ocean's surface, the darkening sky framing it in brilliant shades of violet, pink, and indigo. She smiled revisiting her memories of her days in the sweet trade, her mates, her enemies and her few close friends. Mary Read had disappeared the very day they made land saying she could never live as a lubber. Tucker Gunn migrated south to a place known as Cumberland Island where he had built up his own shipping company and raised a large family on a sprawling plantation. He had passed away as the finishing touches were added to his mansion, or so she'd been told. She thought of Calico Jack Rackham, their brief time together, how they had tried to make a life for themselves apart from piracy and how the pull of one more prize had proven too strong. The day he died, more than one thousand miles away, she knew, though word of his execution didn't reach her until several months later. And so she raised her son, Jacob Rackham, alone while helping her father to manage the affairs of his plantation.

The beautiful sunset blurred and she squinted against another light. She was in her bed. To her left sat Jacob holding her hand, to her right a pair of blue eyed young men, her grandsons. They were saying something, but all sound was muffled. She smiled, and squeezed Jacob's hand; it had been a good life. The gold coin slipped from her fingers . . . and she was gone.

Jacob Rackham inherited his grandfather's lands, and enjoyed prosperity and social status well into his old age. On the fortieth anniversary of his father's execution, he erected a headstone in the family's cemetery, next to his mother's marker with the name *Calico Jack Rackham* etched into its face. The tribute would have pleased Anne Bonny.

~JUNE 27TH, 1776~
DOWNINGTOWN, PENNSYLVANIA

DAVID EBRIGHT

⌒24⌒
PATRIOT

⌒I DARESAY, JOHN this is a truly remarkable document. Thomas has done a most splendid job indeed." The old man shuffled the papers one more time and removed his spectacles before leaning forward in his seat. "Help me over to the window if you please, there's a good fellow," he said as he struggled to his feet with his bony hand tucked into the crook of the other man's arm. "Something is amiss. Well, perhaps amiss is too strong a word. There is a point overlooked within this grand pronouncement."

The old man shuffled across the room, the papers gripped tightly between his fingers. He shook his head slowly and then stroked his chin as he moved to the chair next to the window. Perhaps it shall come to me if I relax my mind and watch the comings and goings on the street below. Allow me an hour or two of solitude so I might dredge the recesses of my ancient mind. Maybe I shall discover what it is that may be lacking. We must, you know, get this document as near perfect as possible. The citizenry deserves nothing less than our best effort. I am sure Tom would willingly indulge me and tolerate but a short delay."

"As you wish, sir," said John as he helped lower the old man into the window-side chair. "I shall return within two hours. As you know, I must leave for Philadelphia today. And sir, if I may say, you need your rest if you are to travel to Philadelphia one week from today. "

"I shall take your advice, my friend and appreciate your heartfelt concern. Now I shall read this once more and promise to release this final draft to your care upon your return."

The old man rested in the chair staring at the words on the parchment. A light breeze caressed his cheek through the open window, the lace curtains swayed rhythmically. The ache in his joints subsided under the gentle warmth of the sun. The merchants and mill workers carted their goods along Lancaster Road crossing the shallow Brandywine Creek a few hundred feet west of the center of the bustling mill town, in the shadow of Downing's Inn. He watched as a boy of fourteen loaded grain sacks into the back of a wooden cart. The boy looked up at the old man and waved.

The man smiled and waved through the parted curtains but the scene suddenly changed. Tall masts filled the sky around him. The smell of salt air filled his nostrils and the street noise changed to something more raucous. He was outside now, standing next to a half-loaded cart. The young boy was gone. There was the wharf to his right, guarded by Redcoats. A brightly colored bird with very long tail feathers circled above his head. Two young men walked toward him, between them, holding their hands, was a pretty girl with long blonde hair, the three all dressed in strange clothes. All of them wore short pants with outside pockets and shirts without sleeves or collars and strange looking shoes. The girl wore black spectacles that hid her eyes and she smiled as she spoke to her two companions and the long-tailed bird landed on her shoulder.

"Good afternoon, sir," said the shorter of the two young men.

The old man nodded.

The girl spoke up, removing her glasses to reveal stunning green eyes. "It's so good to see you! We're here to remind you of an important conversation from a long time ago back in Port Royal."

"Port Royal? Why I left Port Royal more than a half-century ago," said the old man, clearly shaken.

"We understand," said the taller of the two young men. "It's just that a history-making document is about to be signed and you're trying desperately to remember a phrase that you believe should be included. We want you to remember because it **IS** important and it has to be part of that new manuscript."

"How do you know such things? Where am I?" asked the old man.

"You're sitting in a chair in Pennsylvania looking out a window but you're seeing us and Port Royal, Jamaica. A long time ago, you helped save my life and assisted us in the rescue of a well-known pirate and his crew so they could live the rest of their days in freedom as good citizens. Before that, we had spoken about the Maroons and you made a very important point that day. You have to remember it," said the tall one.

"The pirate was Calico Jack Rackham and you were all from the future," said the old man. "I still have your timepiece, Jack."

"You remember my name," said Jack with a smile. "Now do you remember what you told me that day on our way to the shanty?"

"Yes I do. I said …"

Jack interrupted. "Don't tell us . . . just be sure to add those words to the document."

"I will. I …" but they were gone. The old man smiled at the memory of his friends and looked down at the age spots on his vein-covered hands. It had been a life changing adventure and it had brought him here to a new country, one ready to declare its independence, and he had played a part in the effort leading up to the birth of a free nation.

He stood and eased his way to his desk and picked up his quill and jotted down a few words in the margin of the draft. When he finished he removed a small box from the top drawer and put it in his pocket. Minutes later John returned.

"Sir I trust you have completed your review. I must make haste to Philadelphia as you know."

"Yes, John you must be on your way. I remembered what I wanted Thomas to incorporate and here it is," said the old man as he reached out with the rolled up papers.

John looked at the parchment. There was a slash interrupting the sentence following the opening line of the second paragraph - *We hold these truths to be self-evident* and in the margin, he found six added words connected to the slash with a solid line with the words - *that all men are created equal* – inserted.

"This is excellent, sir. I am sure that Mr. Jefferson will be anxious to add this most potent phrase," said John. "Six words of such powerful meaning if I may say."

"Those few words came to mind from a conversation I had with some very special friends long ago, when I was but a lad in Port Royal, Jamaica." The old man sighed and waved his hand as if now dismissing the memory. "John, I have also sealed this note authorizing you to sign our Declaration of Independence in my place. I am afraid that the heat and distance might get the better of me should I attempt to travel to Philadelphia in my condition. Please be so good as to fulfill my duties at this historic gathering."

"I would be most honored, sir."

"Thank you, Mr. Hancock. I believe I shall now return to my comfortable chair at the window and relax in the sun and breeze for another hour or so, my friend. Enjoy safe travels."

Bennett Tinnermon eased himself into his chair once

again and removed an unusual timepiece from his pocket and examined it. Cradling the twenty first century dive watch in his hand, he closed his eyes and smiled, his breathing steady but shallow. He was fourteen again and surrounded by his friends Jack, Kai, Rachel and Q as he returned … to *Gallows Point.*

OTHER BOOKS BY DAVID EBRIGHT

BAD LATITUDE *A Jack Rackham Adventure*

RECKLESS ENDEAVOR *A Jack Rackham Adventure*

COMING SOON . . .

Jacob & Augie Explore The Wonderwood

Learn more about David Ebright and the adventurous worlds
he creates at:

STAUGUSTINEPUBLISHING.COM

JAXPOP.BLOGSPOT.COM

JACK RACKHAM ADVENTURES READERS & FANS
@facebook.com/groups/53041954622/

www.ingramcontent.com/pod-product-compliance
Lightning Source LLC
Chambersburg PA
CBHW071500110726
47908CB00003B/679